Praise for the

"Christie Ridgway writes with the perfect combination of humor and heart. This funny, sexy story is as fresh and breezy as its Southern California setting."
—Susan Wiggs, *New York Times* bestselling author

"Delightful."
—Rachel Gibson, *New York Times* bestselling author

"Tender, funny, and wonderfully emotional."
—Barbara Freethy, *USA Today* bestselling author

"Pure romance, delightfully warm, and funny."
—Jennifer Crusie, *New York Times* bestselling author

"Smart, peppy." —*Publishers Weekly*

"Funny, supersexy, and fast paced . . . Ridgway is noted for her humorous, spicy, and upbeat stories."
—*Library Journal*

"Christie Ridgway is a first-class author."
—*Midwest Book Review*

"Christie Ridgway's books are crammed with smart girls, manly men, great sex, and fast, funny dialogue. Her latest novel . . . is a delightful example, a romance as purely sparkling as California champagne." —*BookPage*

"Ridgway delights yet again with this charming, witty tale o̶ ̶ ̶ ̶ ̶ ̶ ̶ ̶ ̶ ̶ ̶ ̶ ̶ ̶ he characters sympa-
t̶ ̶ ̶ ̶ ̶ ̶ ̶ ̶ ̶ ̶ ̶ ̶ ̶ ̶ he sexual tension be-
t̶ ̶ ̶ ̶ ̶ ̶ ̶ ̶ ̶ ̶ ̶ ̶ out with tremendous
s̶ ̶ ̶ —*Romantic Times*

Titles by Christie Ridgway

HOW TO KNIT A WILD BIKINI
UNRAVEL ME
DIRTY SEXY KNITTING

CRUSH ON YOU
THEN HE KISSED ME

Then He Kissed Me

CHRISTIE RIDGWAY

BERKLEY SENSATION, NEW YORK

THE BERKLEY PUBLISHING GROUP
Published by the Penguin Group
Penguin Group (USA) Inc.
375 Hudson Street, New York, New York 10014, USA

Penguin Group (Canada), 90 Eglinton Avenue East, Suite 700, Toronto, Ontario M4P 2Y3, Canada
(a division of Pearson Penguin Canada Inc.)
Penguin Books Ltd., 80 Strand, London WC2R 0RL, England
Penguin Group Ireland, 25 St. Stephen's Green, Dublin 2, Ireland (a division of Penguin Books Ltd.)
Penguin Group (Australia), 250 Camberwell Road, Camberwell, Victoria 3124, Australia
(a division of Pearson Australia Group Pty. Ltd.)
Penguin Books India Pvt. Ltd., 11 Community Centre, Panchsheel Park, New Delhi—110 017, India
Penguin Group (NZ), 67 Apollo Drive, Rosedale, North Shore 0632, New Zealand
(a division of Pearson New Zealand Ltd.)
Penguin Books (South Africa) (Pty.) Ltd., 24 Sturdee Avenue, Rosebank, Johannesburg 2196,
South Africa

Penguin Books Ltd., Registered Offices: 80 Strand, London WC2R 0RL, England

This is a work of fiction. Names, characters, places, and incidents either are the product of the author's imagination or are used fictitiously, and any resemblance to actual persons, living or dead, business establishments, events, or locales is entirely coincidental. The publisher does not have any control over and does not assume any responsibility for author or third-party websites or their content.

THEN HE KISSED ME

A Berkley Sensation Book / published by arrangement with the author

PRINTING HISTORY
Berkley Sensation mass-market edition / January 2011

Copyright © 2011 by Christie Ridgway.
Excerpt from *Drunk on Love* by Christie Ridgway copyright © by Christie Ridgway.
Cover art by Andre Blais/Shutterstock.
Cover design by Lesley Worrell.
Interior text design by Laura K. Corless.

ISBN: 978-0-425-23917-9

BERKLEY® SENSATION
Berkley Sensation Books are published by The Berkley Publishing Group,
a division of Penguin Group (USA) Inc.,
375 Hudson Street, New York, New York 10014.
BERKLEY® SENSATION and the "B" design are trademarks of Penguin Group (USA) Inc.

PRINTED IN THE UNITED STATES OF AMERICA

10 9 8 7 6 5 4 3 2 1

*I raise my glass to all the women
who have served as sisters in my life—
I found you in carpool lines,
in gymnasium stands, in writers groups.
Thank you for sharing the laughter and the tears!*

We are all mortal until the first kiss
and the second glass of wine.

—EDUARDO GALEANO

1

Leaning against the driver's door of a black stretch Cadillac, Stephania Baci crossed her arms over her pin-tucked white shirt and practiced pleading her case to a stern-faced judge wearing robes as dark as her own tailored jacket and trousers. "Put yourself in my shoes," she murmured, glancing down at her stiletto-heeled half boots, ego-boosters bought for just this occasion. "Who wouldn't commit a crime when faced with chauffeuring an ex and his new fiancée on New Year's Eve?"

Forty feet away, the double doors to the Valley Ridge Resort opened. Even as her heart took an elevator plunge, she shot straight from her slouch. It wouldn't do for her posture to telegraph her low mood. The calm mask she'd donned tonight along with her limo driver's uniform was supposed to camouflage messy emotions—and hopefully smother any stray compulsion to carry out a high crime or misdemeanor.

A lone figure swept onto the portico, his long black overcoat swirling around his calves as he moved into a shadowy corner. Though her nerves were still jitterbugging, this wasn't the male half of the pair she was contracted to drive this evening. The tall man whose outline she could barely make out was wholly unfamiliar.

She ducked her head and studied him through the screen of her lashes, for some inexplicable reason intrigued. But the broad-shouldered silhouette didn't surrender any secrets. When a breeze kicked up, the only new information she established was the length of his hair: long enough to be ruffled.

Nothing to pique her interest. No excuse for her still-chattering pulse, unless it was that faint note of expensive cologne that reached her on the next gust of air.

Stevie and rich men didn't mix with success.

The resort's doors opened once more, pulling her attention away from the stranger. Again, it was not the couple she was anticipating that strolled onto the covered porch. As this pair came closer, Stevie responded with an automatic smile.

"Rex and Janice!" Contemporaries of her late father's, she'd known the husband and wife all her life. "Happy New Year."

Rex beamed. "Back at you, Stevie. I take it the boss has to work the New Year's shift tonight?"

"Right." She didn't add that, with the holidays nearly over and winter being the wine country's off season, there was little work for herself or her part-time, as-needed-only employees of Napa Princess Limousine. The two would guess as much. Their town of Edenville, in northern Napa Valley, was populated by just over six thousand friendly—read: nosy—souls.

"I heard about your sister," Janice said next, as if to prove Stevie's last thought. "Allie broke her foot?"

"This morning. She had surgery this afternoon." Stevie glanced over at the shadow in the corner, wondering if she imagined his attentiveness to their conversation. "Penn's keeping her in Malibu for the next few weeks. She'll be close to the surgeon, and unlike the Baci farmhouse at the winery, their beach place is single story."

Rex and Janice made sympathetic noises. "That means you and Giuliana will have to pick up the slack, I suppose. Besides her PR duties, doesn't Allie handle all the details for the Tanti Baci weddings?"

"Mmm-hmm." The comment barely registered as Stevie couldn't shake the odd sense that Mystery Man continued to focus on them. The frowning glance she shot his phantomlike presence could neither confirm nor deny the feeling—yet it corroborated that odd awareness she had of him. She could swear she felt the intent of his return gaze, and the back of her neck prickled as a fight-or-flight spike of adrenaline kicked into her bloodstream.

The consequence of too much vampire fiction, she thought, suppressing the urge to cross herself as she waved Rex and Janice on their way. Not that she really believed in such dark creatures. No man could pierce one of Stevie Baci's veins and suck her blood.

The doors to the resort opened again, and the two now walking through made that statement fact. It was Emerson Platt and the woman who wore his ring on her finger. Given how abruptly he'd broken off his two-year relationship with Stevie—and the words that he'd used to do so— she should have been mortally wounded. Instead, she was still breathing, wasn't she? Her heart still beat.

She glanced toward the portico's corner again. It was pumping weirdly hard, as a matter of fact.

"Stevie." In a stylish tuxedo, the golden child of U.S. Senator Lois Platt moved down the portico steps, his fiancée's hand clasped in his. "You're already here."

"Can't keep the client waiting," she replied, switching her focus to a spot just left of Emerson's elbow. As tempting as some misdeed tonight might be, she knew that maintaining an unruffled façade was in her own best interest.

Why give her ex the satisfaction of knowing he'd dented Stevie's psyche and battered her self-esteem? To that end, she'd created a mental picture of the bride-to-be, complete with a wart on her nose, receding chin, and sausagelike cankles. Just in case her image didn't actually match the original, she'd decided against even passing her gaze over the other woman.

Spinning on her dominatrix boot heels, Stevie reached for the passenger door handle. It was cold under her fingers. Locked.

An anxious heat rose on her neck as she drew the remote from her pocket. "Just a moment," she murmured, fumbling with the buttons.

Bleeps. Clicks. Double bleeps. The lock stayed stubbornly seated.

The burn on her face intensified. She felt eyes on her: Emerson's, the warted bride's, and especially those of Mystery Man, which only made her fingers more clumsy. "In a second," she said, her voice tight, "I'll have you out of the cold."

She didn't need to see Emerson to hear the tender concern that entered his voice. "It *is* really cold," he said. "Roxanne, sweetheart, will you get too chilled on a winery crawl tonight?"

When he'd been with Stevie, icy temperatures would have had him exhorting her to man-up and deal. But with Roxanne . . . what? Was he afraid his darling's endearing wart would freeze and fall off?

Emerson's shoes scraped on the pavement. "Did you say something, Stevie?"

Oh, God. Had she said that out loud? Her head swung around in order to deny the charge—and only at the last second did she remember her vow not to look upon the other woman. She turned away from the glimpse of silver-spangled skirt and breathed a sigh of relief as she heard the telltale snap of the limo's locks releasing.

With a professional flourish, she opened the door, making a last-minute inspection of the interior. Low lights, miles of leather cushions, two miniature crystal bud vases holding tiny white roses, a bottle chilling in a bucket. Harry Connick, Jr., crooned through the speakers.

Emerson and Roxanne would have their romantic New Year's Eve.

And Stevie, once seated behind the wheel with the privacy screen secure, would have her dignity intact and her cool façade unthreatened. After tonight, she'd make sure there was no reason that their path and hers ever crossed again.

"Go ahead," she urged the couple with a gesture. "Please get in."

A pair of glittery silver pumps paused beside her black boots. A light touch brushed the sleeve of her coat.

"I don't think we've been formally introduced," the other woman said.

Stevie stared at the diamond flashing on the slender hand touching her arm but didn't look up as Emerson cleared his throat. "That's right," he said. "Stevie—Stephania Baci, this is . . . uh, Roxanne."

"Princess Roxanne," Stevie corrected. Princess Roxanne Karina Marie Parini of Ardenia, a constitutional monarchy that rubbed shoulders—geographically speaking—with its cousin in style and language, Luxembourg. Stevie's ex hadn't dropped her for some generic other woman, but instead for European royalty—of a microstate, yes—but European royalty all the same.

She'd *better* have a wart.

"Roxy," the woman said now. "I'm half American, I was mostly raised in America. Roxy is just fine." That diamond-toting set of fingers touched Stevie's sleeve again. There was the delicate sound—slightly nervous—of a clearing throat. "Especially as we'll be working so closely together."

Startled, Stevie forgot her promise and looked up into a pretty face surrounded by honey-gold hair. "Huh?"

"On the wedding."

"Huh?" Stevie said again. "What . . . what are you talking about?"

"Giuliana called us this afternoon," Emerson explained, in that hearty tone she remembered him using for breaking dates and conveying other bad news. "She wanted to be the first to tell us about Allie."

"She had surgery," Stevie said, still puzzled.

"Yes." More Mr. Hearty. "And Jules assured us that our wedding at the Tanti Baci winery—your family winery—at the end of the month will not be affected."

"Surely not," Stevie agreed. Six months ago, at Allie's instigation, they'd started offering the original founders' cottage as a venue for couples to exchange their vows. They'd been desperate for any revenue stream to keep the ailing family business afloat—still were, as a matter of fact—and the nuptials had taken off in a modest manner thanks to her younger sister's hard work and some well-timed TV promotion. "Your day will go as planned, I guarantee it."

"Exactly what Giuliana said." Emerson nodded. "Roxanne and I are sure you'll step in and do a fine job as our event coordinator."

"What?" Stevie's eyes widened. Event *coordinator*? Of course she knew that Allie had assumed more control over details of the ceremonies and receptions as time went on, but . . .

A new male voice entered the discussion. "We all look forward to working with you."

Stevie's gaze jerked to the man who'd come to stand behind the princess. It was her pseudovampire, her Mystery Man, the shadow from the corner of the portico. In the light, he held no more secrets. Now she saw him as thirty-something and dark-haired, with handsome, chiseled features. Under his overcoat—cashmere?—he wore a tuxedo three times more elegant than Emerson's. He gazed on her with an attitude that struck her instantly as ten times more entitled.

There was no explaining it; no single precedent or simple reason for some man to at an instant make her feel as exposed as a raw nerve, but there it was. Everything about him rubbed her the wrong way, including his smile, set so clearly on charm.

Her hackles rose. "Do I know you?" she asked, the tiniest edge to her voice.

A shallow dimple scored one lean cheek. "Definitely going to be fun," he murmured.

Underneath the starched cotton and black wool of her own clothes, a heat rash prickled her skin, but she kept her words cool. "Your name is . . . ?"

"Jack."

"Jack," she repeated. Then, in response to the arrogant, amused gleam in his eyes, she raised a brow. "LaLanne? O'Lantern? In the Box?"

He had a husky laugh.

As it feathered down her spine, Stevie decided to ignore him and address the more salient issue. Turning back to Emerson, she attempted to force out the question. "Let's get this straight. Are you . . ." But she couldn't say it. She could barely *think* it. Hadn't she just promised herself that after tonight she'd have nothing whatsoever to do with her ex again?

Curling one hand into a fist, she tried once more for clarity. "Are you certain that Jules told you that I . . . that I . . ."

"Yes." It wasn't Emerson who answered. The handsome stranger with the I-own-the-world attitude was looking at her again with those knowing eyes. "Your sister promised that it's you who'll handle each and every fine point of the upcoming Parini-Platt nuptials."

~

With her clients inside their first stop of the evening, the Von Stroman winery, Stevie closed her eyes against the glare of the icicle lights dripping from its Alpine-inspired eaves. The back of her head bumped the cushioned rest and she tried visualizing herself removing the tension that clung to her spine like ivy climbing a trellis. She would never get coiled up like this again, she vowed.

New Year's Resolution #1: Stay away from men. Because if she'd avoided the species from the very beginning—

The passenger door popped open. Her nervous heart jolted, and she slapped a palm over it as she swiveled right. A body dropped into the seat beside hers.

"Surprise!" Her friend Mari Friday grinned at her, smile the same white as the uniform shirt she wore, a twin to Stevie's. "I'm parked right behind you."

A glance back confirmed a second limo had pulled up to her rear bumper. Mari moonlighted with Stevie's friendly competitor, Golden West Limousine, on occasion. "You scared me! I almost jumped out of my clothes."

"Hah. I'd like to witness Emerson's reaction to that."

Stevie slid a look toward the winery entrance. "You saw him?"

"Oh, yeah. And I demand a simple answer to a simple question. Why the hell do you have your unworthy ex and his princess bride in your backseat?"

Stevie hesitated.

It caused her friend to roll her eyes. "I get it. You don't want him to know he broke your heart."

"He didn't break my heart!" Stevie denied. Too loudly? "Look, Mari, if he wasn't embarrassed to book my services, how could I possibly refuse to provide them?"

"By saying, 'You're a smarmy two-timer and I wouldn't chauffeur your lying ass on a bet'?" the other woman suggested.

Except Emerson hadn't lied. He'd been honest—brutally—about why he'd broken it off with Stevie. The two-timing part wasn't true, either. He'd dumped her eight months ago and weeks had gone by before he'd been spotted in the area wrapped around another woman. It had taken even more time for word to filter back to her that Emerson's new honey had a "Her Highness" attached to her name.

The people of Edenville had wanted to protect her. They had a habit of that when it came to the Baci sisters, and it only made the situation more humiliating. By taking the job tonight, she figured she'd shut down the pity party the whole town had kept going in her honor.

She was proving to them she didn't need it. That nobody, no how, could upset Stephania Baci's equilibrium. She was the brash Baci sister. The tomboy her mother had despaired about.

Stevie, where's your hair ribbon?

Is that grease on your dress?

Boys want a girl who acts like a lady.

"So who's the other guy?"

Once again, Mari gave Stevie a jolt. "Uh . . . other guy?"

"Tall, dark, and dashing?" her friend qualified. "Don't tell me you didn't notice."

She'd noticed. From the moment he'd stepped out of the resort. But tall, dark, and dashing didn't make up for rich, self-important, and rude. "He's haughty."

"I'll say," Mari agreed. "My sister gave me a Hottie-of-the-Month calendar for Christmas and I bet he's in there."

Stevie frowned. "Haughty, not hottie."

"That's what I said."

"I . . ." She shook her head. "Never mind."

"Just tell me his name," Mari urged. "I'll find out his phone number myself."

Another frown dug between Stevie's brows. Her friend had a headful of blond spiral curls and a black book that rivaled any Hollywood bachelor's. But it was Stevie who had spied tall, dark, and dashing first, and didn't that give her . . .

No. Hottie, true. But the haughty got him permanently expunged from her own Bachelor Book, if she'd actually had one. And not to forget, there was that very recent resolution she'd just made. *Men are off-limits.*

"I think he's with the princess," Stevie said to her friend.

When she'd told her clients they had to get moving or miss their tasting appointments, he'd climbed into the back with Emerson and his fiancée. "His name's Jack."

Mari gasped. "Jack! Of course! 'Jack' is Prince Jacques Christian Wilhelm Parini. I read about him in one of those magazines at the hairdresser's—you know, the pulpy ones with paparazzi pics of movie premieres and Euro trash boogeying down in flashy discotheques. He's some kind of notorious playboy and the princess bride's big brother."

That made sense. He struck Stevie as a royal pain-in-the-ass because he *was* a royal pain-in-the-ass. She loved being right.

Though she should have made the Jacques-Jack connection on her own. Blame it on her ex anxiety. She knew of the man, not from a magazine, but because he was college friends with the Bennett brothers, neighbors since birth and not-so-silent partners in the Tanti Baci winery. Liam and Seth, she recalled, knew Jack through the UC Davis Viticulture & Enology program and had mentioned during one of their regular poker nights that their old buddy was coming for a visit.

"It's a small world of wines," Stevie murmured.

"Yeah, and—" Mari's curls swung in an arc as her attention shifted to the side window. "Oops, gotta go. My peeps are ready to move. Happy New Year!"

She was gone in a blast of chilled air, leaving Stevie alone once again. Mari wasn't soothing company, but she missed her anyway, because now there was nothing else to think about besides that little threat she'd been putting off contemplating.

Your sister promised that it's you who'll handle each and every fine point of the upcoming Parini-Platt nuptials.

Closing her eyes, she groaned. Had Giuliana really made that guarantee? Could she actually expect Stevie to honor it?

The passenger door clicked open a second time. Stevie,

eyes still shut, blessed her buddy and the distraction she'd prove to be. "Mari. Thank God you're back. I—"

Her throat closed as heat prickles took another dash across her flesh and that weird hyperawareness she'd experienced at the resort tightened her belly. Opening her eyes, she saw a long male body fold onto the seat beside her. "Jack," she said.

He smiled at her, the wattage bright enough to bring up the temperature in the front seat. "You remember my name."

And his scent. It reached her again, subtle and smooth, a top-shelf cologne, one ounce likely costing more than her new boots—and probably her monthly rental check as well.

"What are you doing here? You belong there," she said, jerking her thumb toward the winery.

"I belong wherever I want to belong," he answered, smiling that easy smile he had as his body slid nearer to hers on the bench seat. "Just like I do whatever I want to do."

Stevie crowded close to the driver's door. It didn't stop his left thigh from grazing her right, his knee from bumping hers. One long finger reached out to adjust the heater that she'd left running.

Forcing her gaze off his lean hand, she narrowed her eyes at him. "And what you want to do is . . . ?"

Her suspicious tone didn't appear to offend. He relaxed against the leather seat, sliding an arm across its back, obviously comfortable in his own privileged skin. His charming smile deepened. "Nothing for you to worry about. I only thought we might take these few minutes to get better acquainted, *ma belle fille.*"

Not for a winter's worth of bookings would she let him know that just for a second—a nanosecond—she had found the soft foreign phrase as disarming as he most certainly intended. Even as her insides recovered from their quick melt, she made her expression blank and raised both brows in inquiry, all tomboy bumpkin.

His smile was rueful, his shrug European. "What can I say? I know five languages and how to compliment a beautiful woman in each and every one."

Wide-eyed, she pretended to appear impressed. "Wow." Then she dropped the innocent act. "And to think I only know how to say screw you in Italian, Spanish, and Portuguese."

He blinked, then laughed.

"Oh, and in English it's fu—"

Leaning forward, he clamped his palm over her mouth. At the contact, they both froze and the smile on his face died. Her lips tingled, her skin burned, another shot of adrenaline punched into her bloodstream. *Fight or flight.*

Uncertain which order to follow, her body twitched.

His hand dropped.

They stared at each other.

Refine that New Year's resolution, Stevie thought, despising her breathlessness. *Stay away from* this *man.*

She cleared her throat. "You should go back to Emerson and your sister." *Please go back to Emerson and your sister.*

His gaze didn't move from her face. But he settled back in his seat, and after a moment, humor gleamed once more in his eyes.

"What are you laughing at now?" she demanded.

He shrugged again. "Me, maybe."

Nothing felt the least bit funny to Stevie. She sent him another suspicious look, but his attention had shifted to a small item he was withdrawing from his jacket pocket.

A crystal bud vase.

A familiar crystal bud vase.

"That belongs in the back of the limo," she said, puzzled.

He glanced up. "I thought so. I found it outside. It must have fallen from the car."

Frowning, Stevie accepted it from his outstretched

hand, careful to avoid another touch. Then she held it toward him. "If you wouldn't mind, you can return it to its place in the back."

His tall body didn't budge. He regarded her with another of those faint, almost-mocking smiles. "I wasn't kidding, you know."

"About what?"

"Until the end of the month, I'm going to be your new best friend—"

"I don't think so."

He shrugged and that shallow dimple flashed again. "All right, have it that way. I'm going to be the fly in your champagne. The thorn on your rose."

Champagne and roses. He was just that kind of guy, she supposed, barely suppressing a snort.

"Point is, I'm sticking close, *mon ange*."

Again with the French. Rolling her eyes, she ignored a second surge of traitorous warmth in her belly. "Why?"

"Why?" His smile disappeared; his expression turned coldly serious. "To ensure, of course, that you don't sabotage my sister's wedding."

At daybreak on January first, Stevie let herself into the house where she'd grown up on the grounds of the family winery. An ancient sweatshirt of Allie's hung on the bent-wood coatrack by the front door and next to it dangled a ball cap with the *Build Me Up!* logo from Allie's husband's top-rated home renovation television show. The interior was silent and chilled. Only Allie and Penn lived there now—and part-time at that.

Stevie winged a healing thought toward her younger sister, imagining her recuperating in the newlyweds' house on the sand in Southern California. It was too early to check in on the patient just yet. As for her older sister—some vestige of holiday spirit had prevented Stevie from making a six A.M. call to Giuliana, presumably still snoozing in her bed at her rented condo. Jules was no early riser.

And Stevie needed something besides coffee before she went toe-to-toe with the oldest Baci sibling about that "promise" she'd made to Emerson and the princess bride.

It had been a tumultuous previous twelve months, Stevie

acknowledged, as she wandered through the downstairs rooms. Their widowed father had died of cancer. The sisters had discovered the winery was in dire financial straits. And then Allie had fallen in love with Penn Bennett— illegitimate half sibling of the Bennett brothers the Bacis had grown up with—and married him last summer. Stopping before the overstuffed bookcase in the family room, Stevie ran a fingertip over her old favorites.

With all that upheaval, it was no wonder she needed grounding before facing the new year and this new dilemma regarding the upcoming wedding. Certain she'd find that stabilization here, she felt the tightness across her shoulders relax. Again her hand hovered over the books that had been the close companions of her childhood: an illustrated anthology of fairy tales, a compilation of Hans Christian Andersen's stories, a now-ragtag collection of books about princesses and dragons and brave knights. How many times had she and her friends holed up in the ramshackle cottage on the winery grounds and lost themselves in romantic tales of the past?

Closing her eyes, she picked a book at random, then tucked it under her arm and left the farmhouse to stroll in the direction of the one-hundred-year-old home of the original winery founders. Though Anne and Alonzo's first residence had been renovated as the centerpiece of the winery weddings, to Stevie, nothing could change what it had always been for her.

Part fort, part clubhouse, all comfort.

Still, the gravel she scattered sounded eerily loud in the early morning. The narrow lane led not only to the cottage, but also to the wine caves and visitors' parking lot. No one was about so early on the holiday and the heavy overcast darkened the green of the eastern hills. The surrounding acres of Baci land were covered in dormant vines. Devoid of any foliage, they stood side by side like spindly, twisted grave markers. Life wouldn't show on them again until spring.

She shivered, cold tracking down her spine as if warning of some dire danger ahead. "Stop being such a wuss," she whispered aloud as Anne and Alonzo's cottage came into view. Single-story, whitewashed adobe. A wide front porch and carved double doors. A stone chimney showed at the roofline, matching the massive river-rock fireplace in the main room that was said to have been built by Alonzo's own hands. Inside, Stevie would find the steadiness she needed.

Eager now, she hurried forward. With one knee-length, bright red rubber boot on the first shallow step, motion on the porch caught the corner of her eye. She started, dropping the book under her arm and jolting back. Her feet stumbled over themselves and she went down, landing on her ass.

Gravel dug into her behind through her jeans. Surprise had stolen her breath, but air found its way back to her lungs as she watched a pair of expensive running shoes advance into her line of vision. Stevie silently cursed the man inside them, and then ignored his outstretched hand as she rose to her feet.

With a glare at him, she brushed off her backside and yanked down the thick fisherman's knit sweater she wore. "I ran the hurdles in high school track," she said. "Played basketball. Was a linebacker on the powder puff football team—you know, the one who sacks the quarterback? The only person who's ever knocked me on *my* butt was Belinda 'The Brute' MacGraw."

"The Brute," Jack Parini, *Prince* Jack Parini, murmured. "That's kind of cruel."

Stevie narrowed her eyes. "She nicknamed herself."

"Ah." He nodded. "Guess they grow the girls tough around here."

"Absolutely." And Stevie, despite that one hit of Belinda's, was the toughest of the tough. Didn't she have the masculine name, the business that was all about cars, the past history of lost ribbons and ripped party dresses? On occasion she might wobble on her feet, she'd admit to that, but even Emerson hadn't managed to leave much more than a bruise.

If that.

So the prince wasn't going to shake her up any further, either. "What are you doing here?" After his big warning about his sister's wedding the night before, Emerson and Roxy had returned to the limo and he'd climbed into the back with them. At the next winery stop, Jack had gone off with another group and she'd been grateful.

"I was out for a walk," he said now, and then turned to glance over his shoulder. She noticed he looked as good in running pants and a long-sleeved microfiber shirt as he did in a tuxedo. "I'm staying with the Bennetts and there's a path—"

"I know, I know," she said. Their winery property adjoined that of the Bacis. Years ago, Liam and Stevie's sister Giuliana had worn a path between the two places that ran as deep as the wounds they'd left on each other's hearts. "It's early."

"I don't sleep much."

She hadn't last night, either. Her dreams had been an exhausting compilation of frustrating or frightening elements—twisting roads and steering that wouldn't respond; an urgent appointment at an address she couldn't recall; a beautiful man watching her trip down a flight of stairs, leaving a single shoe behind.

Now she remembered who that beautiful man looked like. Bending over, she retrieved her fallen book and then dug her key ring from her jeans pocket. Brushing past Jack, she successfully mounted the steps. "Have a nice day."

Not taking the hint, he was at her shoulder as she unlocked the cottage's front door. "What is this place?" he asked. "It looks like something from a fairy tale."

"It's the venue for the winery weddings. My sister Allie's trolling the Internet for a unicorn to graze in the front yard." Stevie released a small sigh and turned to face him. "I suppose you'd like to see inside."

He stepped back, eyebrows high, palm rising to his heart. "What was that sound? Did you just drop the chip on your shoulder?"

"Very funny." Not at all, really. Because she wasn't the kind who carried a chip around men. She was a guy's girl—the kind who was offered the extra ticket to the 49ers game. The one forced to wince at the dirtiest of jokes because the assembled company forgot that she was female. The pal a man called on Sunday afternoon to help him flush a radiator. With men, she was at ease.

Jack Parini threatened that. Around him, she felt too . . . female. Merely breathing in his body heat and the subtle scent of his masculine soap sent a flush rising up her neck and cheeks. She spun back, pushing open the door to hide her unfamiliar discomfiture.

He followed her inside.

Stepping farther from him, she went into tour guide mode. "A hundred years ago, Liam Bennett and Alonzo Baci were partners in a silver mine. When the ore played out, they invested in land . . . this land. Alonzo had learned about grapes and winemaking growing up in Italy, so they created the Tanti Baci winery."

"Meaning 'many kisses,'" Jack translated.

She shot him a look. "That's right. You know all those languages."

His smile was unrepentant. She remembered Mari claiming he had a playboy reputation, and with that beautiful face and devil-may-care smile she could well believe it. His gaze roamed around the room, a spacious area that had the massive fireplace on one wall but was otherwise filled with honey-colored craftsman-styled pews set on the gleaming hardwood floor. Seventy could sit comfortably here. A door led to a hall down which a groom's waiting area and the luxurious bridal boudoir were located.

"This house was . . . what?" he asked. "Liam and Alonzo's bachelor pad?"

"No. Alonzo built this for his bride, Anne. The San Francisco society beauty that both he and Liam courted."

"Alonzo won her then."

Stevie nodded. "And though the Bennetts and the Bacis have survived generations of intertwined business dealings since, there's always been a feud at some level of simmer between those of us who live here and those in the big house over there." She pointed in the direction of the Bennett property.

"Hmm." Jack strolled toward her. "Maybe that explains why you bristle around me. You're a Baci, and since I'm temporarily living at Liam and Seth's, I'm a stand-in Bennett. Maybe we're this generation's feud."

"I don't bristle!" she said, but she did just that, backing up as he drew closer. "And Liam and my sister Jules have the feud thing sewn up." Her butt hit the back of the last pew.

"Ah." Toe-to-toe with her, his hand reached out to play with the ends of her blunt-cut hair. "We aren't enemies, then?"

She tried swinging away from him, but his fingers tightened on the strands. They didn't have nerves—else they'd cry when cut, right?—but she could swear the sensation of his touch was flowing to her scalp and from there cascading like a warm waterfall over her body.

"We aren't anything," she choked out.

"No?"

"No. I'm no threat to your sister's wedding. I'm not your enemy." She sidestepped, her hair tugging free of his hold. "I don't know you at all. We're strangers."

"From the first moment you saw me, you've acted as if I rub your fur the wrong way."

He had that right. Around him, she felt twitchy and feline, half of her wanting to spit in his face with the other half wanting to draw her claws down his back . . . his bare, muscular back.

"Look, I'm not into politeness for the sake of being polite," she said. It was one of the reasons why she hadn't fit into Emerson's world. "I call things like I see them."

Jack Parini was close again, his expression revealing only a mild combination of curiosity and amusement. "And, *mon ange*, how exactly do you see me?" he asked, a faint smile curving his mouth.

She shook her head. "I can't say. I told you, we're strangers. For all I know you're a thief, a murderer, a kidnap—"

The last syllable dropped to her belly as his hands closed over her shoulders. He jerked her close, his gaze hot, his body hot, his hands hot on her through the wool of her sweater. Stevie's pulse skittered. There it was again, that shocking and unprecedented physical response, like nothing she'd experienced before.

Nonplussed, she stared up at him. Inky lashes surrounded his eyes that were a chilly gray instead of chocolate-dark like her own. The nostrils of his straight nose flared and his fingers flexed, holding her tighter.

"W-what?" she asked.

His eyes glittered like ice. "Or maybe I'm the kind of man who takes advantage of a woman alone."

She could tell he was angry, and his sudden change in mood sent the blood speeding through her veins, laced with yet another dose of high-octane adrenaline. Her belly tightened and the surface of her skin became ultrasensitized. Perversely, she felt her mouth soften, as if in anticipation of a kiss.

Instead of being scared, she was turned-on, she admitted to herself as her tongue licked over suddenly dry lips. His fingers tightened, and she twitched in his hands.

Her movement broke the tension. His grip loosened, his eyelashes dropped to shutter his gaze, and he stepped back, arms dropping to his sides. With a roll of his shoulders, his tight expression disappeared.

Just like that, the elegant, careless playboy prince was back, leaving her nerves singing, stretched tight by desire . . . and frustration. God, she'd wanted that damn kiss.

"That's right," he finally said, his voice cool. "You don't know me at all."

And then he turned and strode out of the cottage, clearly communicating that he didn't give a flying fig if she ever would.

"Hell," she whispered to herself, her skin still throbbing where his hands had been on her. She'd got up that morning thinking her biggest dilemma was getting out of involvement in Emerson's wedding, but now she thought a greater problem might be in *for*getting—about the disturbing and dangerous Prince Jack Parini.

~

Jack Parini had sworn to himself he wouldn't say a word, but only a mile had passed before he turned to his former college roommate and current running partner. "Tell me everything you know about Stephania Baci."

Liam Bennett shot him a look, the beginning of a smile curving his mouth, though his footsteps didn't falter as they traveled at a steady pace along the rural lane. "Woman trouble on the first morning of the new year, Jack? I should have figured you had a reason for rousting me for a run besides working off your ugly beer gut."

"It's too bad the five miles won't do a thing about your creeping bald spot," he shot back, glancing at his friend's full head of hair.

"Is that any way to talk to the person you're trying to pump information from?"

"Forget it," Jack said, not sure which annoyed him more, his own weakness or Liam's amusement at his expense.

"It's especially funny," the other man continued, "because Stevie Baci called just thirty minutes ago and put to me that exact same question."

"Odd." Jack feigned puzzlement. "You'd think she'd know all about herself."

"Ha ha. Of course I mean she asked about you."

"Ah." He dropped behind Liam as a truck passed. "What did you say?"

It came out casual, barely interested, which was exactly how he felt. A decade ago, he'd stopped giving a rat's ass what other people thought about him, up to and including most of his family. Ugly gossip, whispered innuendo, and a notorious reputation followed wherever he went, and he didn't bother anymore with dodges or corrections. Hell, some of it was deserved.

For example, he couldn't deny how offhand he generally treated the XX half of the population—which made his keen curiosity about Stephania Baci perplexing. Something about that woman got under his skin. Of course, there were those coltish legs. The spectacular ass. And she had an interesting, angled face with soft hair that curved around her jawline to brush her slim neck. Her mouth couldn't be overlooked, not with those full, rose-colored lips that just begged for attention.

Definitely the mouth.

For all I know you're a thief, a murderer, a kidnapper.

He felt himself tense. "What exactly did you tell her about me?" he asked again, his voice sharper this time.

His friend glanced over, and there might have been a touch of sympathy in the look, which Jack didn't appreciate. He didn't goddamn need it.

"Nothing much," Liam said. "That you're sixth in line for the Ardenian throne—"

"Seventh," Jack cut in. "My oldest brother has another baby." Their father had three sons by his first wife, Nadia. She'd died two years before Jack's mother, Rayette June Crawford, a beauty queen from Fiddlecreek, Georgia, had traveled to Ardenia with a passel of her pageant buddies. The king had spotted the Miss Peaches & Pralines during her tour of the family's castle in the capital city.

What Wilhelm wanted, Wilhelm expected to get, a trait he'd passed on to each of his children. Jack didn't know what he and his sister, Roxy, had inherited from their mother. Perhaps the ability to offer a bless-your-heart smile while simultaneously wishing the recipient would roast in hell.

"Anything else?" he asked.

They came to a crossroads and he followed his friend to the right, toward the town of Edenville. They weren't on a main road, but he had a good sense of direction. Even without one, it was hard to get lost in the Napa Valley, what with the Mayacama Mountains on the western side and the Vaca Mountains to the east. All around them, though, were vineyards. At this time of year, despite their sheer numbers, the vines looked almost . . . lonely without the adornment of foliage or fruit.

In a few weeks, he remembered, wild mustard plants would add their splash of golden yellow between the rows. But now there was nothing but the stark beauty of the sleeping vines.

He was lagging behind his running buddy and his legs protested the burst of speed necessary to catch up. "Too much time at a desk," he commented, coming shoulder-to-shoulder with Liam once more.

"I mentioned that to Stevie. That you've spent the last ten years doing anything but winemaking."

In Jack's college years, when he'd first met the Bennetts, he'd intended to work in the family's Ardenian vineyards post-graduation. It was all he'd ever wanted. "I won't ever go back to Ardenia," he had said.

Though after a couple of years of near self-destruction while partying in various European capitals, he'd woken up with one hangover too many and decided to halt the nonstop clubbing and get an actual job. Even then, though, he'd bounced around Paris, Brussels, New York, and finally Atlanta, working with numbers, of all the crazy-ass things.

"Yeah, but that doesn't mean you need to stare at spreadsheets for the rest of your life."

Jack shrugged. "I quit my last job. I'll figure out the next thing after Roxy's wedding."

"I told Stevie that, too." Liam wiped the sweat from his forehead with the sleeve of his faded Aggies sweatshirt. "There's no more devoted older brother than you."

Jack released a short laugh. "You know I'm no saint," he answered, deciding that he needed to put in more miles each week, if after a mere twenty minutes his chest felt tight. "I owe my sister, big."

Which was why, when he'd picked up on her concern about Stevie's involvement with the upcoming wedding, he'd gone on instant alert. It had only taken a probing question or two to uncover the source of her disquiet—the other woman was Emerson's ex. "You know why I'll do anything to ensure Roxy's happiness."

"What's going to make *you* happy, Jack?"

He ignored the question because he figured a full night's sleep was as elusive as a cessation to the grinding guilt that still wore away at him. And years ago he'd given up on finding someone who'd unconditionally believe in him.

"Jack?" Liam prodded.

"What makes me happy never changes," he said, a bullshit answer sliding out smoothly. "A good bottle of cab and a hot chick."

Which had him thinking of Stevie Baci again—and this time he let himself, because why not indulge in the pleasant distraction? That's what women were to him. He imagined a fire, glasses of ruby red liquid, her slender body wrapped in a silky robe and nothing else. When she sipped her wine, a drop would cling to her bottom lip and he'd lower his head to lick it from her mouth . . .

The toot of a car horn startled him from his fantasy and he stumbled, nearly falling into the path of a second car. "What the hell . . . ?"

"Your brother-in-law to be," Liam said. "That a new BMW he's driving?"

"Yeah." He gazed after the sleek model speeding away.

"Emerson seems to have a short attention span when it comes to cars . . ." Which brought him right back to Stevie. The truth was, he had a perfectly legit reason for asking Liam about her. She'd been the woman on Emerson Platt's arm before the man had fallen for Jack's little sister. And that past history should be his sole focus, because really, it was ridiculous to pursue a woman who'd taken a dislike of him. When it came to sex, he didn't like to work that hard.

Still, he aroused her as much as she did him, though she would be unwilling to admit it, he was sure. There was only so much she could hide, however. With his hands on her he'd seen the heat of want in her eyes and that exciting thrum of her pulse against the thin skin of her throat.

Anger had been coursing through him at the time, but still he'd wanted to bend his head and soothe that flustered beat with his tongue. Or use his mouth to make a mark there, just because he could. Because he knew, despite herself, she'd let him.

Merde. There he went again, pondering the woman's prickly, sexy appeal, when instead he should only be considering the threat to his sister's wedding plans if Stevie got it into her head to go ex-girlfriend on Emerson during the next few weeks.

So find another focus, Jack, he warned himself, staring down at his running shoes.

That's when he plowed into Liam.

He lurched back to keep his balance, blaming the brunette dominating his thoughts. "Damn woman," he muttered.

"What's that?"

"Doesn't matter," he muttered again. She was gone. Out of his head.

"I just bought this," Liam said. "What do you think?"

Jack looked around, orienting himself. The lane they'd been running on had T'd into the two-lane highway that bordered the eastern mountains of the valley. Another quarter mile along it and they'd meet the turnoff to the main street of Edenville's small downtown.

Here, though, was the seam between farmland and commercial enterprise. On the other side of the road was a gathering of utilitarian structures: a car repair service, some anonymous corrugated metal buildings, a stand of no-frill duplexes, while where he and Liam stood was a small, established vineyard.

Small? Established? It was postage stamp–sized, really, maybe two acres, and it was obvious that the fall's fruit hadn't been harvested. The detritus of untended grapes and withered leaves lay at the base of the vines in graying heaps.

He shot a look at his friend. "You bought this? Why?"

Liam shrugged. "The old man who owned it died last year and it finally came up for sale. I admired what he was trying to do—develop an artisan cabernet sauvignon from a single small vineyard."

"It's the size of my fingernail." Not to mention one hell of a mess.

"Makes it more of a challenge, don't you think?"

Jack looked back at Liam. The Bennetts ran a successful large winery and had other thriving business concerns as well. "You're serious? You're going to make a boutique wine?"

"Thinking about it." He reached into the pouch of his sweatshirt to withdraw a set of keys, and tossed them to Jack. "Why don't you look around, give me your opinion."

"I haven't had anything to do with winemaking since college graduation," he protested.

"A good reason to start small."

Jack looked down at the keys in his hand. "And these are to?"

Liam pointed to a building on the far side of the vines. Jack laughed. "A castle?" Because that was its style, complete with battlements, though it wasn't any bigger than a small family home.

"The winery. Old Arnie had his quirks."

Still staring at the stone building, Jack felt Liam turn away. "What are you doing?"

"I've got to get back. Take your time. Look around."

"You're just going to leave me here by myself?"

"If you want company, you can always take a stroll across the street," Liam answered, nodding toward the structures across the way. Then he jogged off in the opposite direction.

Something told Jack not to look. But he didn't hold out any longer than he'd held out asking about Stevie Baci two and a half miles back.

She was there. He caught a glimpse of her in the space between two metal buildings, where a gleaming black limo sat, the driver's door open. Changing his position gave him a better view. With her back to him and one foot on the running board, the woman he'd banished from his thoughts leaned across the roof, rubbing a cloth along the lacquered finish. The breeze shifted and he figured she had the stereo playing because he heard Def Leppard's heavy metal libido-stirrer, "Pour Some Sugar on Me."

She still wore those red rubber boots over her skin-tight jeans, but the sweater was gone, replaced by a form-hugging blue T-shirt. The hem of it rode up as she leaned farther over the top of the car, baring that sweet spot between her waist and a low-riding band of denim.

Had he mentioned skin-tight jeans?

She was a concern. A possible threat to his sister's future—no matter that she denied it. But also a hot, sweet temptation that with each passing moment buried itself deeper beneath his skin.

And there was nothing the least bit legitimate—or even casual—about the way his palms itched to slide along the curve of her perfect—perfectly naked—ass.

3

The first day of the new year was well into the afternoon when Stevie ran her older sister, Giuliana, to ground. Even then, it took recognizing Jules's spill of dark hair. The flowing mass obscured her face as she sat with her head cradled on her forearms at a corner table in one of Edenville's many coffee bars. In the Napa Valley, places that doled out caffeine had nearly as high a per-capita rate as those that poured wine every day from eleven A.M. to four P.M.

Her sister's rag-doll pose halted Stevie for a moment, but then she made herself march forward. It was absolutely imperative to confront Jules about her promise to Emerson and his bride-to-be. Her sister *must* agree that someone else take charge of the upcoming wedding.

Stevie yanked out a chair, and the loud screech of legs against the floor caused Jules to jerk. Her head slowly rose.

"Ooh." Stevie winced. The greenish pallor and heavy-lidded gaze were not a normal Jules appearance. "You must have tied one on last night, huh?"

Which was only odder. The oldest Baci sibling rarely let anything get the best of her.

Sinking into the seat opposite, Stevie nudged the large latté mug on the table closer to her sister's lifeless hand. "We need to talk."

Jules's head dropped back to her arms. "Not now," she mumbled.

"Giuliana—"

"Go 'way." Her fingers twitched in a slight shooing motion. "Later."

Except there was no time like the present, Stevie decided. Jules in the vulnerable state of hangover might be easier to reason with. Better yet, she might quickly accede to Stevie's demands just to get rid of her.

"This will only take a minute," she started, then broke off when a large body slid onto the chair beside her sister. Her jaw dropped. "Kohl?"

With a light touch, startling from a guy who was over six feet of wide shoulders and muscled thighs, he tucked Jules's hair behind her ear. "A scone," he said, his usual growl of a voice soft. His eyes were only for the near-comatose woman. "You need to eat something," he told her, placing a thick plate on the table.

Stevie stared. Kohl Friday was the vineyard manager at the family winery. An Iraq War veteran, since his return to civilian life he'd been most notable for his deep silences and more-than-occasional barroom brawls. He'd been a hothead since childhood—who could blame him after being saddled with the first name Kohlrabi by his hippie parents?—but lately you could practically hear his personal time-bomb ticking.

Yet now he seemed . . . tender toward Jules.

"C'mon, honey," he urged.

Honey? Stevie shook herself as her sister once again lifted her head. This time Jules straightened to a sit, and then managed to bring the latté mug to her lips.

"Good," Kohl said in quiet approval. "Now a little food."

She was chewing her second bite when Stevie got over her surprise enough to remember her purpose. "Look, Jules," she said, "we need to have a conversation."

The new Kohl sent her an old-Kohl dark look. "She's not up to a talk."

Okay, she'd known him all her life and he was the older sibling of her good friends Mari and Zinnia, but he wasn't *her* big brother. Not to mention that Stevie had resolved that men were not going to impact her in the new year. "This is between me and Jules, and—"

A phone trilled. Giuliana fumbled in the kangaroo pouch of her hoodie and yanked out her cell. "Allie," she murmured, staring at the screen. With a toss, she passed the phone to Stevie.

"Hey!" she started to protest, then subsided. The fact was, the situation involved Stevie, Jules, *and* Allie. Surely her younger sister would side with her on this issue.

It took a few minutes to get an update on her sister's condition. Allie's husband Penn had already reported on the success of the day before's surgery, but it was good to hear Alessandra's own voice. She sounded remarkably chipper, but since her marriage, she'd been almost annoyingly happy. Her mood dipped, though, when Stevie played snitch and said their older sister was hungover with a capital *H*.

"Jules?" Allie's voice sharpened. "Our family paragon?"

"Yep." Though she understood her sister's doubt. Since birth, Giuliana had been the proverbial perfect child, just as Allie had always been the pampered baby sister.

Leaving Stevie relegated to the role of family screw-up.

Their mother's voice echoed in her head.

Can't you keep clean for five minutes?

Lower your voice, Stephania.

Boys want soft, sweet girls.

Pushing the old memories out of her head, she refocused on the present. "But that's beside the point. The real problem is, Allie, that our sister told Emerson and his fiancée that *I* would take over your wedding duties."

There was a moment of silence on the line, then a quiet sigh. "Well, who else is there?"

Panic washed heat over Stevie's skin. "Who else? Anyone else but me!"

Another sigh. "I feel terrible that I can't do it, but the doctor says—"

"Not you," she interrupted, feeling guilty. "And no need to apologize. But Jules could . . ." She let the words die away as she glanced over at her sister, with her ghastly complexion and exhausted eyes.

"She's running the vineyard," Allie reminded her. "All the administrative tasks, including inventory and supplies, overseeing payroll, keeping the wine club going. While you are—"

"Don't say it," Stevie said, guilty all over again. She wasn't doing anything for the one-hundred-year-old Tanti Baci winery. Alessandra had been in charge of the PR end for years, and after their father died, Giuliana had returned from Southern California to take over his duties. While Stevie . . . In the past few months, Stevie had contributed exactly zero beyond pouring wine at the occasional tasting. The rest of the time she worked exclusively at her own business, Napa Princess Limousine.

Which was in its fallow season.

"Don't make me do it," she whispered.

Allie's voice filled with sympathy. "I know you don't want to deal with Emerson."

"It's not him."

"No? Then what? Who?"

Jack. His name popped into her head. *He* popped into her head, his handsome face, his elegant body, the way his touch made her toes curl in feminine surrender and her fingers into defensive fists. *Mon ange*, he'd called her. *My angel.*

That devil.

That dangerous devil.

"Never mind," she said, dropping her forehead to the

heel of her hand. Stephania Baci liked nothing less than the smell of defeat, but right now it had the scent of fair trade coffee beans. Her voice sounded as miserable as she felt. "Don't worry about anything. Just get well and—"

"I'll take care of the wedding."

Stevie lifted her head to look at the Corpse that Spoke, aka Giuliana. "What? Wait . . ." She took a minute to end the conversation with Allie, promising to call later, then studied her older sister from across the table, trying not to let her hopes rise too high. "What did you just say?"

Jules appeared marginally better. She patted Kohl's hand as he tried to ply her with another piece of scone. "I'm fine," she told him, then met Stevie's gaze. "And I'm sorry. I didn't see another way at the time."

"There *isn't* another way," Kohl said, his voice firm. "You've got too much on your plate already, Jules."

She ignored him. "I'll juggle one or two things, and—"

"I'll do those one or two things," Stevie offered quickly. "I can take over the . . . the . . ." Her mind went blank.

Kohl frowned. "You've never been involved in the winery business. You can't take over your sister's responsibilities."

"Sure I can." Though she couldn't actually discuss her sister's responsibilities with any specificity.

His eyebrows drew together. "Stevie—"

Jules put her hand on his arm to quiet him. "Shh. We'll figure it out later."

"Now. We'll figure it out right this minute," Stevie said. It would assuage her guilt if they nailed down the details immediately.

"All right," Jules agreed. She leaned forward, both elbows on the table as Kohl kneaded her shoulders with one big hand. She let out a little moan. "Oh, that's wonderful."

"Wonderful" summed it up for Stevie as well. Once they hashed this through, she would call Emerson personally and inform him of the altered arrangement, ensuring the new year would begin just as she'd meant it to.

Free of men.

"What the hell are you doing, Friday?" a low voice demanded.

A low, *male* voice—and a definite bad omen. Without looking up, she groaned to herself. Why did Liam Bennett, long-time neighbor and Jules's personal nemesis, have to show up now?

Stevie glanced over her shoulder, taking in the set of his jaw and the way he was focused on Kohl's hand on her sister's body.

"So you *did* get her drunk last night," Liam accused the other man.

Kohl stiffened. "I—"

"It's none of your damn business what Kohl and I did last night," Jules said, a flush of pink on her cheeks chasing away the last of her pallor.

"I was talking to Friday and not to you," he snapped, sparing her the briefest of blazing glances.

"You were talking *about* me," she retorted, jumping to her feet. "And I won't have it."

Liam stared down his nose at her. "You've never been able to stop me. From anything."

Jules's face went redder, then the color leached away. She swayed.

Uh-oh, Stevie thought, half-rising.

But her sister's spine steeled. "Including from becoming an icy-hearted robot."

And with that, she stormed out of the café, Kohl following in her wake. Three seconds of silence passed, then, muttering an oath, Liam shoved his hands through his dark blond hair and exited himself, turning in the opposite direction of the vineyard manager and Stevie's sister.

"Okay, then," she murmured, dropping her head to her arms, mimicking Jules's earlier sprawl. It seemed a fine way to sit when absorbing the depressing realization that the only thing she'd gotten out of the brief meeting was an abandoned latté and a bad feeling about a love triangle in the making.

~

After her frustrating day, Stevie looked forward to the evening. It was her turn to host poker and darts night, and surely the event would put her in a better mood. A few hours of relaxation might even aid in figuring out her next step in untangling herself from the wedding business.

While the early arrivals congregated by the beverage tub stocked with ice and beers on the narrow sideboard in the duplex's dining alcove, she set out the deli meats, breads, and chips. The first guy she'd ever punched—Ben Copeland, first grade, for trying to steal her bag of homemade snickerdoodles—was talking.

"So then the farmer's daughter took the bull by the horns and—"

She grabbed a sourdough roll from the pile and threw it, bouncing it off Ben's forehead.

"Hey!" He turned to her in surprise. "What's gotten into you?"

"The joke?"

He continued staring at her, wearing a befuddled expression, looking just as he had when her fist had met his solar plexus that day by the swings.

She huffed. "I can see the punch line that's coming, okay? It's not appropriate for mixed company." When his eyebrows rose in continued bewilderment, she huffed again. "Ben, I'm a girl."

"Oooh." The light dawned over his face. Then his gaze slid down her figure. "Wow, I think you're right."

She promised herself she wasn't blushing. Still, her face felt hot as she noticed the other guests—J.D. and Chuck— were now also staring. Maybe she shouldn't have worn the new bad-girl boots. Or the thin, pale-pink wrap sweater that she'd been given by Allie and Penn that V'd so low in front. Or her favorite dark jeans, which were just a smidge tighter after all the holiday dinners, parties, and Christmas cookies.

"Double wow," J.D. agreed, his focus on her cleavage. "You look, um, different."

Chuck cleared his throat. "You clean up real good, Stevie. Why don't you always dress like that?"

Face definitely burning now, she marched into the kitchen in order to get away from them and the knowledge that she usually wore her jeans with the ripped knees and a sweatshirt with bleach stains on poker and darts night. There, she leaned against the countertop and massaged her temples. What had prompted her to change her uniform? With Emerson's wedding in the offing, now was not the time to appear different in any way. It was important to assure everyone—including herself—that she was her usual, tough, tomboy self.

Instead of returning to the party, she exited the kitchen and rushed to her bedroom. Her favorite jeans were a little tight, too, but she did a few deep knee bends after yanking black sheepskin Uggs onto her feet. Though her lucky sweatshirt was in the laundry basket, she replaced the feminine sweater with a waffle-weave Henley as dark as her boots. It was securely buttoned to her throat.

That the guys didn't notice the costume switch made her breathe easier. It put her in such a light mood that she slid a double batch of the pizza rolls that were Ben's favorite into the oven. "I'm almost done here," she yelled from the kitchen toward the dining table where they played cards. "Go ahead and deal 'em up. I'll be out in a second."

J.D. stuck his head into the room. "Let's wait for the Bennetts."

Stevie froze, her hands stuck inside lobster-shaped oven mitts. "I thought they weren't coming tonight. They . . . they have a house guest."

Jack Parini. Why couldn't she stop thinking about him? And why did the thought of him at the party make her regret changing from the pretty-in-pink sweater to the funereal black Henley?

"They're coming." At the sound of the doorbell, J.D. grinned at her. "Bet that's them," he said, disappearing from sight.

Stevie pressed the quilted lobsters belly-to-belly and breathed deeply as if in the yoga class her friend Mari always encouraged her to attend. *Don't rush out there*, she told herself. *And don't let Jack Parini see how he makes you anxious.*

"Hey, Stevie," a man said, stepping into the kitchen.

Shrieking in surprise, she jumped, pressing the orange mitts to her heart.

Seth Bennett, Liam's younger brother, stopped short. "Geez, Steve. Are you all right?"

"I'm fine." She scowled at him. He was wearing his lucky poker duds, too, and his blond and blue-eyed good looks were enhanced by the pale blue polo that had "Boalt Law" embroidered on the chest. The salsa stain on the sleeve from the time J.D. dumped the bowl over his winning seven-high hand barely showed. Seth was the best bluffer of them all.

"Then why so jumpy?"

Her own poker face had definitely slipped. "I told you, I'm fine." She turned away to pull the cookie sheets from the oven. "I just didn't expect to see you, Liam, and Jack tonight, that's all."

"Jack didn't come with us," Seth said.

"Oh." And at that her traitorous mind was on its own again, wondering just exactly who he *was* with tonight. Likely some other woman, one comfortable in pink sweaters and around men who called them *mon ange* with the all-smooth self-assurance of a . . . of a European prince.

She could still hear the words in his lowered voice, the phrase holding both a hint of humor and a larger dose of let's-keep-this-light. Last night in the limo, he'd been serious about not taking anything seriously.

Yet that composure had fallen away in the cottage this morning. He'd jerked her up against him, his fingers tight on her shoulders, his hard belly pressed against hers, the tips of her breasts brushing his chest with each of her unsteady breaths.

Thinking about it now made her hot. Beset once more by that instantaneous, surprising, confusing desire. Instinct told her that to get back to normal she had to never touch, smell, or share space with Jack Parini ever again.

". . . definitely not yourself," Seth was saying.

"What?" She forced her focus on him, feeling annoyed. "I don't know why you'd say that."

He laughed. "There's a reason you drop forty bucks every two weeks. You bluff for shit, Steve."

Her frown deepened. "Sometimes I win."

"Only because J.D. can never remember if a flush beats a straight or vice versa." He leaned against the countertop and crossed his arms over his chest. "But the giveaway tonight was the fact that I just told you about the key and you didn't blink."

"What key?"

"See, you weren't listening at all. I found an old key in a safe deposit box. We're still uncovering stuff since Dad's death." He grimaced. "Though this seems like something he'd forgotten about, not a secret he'd been keeping, like . . ."

He didn't need to finish that sentence for her. Calvin Bennett had died of a sudden heart attack six months before her own father. After his death, the fact that he'd fathered two illegitimate children had come to light. A son, Penn, who had met and married Allie during his first visit to his half siblings. There was a daughter whose whereabouts remained unknown.

"It's an old-looking skeleton key attached to a tag that reads 'Baci.'" He wiggled his eyebrows. "Maybe it's a key to the treasure."

She stared at Seth, aware he was teasing but still jolted by the thought. "Why would your family have it after all this time?"

"Don't know." Seth shook his head. "Don't really know what it opens."

"Still . . ." Stevie swallowed, wondering if it could possibly be part of the Anne-Alonzo-Liam legend. All her life she'd been enthralled by the stories of the three, of the treasure and of the decision the society debutante had made to marry the scrappy immigrant instead of the well-connected rich guy. Smart girl. According to her father, the spirit of Anne and Alonzo's great love affair survived beyond the grave.

"Seth . . . have you ever, even for a second, wondered if the legend of the treasure and the ghost story are true?"

He laughed. "If I didn't think you'd take me down for it, I'd say you have the goofiest—and biggest—sentimental streak in Napa Valley."

Embarrassed, she turned away to fuss with the pizza rolls. "Forget I said anything," she muttered.

"I didn't say I don't believe in ghosts. I didn't say there definitely isn't a treasure."

Stevie didn't look up from the platter she was arranging. "So you believe the treasure's real?"

"Real?" Seth asked. "Well, I don't— Hey, Jack."

Huh? Stevie thought. What did *I don't heyjack* mean?

And then she knew exactly what it meant, because her skin prickled in that predators-in-the-proximity manner it did around only one person. One man.

Jack. On a deep breath, the faintest note of his expensive scent entered her lungs.

"Hey, back," she heard him say to Seth. "What's this about a treasure?"

Stevie stayed turned away. There was no need for her to look at Jack or to answer him. She shouldn't do either if she wanted to appear normal. To *be* normal.

Damn it, she *was* normal, she thought, cursing her reluctance. Stevie Baci. Tough girl.

And then Seth stepped up to the plate, thank God. "We told you how the original owners of Tanti Baci, Alonzo and

Liam, had a falling out over Anne. But there are those who say that argument was aggravated by some silver that went missing—the last load from their mine."

"Yeah? Raw ore?" Jack asked.

"Or maybe it was crafted into some sterling pieces or perhaps a set of silver and gold diamond-encrusted jewelry. Take your pick." Seth added, "In any case, even though it went missing, the rumors persisted. Every now and then we still catch people—kids usually—with shovels and flashlights digging holes around the property."

"I'm not surprised," Jack said. "Hidden treasure . . . hard to get more romantic than that."

"Unless it's ghosts," Seth said. "Stevie's the expert on that Baci legend."

His death, she promised herself, would be as slow as the heat crawling up the back of her neck. "Shut up, Seth." She used her most pleasant voice.

"Keep talking, Seth," Jack countered.

"Not me," the other man replied. "I want to live to taste my first beer of the evening. I'll leave you to persuade the lady."

The rat left the kitchen.

His royal friend didn't.

She sensed him drawing closer, but she kept arranging and rearranging the stupid pizza rolls on the platter as if it were a Rubik's Cube. Then Jack touched the back of her arm.

Her hand jerked. Hors d'oeuvres scattered.

Holding the tongs like a weapon, she whirled to face him.

Wearing a rueful smile, he lifted his hands in surrender. "Honest, officer, I didn't mean to startle you." He wore that charming smile. It was the *mon-ange* Jack who stood before her now, the one who wasn't serious about anything.

Still, it was a struggle to control her breathing, and her self-consciousness grew. While she had on her ratty poker duds, Jack Parini wore a slick pair of dressy jeans and a tissue-thin white shirt with buttoned pockets. He'd rolled up the sleeves to reveal hair-dusted forearms.

"My mind was elsewhere," she lied, hoping it would cover her extreme reaction.

"On those ghosts perhaps?"

She was shaking her head before he'd finished. "Seth was just joking around."

"About . . . ?"

Oh, what did it matter? "My dad told us a story when we were kids." She sidestepped to put a little more distance between herself and the prince and refused to believe she was blushing again. "If you bring your true love to the cottage, the ghosts of Anne and Alonzo will appear."

"Ah, damn." Jack snapped his fingers. "There goes that dream."

"What?"

"You. Me. We were there this morning, and unless you're accustomed to seeing specters and so didn't react, I'm guessing neither one of us had a sighting." He shook his head as if in regret. "Meaning no true love."

She rolled her eyes. "Like you were hoping."

"*Bien sûr, mon ange*. I'm a man full of hope."

She wouldn't let the French get to her. "Full of something anyway."

He laughed, then stepped closer to run the back of one knuckle down her cheek. "You look overheated."

"I had the oven on. Making stuff for poker and darts night."

"Yeah." He let his hand drop, then nodded toward the dining room. "Nice men out there."

"Good friends." J.D. worked at the local grocery store and Ben was trying to make a go of a tire business. Chuck was a landscaper. "Maybe not up to your flashy standards, but—"

"I said they were nice. And worried about you, by the way."

The distraction of him still so close made it take a few

moments for his words to sink in. "What? They don't worry about me."

"It's the upcoming wedding. They don't like seeing you upset by it."

Her spine went rigid. "I'm not upset by it!" This civic pity party was supposed to have ended with her New Year's evening of chauffeuring. "Didn't I drive him and his princess bri—your sister around all last night?"

Jack shrugged. "Don't tell me, I'm just reporting. From what they said, though, it seems the whole town is certain your ex's nuptial event has shaken you up."

Her fingers curled into fists. "Who said that? I'll shake *them* up. I'm perfectly fine, damn it. Not affected by the wedding. No threat to your sister's big day. *Perfectly fine.*"

"Has anyone ever mentioned you're a terrible bluffer?"

"Never." She muttered the lie.

He grinned. "Oh, baby, I can't wait to play with you."

Her face flamed and her gaze shot to his.

"Play poker." His grin widened. "Damn, I was right. You're fun."

She wasn't fun. She was tough. Strong. Full of pride. And this stupid rumor that she was pining over Emerson Platt had to stop.

She could think of only one sure way to make that happen. Closing her eyes, Stevie inhaled a deep, calming breath. The single thing she couldn't stand more than the edgy way she felt around Jack Parini was the idea that people pitied her. So . . .

"Monday. Nine A.M., at the Tanti Baci winery," she said. "You, Emerson, and your sister need to be there to go over the details of those end-of-the-month I dos with the event coordinator."

Taking another deep breath, she leapt. "Who is me."

"I wish you'd reconsider," Jack said, watching his sister pace the small room they'd been shown into at the Tanti Baci administrative offices. She'd nagged him into leaving for the appointment fifteen minutes too early, so it was no surprise that Stevie hadn't yet arrived, nor the groom, who was stopping in at the headquarters of his commercial real estate business before the meeting.

"Reconsider what?" Roxy asked.

"There was no reason to rush into marriage. How long have you known this guy again?"

She paused, a stubborn expression coming over her face before she restarted her prowl of the room. "It's irrelevant. The moment I realized I was in love with him, I decided I had to reach for my future happiness with both hands."

Jack shifted in his chair, his sister's conviction making him uneasy. Eleven months ago she'd been a mouse, quietly going about her life working for a San Francisco nonprofit. Then . . .

But he didn't want to think about that. He only had to

deal with the repercussions—which were that his sister had set her sights on Emerson Platt and was now engaged to marry the man.

He frowned at her. "Well, at least you and Emerson should choose a different location for your wedding." Taking into account her nervousness over Stevie's involvement and despite Stevie's denials, it only made sense.

Roxy paused a second time. "Are you kidding? The invitations have already gone out."

"I'm serious." It was such a simple solution, he should have suggested it the moment he understood it was Emerson's ex who would be in charge of the event. "Look at you, you can't sit still."

The room's square footage was made even smaller by what it held: desk, trio of visitors' chairs, and open shelving that displayed some photographs and a collection of bride and groom figurines that must have once sat atop wedding cakes. Yet Roxy had found a path that took her from the shelving to a window and then back again. And again.

"Just change the wedding and reception to some other place," he urged.

"Jack, it's not just the invitations. Venues fill up months in advance." She spoke to him even as she was moving again. "In some cases, years. We were able to book the winery at such short notice because of the season and because it's newly opened for events."

"Oh." He watched her stop in front of the shelves and her hand reached toward one of the small bridal couples. In a casual move, he rose from his chair and joined her. Roxy's arm dropped and he pretended it was a photograph that had drawn him to her side. "I guess those are the Baci girls," he said.

He didn't need Roxy to confirm, because the answer was obvious. All seemingly aged under ten, they shared the shot with a kiddie pool filled with grapes. The smallest sister, curly-haired, stood in the center holding up the hem of her dress as she smiled at the camera. The oldest girl had a hand on her littlest sister's shoulder as if to steady her.

And then there was Stevie.

Jack had to bite back his grin. The photographer had caught her mid-jump. She looked as if she'd cannonballed into the grapes a few times already. There was juice staining her feet and ankles below rolled-up jeans. Her dark hair was floating around her and it was certainly more smushed grapes smeared along one cheek. Unlike her sisters, she wasn't looking at the camera. Instead, her gaze was on a dark-haired woman standing to the side, as if she'd just come upon the scene. Stevie's small face was stamped with guilt.

"That has to be Stevie's mother," Roxy said.

"Yeah." The resemblance was remarkable. She'd grown up to be as beautiful as the woman who had given her birth. And, God, yeah, Stevie *was* beautiful. He couldn't decide what attracted him more, though: her brash bluster or her long-legged body. Every time he told himself to stay clear of her, she'd show him another side—a distinct lack of talent for poker, a surprising ability at darts—that drew him closer despite himself.

"You like her."

Jack turned his head to look at Roxy. She was stroking a fingertip over the filmy veil on one of the toy-sized brides, her expression tense. Yeah, he wasn't wrong about Stevie's involvement making his sister anxious. His gut clenched. "Rox, don't have the wedding here."

"I have to."

"No, you don't. Move it. Move the whole damn thing to Ardenia."

"Papa—"

"Will pay whatever it takes, you know that." He regretted the words the moment they left his mouth. The memories they evoked . . .

Roxy put her hand on his arm and he knew she'd followed the dark train of his thoughts. "Jack. Imagine this instead. At the castle in Ardenia, Mom in charge of my wedding."

He groaned. "*Gone with the Wind* meets a Disney princess movie premiere." There'd be parasols and diamond-studded crowns. Southern food, elephant processionals, and probably seven dwarves, too. His mother had never met an excess she'd didn't like, and the thought of that was enough to make even a bystander shudder. "Okay, maybe you are better off with Stevie."

"I think so," Roxy agreed. "Despite the fact that she and Emerson share a past. I should be able to handle that. I *can* handle that." Then his sister hugged herself, and she resembled once more that little mouse she'd become a decade ago.

It shredded his gut. He hated seeing Roxy doubt herself or the man she'd fallen in love with. He'd kill Emerson if he hurt her. And as for Emerson's ex . . . Well, this was a guarantee he could make. "Don't worry about Stevie. I'll handle her."

At those words, the woman herself crossed the threshold of the room. He stepped back in surprise, his shoulder hitting the lowest shelf, sending one of the bridal sets to the floor. Roxy bent to pick it up as he stared at Stevie. She'd found yet another way to surprise him.

She was dressed in black again, high-heeled boots, black tights, a scrap of a black skirt, but on top of that was a powder-pink, skin-tight sweater that made her flesh look pearly and that highlighted cleavage he hadn't anticipated with those boyishly long legs and slender hips.

She'd been hiding full breasts beneath oversized sweaters and tailored shirts. *I'll handle her.*

Christ, he'd just promised that.

The wary glance she shot him as she strode toward the desk made clear that the task wasn't going to be easy. From their first meeting, she'd resisted the idea that he'd be sticking close.

Emerson rushed in next. He went directly to Roxy,

brushing a kiss against her cheek. She smiled, relaxing a little, and then her fiancé leaned across the desk to bestow the same chaste caress on the wedding coordinator.

Jack stiffened, though he noted that Stevie herself didn't react, appearing as unruffled as if her ex's lips on her skin was an everyday occurrence. Hell . . .

What if it was?

At the thought, his muscles tightened and a white-hot spear jabbed his gut. It felt like—anger. Yeah, that was the name of the emotion. It made him mad as hell to be wondering if his sister's fiancé was keeping his options open.

Or still had Stevie on the side.

The flame in his belly crawled up his back and he stomped to one of the free chairs and yanked it closer to her desk. Then he sat. "Let's get this show on the road."

Stevie shot him a look. "Emerson and your sister and I can do this alone. You don't have to—"

"Thorn on your rose," he reminded her.

Her eyes narrowed. "Fly in my champagne."

"Exactly."

The bride and groom took the other two chairs as Stevie opened a folder on the desk, then cleared her throat. "I spoke with Allie first thing this morning and I don't see any looming problems—"

"My mother," Emerson put in.

Stevie continued as if he hadn't spoken. "—except Emerson's mother." Her gaze met her ex's, and they shared a quiet laugh.

The intimacy of the moment rankled. Jack edged his chair closer to the desk. "What does Senator Platt have to do with my sister's wedding?"

"Jack," Roxy started, her voice soft. "Remember there are two involved in this marriage."

"As long as it's only two," he muttered.

Stevie was giving him another of her wary looks. "Though this is Roxy and Emerson's big day, his mother is hosting the rehearsal dinner the night before in the Tanti Baci wine caves."

Dark. Dank. "Perfect."

One of Roxy's hands crept into the pocket of the faux fur–edged jacket she wore as her gaze cut to Jack. "Maybe I should talk to her," she said nervously. "Maybe there's another location . . ."

"You'll like this one," Stevie said. "It's different than you're thinking. Very atmospheric. Romantic."

Emerson laughed. "Steve, remember a couple of years ago when we stumbled across J.D. and the waitress he was dating in that hidden alcove? We thought we were the only ones who knew of it and were—" He broke off, glancing at Roxy.

Though a red flush crawled up her neck, Stevie acted as if her ex hadn't spoken—and spoken of some private moment they'd obviously been pursuing themselves. "There's a beautiful burl wood and walnut table that seats thirty comfortably. We can squeeze a few more in, if necessary."

Jack wanted to squeeze someone's throat. Emerson and Stevie's past history only became more problematic by the passing hour. It made his sister doubt her standing, it made the prospect of the next few weeks torturous, it . . .

Fine. For whatever reason, it made Jack crazy to think of the dark-eyed beauty involved with anyone but him.

I'll handle her.

Hell, yes, he wanted to. He really wanted to.

Making a lap of the room as the wedding couple and coordinator discussed some further details didn't cool his mood. He ended up leaning against the credenza behind Stevie's seat at the desk, and she kept glancing back at him.

As Emerson and Roxy studied some paperwork, he reached past Stevie to pluck a pen off her work space. His arm brushed hers, and she jumped. Then he grabbed her hand. She resisted, as he knew she would, but he held firm.

Turned up her vulnerable palm.

Slowly etched his cell phone number there, as if it was foreplay.

It was, of course. He'd said from the beginning that he was sticking close, yet he'd resisted following up with any real moves for reasons that he couldn't explain, not even to himself. But he was determined to push forward now. "So you'll always know how to reach out and touch me," he whispered to her as he traced the last digit.

Because he was definitely going to stay near enough to touch her. Physical responses couldn't lie, and because of hers, he figured his odds of success in the touching department were pretty damn good. There was no reason to feel guilty about it, either. No laws would be broken—and no one expected Jack Parini to toe any respectable lines anyway.

So, since he couldn't persuade his sister to relocate her wedding, then he was going to be breathing Stephania Baci's same air for the next few weeks. He planned to keep her very, very busy, all the while making sure she didn't have the time, inclination, or energy to stir up any embers with her old flame.

~

Roxy accompanied Emerson across Tanti Baci's gravel parking lot toward his car. The chilly fog made the air heavy and muffled the sound of their footsteps. Glancing over at her fiancé, she wondered if it was today's weather that made him seem both burdened and silent.

Except he'd been frowning and quiet for days. Since . . . New Year's Eve? She hated the weighty quiet between them.

Shivering, she crossed her arms over her chest. Her movement caught Emerson's attention. He was a solid man, six feet tall with the all-American handsome features of a college fraternity president. Which he'd been, at the University of Southern California. His hair was only one shade darker than her own honey blond, and when she'd met him, she could think only that she'd never mistake him in the dark for a whip-thin European with lean hands and a slivery smile.

Emerson—when he smiled—had a grin that drew people like a crackling fire in winter. It thawed them exactly that way, too.

It had thawed her, almost from the very first.

His brows drew together now. "Princess?"

He'd called her that the night they'd met, at a benefit in San Francisco, and it had immediately tripped her heart. Outside of Ardenia, she didn't use her title or live like royalty. Thinking of the attention such notice might garner in her daily life had churned her stomach and she'd stepped back, instantly on guard.

"Princess Leia is who you're supposed to be, right?" the big blond man had gone on to say.

She'd blinked then, laughing a little. "Yes. Princess Leia." The staff of the nonprofit where she worked had attended the charity event at the planetarium that night in costume. Everyone had been invited to dress as characters from a science fiction movie and the entire office was in *Star Wars* gear. Because she had the long hair, she'd been relegated to attending as the female lead of the first film, complete with a white robe and those goofy cinnamon buns on either side of her head.

Once the ice had broken, she and Emerson had spent the rest of the evening together, looking at the exhibits and chatting in a casual manner. Few personal details were exchanged. Maybe it was because of the relative anonymity, but there hadn't been another time when a man had gotten under her defenses so quickly—though that might be due to the fact that she so rarely went out at night and absolutely never dated. Even a month before, she would have made excuses and not attended that particular party, either, but recent events had jolted her from her decade-long somnolent state.

She'd been ripe for life. And love.

"Princess?" Emerson said again now, his frown deeper.

"You were still calling me that two days after we first met," she recalled. "When we ran into each other at that coffee place."

"Because you never told me your name at the planetarium."

"Yes, I did." She shook her head. "You just can't admit to forgetting it."

It was an old, teasing argument, and she hoped it might lighten his mood and bring out one of his sweet grins. Instead, he just sighed and ran a hand over his hair as they came to a stop beside his BMW. "Are you in any hurry to get somewhere this morning?"

The cold found its way to her bones, despite the jacket she wore. "No hurry." She stuffed her hands in the pockets, fingers seeking—but that's right, there was nothing there to find.

When Emerson leaned against the side of the sedan, she mimicked his pose, angling her head to look into his face. His gaze was focused on the distance, but she didn't think he saw the rows of naked vines or the mountains rising behind them.

"Did you, uh, have something you want to discuss?" she asked, trying to hide the nervous quaver in her voice. But she should be happy he wanted to take a few moments alone with her, she reminded herself. The wedding process, the proximity of his family here in Edenville, and the fact that Jack had arrived in town had curtailed their chances for much private conversation.

She swallowed. "You know you can tell me anything." When he was silent another long moment, she withdrew her hands from her jacket and shoved them in the pockets of her wool slacks. There was something at the bottom of the left . . . a glass wine stopper. Every night, the small devices came out along with bottles of wine during the happy hour tasting at the resort where she was staying. Running her fingers over it relaxed her. "Anything, Emerson."

He smoothed his hand over his hair again and moved his head, as if taking in his surroundings for the first time. "It's beautiful here, isn't it?"

Her heart cracked a little. If he appreciated the Baci lands so much, did that mean he felt the same way about the Baci sister he'd once dated? Her fingers tightened on the stopper. "The winery is lovely."

His glance cut to her. "I don't just mean Tanti Baci. I mean the entire valley, the wine country. Maybe to someone who grew up in Ardenia—"

"No, no. There is beauty there, too, of course, but one doesn't surpass the other." As a matter of fact, the wine region of her small homeland was very similar to this. But she and Jack had left Ardenia when she was fourteen and he was twenty-one and some of its fabled splendor had faded from her mind due to time and circumstance. "And when it comes to growing up"—she affected the Southern drawl she'd been steeped in during high school—"did y'all forget I spent so many formative years in Georgia?"

That caused him to crack a smile as he slung an arm around her neck and drew her close enough to kiss the top of her head. "It's one of my life's ambitions to see you shelling peanuts in cowboy boots."

"Cowboy boots and nothing else?" She held her breath.

Emerson dropped his hold on her to put inches of space between them. "It's not time for that kind of talk."

Why? she wanted to demand. It wasn't that they hadn't kissed and touched during their courtship, but once they were engaged, it seemed as if Emerson had put up a barrier between them. It had only seemed to grow stronger and higher as their wedding date drew closer. Her fingers clutched the wine stopper like she wanted to clutch Emerson himself. He was the man she loved, the only man she would ever love, while he looked a million miles away again.

"What is it?" she asked, desperation making her voice a little breathless. "Tell me what's wrong."

He didn't look at her. "I wonder if you'll enjoy Washington, DC. It's a long way away." His gaze found her face. "And you like Edenville, don't you?"

Emerson loved Edenville, that was certain. He'd been based here all his life, though his family had a residence in San Francisco, an hour away, and another in the nation's capital, where his mother had been a U.S. senator for nearly two terms. It was why he'd make an excellent representative for the area—and why she was sure he would be elected to congress in the next election, just as he and his mother planned. After that . . . well, when Lois Platt retired from the senate some years hence, it would surprise no one if her son stepped into her shoes.

Roxy slipped her hand through Emerson's arm and hugged it close to her. "I will love wherever you are."

He pulled away and took a few steps from her. "My mother wants me to hold a press conference before the rehearsal dinner."

"What?" His distance was more alarming than his words. "Why would she want you to do that?"

"Why do you think?" He shoved his hands in the pockets of his slacks and tilted his head skyward. "Local boy marries a beautiful royal princess . . . your mother and father will be here—"

"Without scepters and ermine robes, I assure you." Though, to be honest, it was hard to predict how Queen Rayette would present herself. Roxy made a mental note to extract a promise that her mother would attend all California events crownless. She could envision the pouts already.

"Still," Emerson said. "The press will eat it up and voters will get a kick out of the glamorous aspect of it."

Roxy lifted her arms from her sides. In brown wool pants, boots, and a cream-colored cashmere turtleneck, the most glamorous aspect of her was the diamond solitaire on her left ring finger. "I'm no movie star."

Emerson turned to face her, his expression set in serious

lines again. "Are you worried about the attention? About someone seeing you and wanting to—"

"That isn't an issue!" The mention of it sent her heart thumping against her chest. "What happened was a long time ago and can never happen again. I have no doubts about that."

"Roxy—"

"I won't let that one past event send me scurrying like a mouse to a hole ever again." Her hand slid into her pants pocket and she worried the wine stopper. "I lost ten years of feeling free, but I'm over that now. Completely."

He studied her face. "What if I had never met you?" he asked quietly. "What if you hadn't braved your fears and gone to the first party, practically, in your entire life?"

She shrugged. *Maybe you'd be marrying Stevie Baci at the end of the month. Local boy with local girl, and the voters wouldn't need any trappings of glamour to be ecstatic about that.* But Roxy had gone to the party and the person Emerson was marrying was her.

And she loved him so very much.

He subsided into silence again. Maybe if she had more experience with men, she'd have a better chance of reaching him and what was at the root of what troubled him. But though she had three half brothers as well as Jack, she was much younger than all four. When she left Ardenia for her grandfather's farm in Georgia, she'd gone to an all-girl's Catholic high school and from there to a women's college in California's Bay Area.

The only man who'd gained her trust beyond her family members was Emerson, starting from that very first night. She'd talked and laughed like any young woman and felt safe and secure, as if a light had been lit inside her, one that couldn't be extinguished no matter how dark the night. How close the walls. Though they hadn't exchanged phone numbers, she'd been certain she'd see him again.

Maybe she was more like her father than she'd thought.

He'd glimpsed her mother across a marble parquet floor and instantly decided she'd be his queen. Emerson had handed her a glass of sour and semiwarm white wine from the charity event's cash bar and she'd seen herself in a wedding veil with a glass of something chilled and sparkly.

She'd fallen in love, just like that.

And now she had this terrible feeling she was losing him.

Her fingers wrapped around the wine stopper, she stepped closer to her fiancé. "Emerson . . ."

He turned to her, and his handsome face arrested her all over again. He was hers! He should be hers forever! But with Stevie Baci practically standing between them and the altar, Roxy wasn't certain that Emerson was as certain as she.

Another woman would demand answers or reassurance or both. But Roxy Parini wasn't that strong. When she was fourteen years old, she'd stepped into the sunlight for the first time in five days and told the policeman, "Call me Rocki." It had seemed such a steady and strong nickname. It hadn't stuck. She'd been back to Roxy by the time she'd reached home.

That statement of bravado hadn't been fulfilled until she'd talked with Emerson, laughed with Emerson, managed to meet Emerson in a coffee shop and agreed to go out with him that night on their first date.

Her first date ever.

Where was that courage now?

He glanced at his watch. "I have meetings. I'd better get back."

"All right," she said and watched him unlock his car and climb in.

"You'll get a ride with Jack?" he asked. At her nod, he closed the door. Then his window rolled down. His frown was back.

"Yes?" she forced herself to ask again, hoping, praying,

wishing that this time he'd tell her what had come between them.

"Does your brother have a thing for Stevie?" he demanded.

Roxy shrugged helplessly. As he drove off, she could only hope that Emerson hadn't just actually, finally, articulated what was bothering him—because if it was that, she *didn't* want to know.

5

The click of the door as Emerson and Roxy left the office made Stevie jump. Jack Parini was still in the room—standing just behind her desk chair—and the walls seemed to close around her when the only certain getaway was blocked by a soundproof wooden panel.

Who would rescue her if she called for help?

And she needed help, because her palm throbbed like a new tattoo where Jack had pen-inked his number onto her skin.

She scrambled to her feet just as he shifted, preventing her from escaping the narrow space between the work surface and the wall at her back. Her pulse picked up and a flush rose to the surface of her flesh. It felt like cowardice not to look him in the face, but her gaze dropped anyway, skittering along his black sweater, past his worn jeans, to the toes of his polished black loafers.

"Excuse me," she said to them, her voice tight.

They stepped to the side, and she brushed past Jack. Her shoulder grazed his chest and icy prickles shot down her arm. The sensation seized the breath in her lungs and she had to force her feet to keep moving.

"The Platts are having a dinner party Wednesday night," he said. "I need a date."

She barely registered the words, so intent she was on putting more space between them. "You'll find one."

"Stevie." His voice was low. Soft. "I want you."

The breath halted again in her throat, stuck just as surely as the bottom of her boots to the polished wood floor. Though she was still six feet from the door, her legs wouldn't move. *I want you.*

Damn it. Damn him. To salvage her pride, she'd agreed to playing event coordinator, but not plaything for the princess bride's brother. Yet he enjoyed unsteadying her, and at that realization, annoyance overcame breathlessness. "You're not supposed to say that," she told him.

"What?"

"Don't even try the innocent act. You know what. 'I want you,' you said."

"I do." There was a laugh in his voice. "I have to do this dinner thing Wednesday night and I heard the Platts are a stuffy, staid group. We can liven things up with the sparks we set off every time we touch. It'll be fun."

Again with the fun. Not to mention the sparks. This was so wrong on so many levels that she didn't know where to begin. Exasperated, she gazed at the shelving in front of her, staring without seeing the family photographs and the collection of vintage wedding cake toppers that had been her mother's.

"You look like her," Jack suddenly said.

She glanced at him in surprise. "Who?"

"Your mom." Two strides, and he was standing beside her. His hand indicated the photo of the little girls. "That's the three of you and her, right?"

"At our annual grape stomp. At harvest every year our father would insist we carry on the Baci family tradition, despite Mom's protests." The memory made her smile for a moment, then it died. "She didn't like the mess, and Jules and Allie, dutiful daughters, would follow directions and stay as stain-free as possible. While I . . ."

Not your new shirt, Stevie.

How could you lose another button?

Stephania, you'll be the death of me.

She cleared her throat. "My mother claimed I must be a changeling or that her real middle daughter was stolen by gypsies. She despaired that the tomboy left in her place might never develop any feminine qualities."

"Obviously she was teasing," he replied. "You look just like her. And as for feminine qualities . . ." His hand slid over the back of her hair to settle on the nape of her neck. "We both know you're female to the core."

At his touch, her skin broke out in a rash of goose bumps—and that core he mentioned? It went hot. Melting inside, she stiffened her knees, trying to throw off her ridiculous, helpless response. "I—I don't look like her," she mumbled, hardly knowing what she was saying.

He applied gentle pressure on her nape, compelling her to face the photograph again. "Of course you do."

And Stevie saw it now, when she looked at her mother instead of at that figure-in-action that had been her little-girl self. The same triangular face, smooth hair, long legs. Her mother was regarding her daughters with an indulgent smile—no, she was focused on *Stevie*, the changeling, the child left behind by gypsies, with that fond expression.

"Wow," she said, glancing back at Jack. "I . . ." The rest of her thoughts disintegrated as his hand left her neck and one finger traced the length of her spine. Her body felt like a pincushion, points of sensation spreading from her vertebrae to her scalp, toes, and fingertips.

Again, there was the melting heat below her belly and an empty ache between her legs.

God. His hand lingered at the small of her back, and that empty place clenched. "You shouldn't . . ." She had to swallow and start over. "You shouldn't touch me like that."

"Because it turns you on?"

Heat flooded her again, even as she whirled away from him. She sent out a stern glare. "Come on. Don't talk that way."

There was a lazy smile in his eyes. "But it's true, isn't it?"

She crossed her arms over her chest just in case the physical evidence might show through her bra and thin sweater. "Is this a European thing?" she demanded. "Do Ardenians feel free to talk about . . . to discuss . . ."

"Sexual arousal, sexual attraction, good old-fashioned lust?"

She made a sound that was half despair, half impatience.

He laughed.

"It's not funny!"

"That's what you say," he answered. "But a lot of the world considers Americans' squeamishness about sexual matters amusing. Must be those Puritan roots."

"Not jumping into bed with every man I meet doesn't make me squeamish."

"I was only referring to *talking* about sex, *mon ange*, not actually doing it." He shrugged, a smooth roll of his shoulders that made her feel a gauche fifteen. "But I understand your conflicts. When I visited my grandfather in Georgia, I spent a lot of time with good Southern Baptist girls."

"No dancing, no drinking, no making out?" she guessed.

He stepped near again, the knuckles of one hand edging the curve of her cheek. "No, *mon ange*." Humor threaded his voice again. "Just a lot of praying about indulging in all of the above come Sunday morning."

Meaning those good Southern Baptist girls hadn't resisted him. And despite her New Year's anti-man vow and his obvious playboy expertise, part of her didn't want to, either. But she didn't really know the man, and . . .

His thumb brushed across her bottom lip. His lazy eyes were on her face, his half smile revealing he was totally in control—and that he enjoyed toying with her. Over his shoulder, Stevie glimpsed the photograph on the shelf and she recalled that wild little girl she'd been, the one who'd gone into new adventures feetfirst.

Perhaps her mistake in handling Jack Parini had been in hesitating to assert her own will.

And wants.

Without a flicker of warning, she went on tiptoe and kissed the prince.

It was more flash than sparks.

More explosion than exploration.

He grunted, a sound of surprise, but he recovered quickly. His hands were at her waist, biting her flesh and then yanking her close. His body was as hot as hers, his mouth just as insistent as he slanted his head to take the kiss deeper, harder, more fiery.

Their mouths parted under the pressure, but she moved her tongue first, determined to keep the upper hand. As their tongues met, dueled, one of his big palms slid down her hip to clutch the curve of her butt. She shuddered against his hard chest and slid her fingers through his hair, tugging at the silky strands.

He bit her tongue.

She gasped, lifting her mouth to take in air, then retaliated with a nip to his chin. His head dipped and he had her mouth again, his free hand holding her jaw so she was captive to the onslaught of his kiss.

As if she wanted to get free.

But she wouldn't be at his mercy, either. Her fingers raced down his sweater and she burrowed beneath the soft wool at the small of his back to touch sleek skin. He shuddered, and the flesh burned against the caress of her palm.

Her heart thumped in her chest as she continued trading greedy kiss for greedy kiss. Then he grasped her shoulders and thrust her from him, keeping her at arm's length. His lips were wet.

"You play dirty," he said, his voice hoarse, a glint of irritation in his eyes.

She shook her head, trying to manage her breathing. "You're just mad that I didn't let it be your game." Every tomboy knew she was destined to lose if she let the boys control the field and set all the rules.

His gaze shifted from her eyes to her mouth. "Shall we call a time-out, then?"

She was tingling all over, her breasts felt swollen, and that emptiness between her legs was a keen ache she'd never experienced before. Though her nature was far more brash than cautious, those feminine instincts her mother had despaired of fostering in her were right now waving their aprons and muttering warnings like junior high health teachers.

They told her she should back away, get out of his arms, cross her legs.

She looked Jack Parini coolly in the eye. "Hell if I'll cry uncle," she said, ignoring all that fluttering to move back into his arms.

His hands slid down her back. He gripped her hips and tilted them against him, and she could feel his thick erection pressing her belly. She wiggled against it until he groaned and tightened his fingers to restrict her movement. Frustrated by his unspoken direction, she rose on tiptoe and wrapped an arm around his hips, pulling him tighter to her. Their mouths met.

A laugh, sexy and deep, rumbled in his chest. "What did I start?" he said as they again came up for air.

A fire, she thought, dazed by the sudden influx of oxygen. A conflagration. It was overwhelming, maybe, just a little, but *she* wasn't overwhelmed. The brazen Baci sister hadn't backed down, and it had saved her from . . . from . . .

But Jack Parini was no threat to her.

Never, she promised herself with a fierce frown.

He laughed again, as if he could read her mind and had his own opinion on the subject. That made her annoyed enough to kiss him again, because when kissing him, the upper hand was hers . . .

Until he changed it up. What before had been hot and consuming, he altered now, halting the trade of heavy tongue thrusts to trail his mouth along her jaw and down her neck.

He licked her pulse point.

Her body tensed, hovering on a tight tremor like a tuning fork. His mouth turned even more tender, and she backed up, trying to retreat. He followed, until he had her against the edge of the desk.

Her heart was pumping harder than before, much harder than when they'd been fighting for conquest. She sensed one of his hands leaving her waist, and then it had moved to the desk, the position more confining.

Alarms sounded and the fluttering ladies in her head started advising again even as his lips turned more gentle. He sucked her bottom lip into his mouth and her knees sagged. She was on the verge of something . . . of yielding . . .

And that thought galvanized her. She broke from his hold, sweeping her hand against his arm locked on the desktop. Something tumbled to the floor as he moved back.

His gaze fastened on hers. His expression was tight, his pupils dilated. Then his mouth quirked in that familiar, mocking smile. "Uncle?"

Her competitive spirit tried to rally, but her energy was sapped. She couldn't go another round. Grimacing, she glanced away. "Uncle."

"Wednesday night." Satisfaction filled his voice. "Seven o'clock."

That's when she realized that the Platt dinner party had been on the line. She should have known he'd not been just playing, but playing *for* something . . .

The man was even sneakier than she thought.

The office door opened then closed behind him just as she spied the item that had fallen to the floor. She knelt to retrieve it, surprised to discover it was the smallest of the bride-and-groom wedding cake toppers. She couldn't figure out how it had come to be on the desk, when its place was on the shelf. Returning it to its position, she decided that it was apropos, though. Rather than being the usual nuptial couple, this was a Mexican Day of the Dead version—both bride and groom were actually skeletons dressed in wedding regalia.

A reminder that when she was playing with Jack, she was playing with lethal fire. And to make it even worse, she decided, as she glanced over at the closed office door, she was unsure if she truly wanted rescue.

~

Jack couldn't wait for Stevie to show up at the Platt residence. She'd texted him with the assertion that she would drive herself, and he'd allowed that. But now he hoped like hell she wouldn't ditch him altogether, because he needed something to distract him from the disapproval that radiated from Senator Platt, her husband, Ned, and Emerson's two snobby sisters and respective spouses.

Christ, weren't Americans supposed to have a secret adulation for royalty? Of course, he held dual citizenship himself and his "noble" Ardenian family didn't strike him as any more or less better than Grandpa Crawford's neighbors in Fiddlecreek, Georgia.

"My assistant put together a file on you, Jack," Emerson's mother, the senator, said. "You have quite a reputation, I see, like the little table-and-chair throwing event at that bar in Brussels." She handed him the whisky and soda her husband had mixed at the bar in the spacious "family room." They probably thought of their Napa home in cabin terms, though it had to be over six thousand soaring square feet. And while it was constructed of peeled timber, everything inside it was miles above frontier quality.

He sipped his drink from a crystal highball glass. "You should have gone straight to the FBI," he said with a smile, though there was a burn in his gut that didn't come from the booze. "I've been told they have an extensive file of their own." Which was complete bullshit as far as he knew, but he liked the idea of the senator now wondering if he was part of some radical political group instead of merely a man with a reputation as a dilettante, womanizer, and wastrel, with one very real and particularly ugly episode in his past.

Emerson's brother-in-law, Erik, elbowed Jack, jiggling the ice in his glass. He was a loud, florid man who should get out and play some rounds rather than sitting on his couch watching tournaments on the Golf Channel. "I want to see a file of all those supermodels you dated. Heh heh. Complete with pictures." His voice lowered, but only enough so that the people in the next county couldn't hear him. "Did that Melinda really try to take her life over you?"

"Malia," Jack corrected. "And the last I heard she was out of the hospital but back in Thailand, nursing her crushed heart."

More BS. From what he understood, Malia was preparing to grace the catwalks during Fashion Week in Milan. But the Platts and company put him in the mood for lies. It was a habit of his—bad, he supposed—that the more someone lifted their eyebrows at his past, the more he was driven to feed their sordid assumptions.

Guilt didn't give him a single pinch for spreading stories about Malia, either. Not after her publicist had planted those rumors that the beauty's overdose had been a response to her unhealthy love affair with Jack, rather than blaming it on her real obsessive relationship—the pills that kept her six feet at 102 scrawny pounds.

On his other side, Roxy touched his arm. "Jack," she admonished, wearing a nervous smile. "Let's talk about something else, everyone. Who here makes New Year's resolutions? Or do you avoid them altogether?"

"By all means, let's discuss another topic," Senator Platt said, gesturing for the company to find themselves seats on the grouping of heavy, dark-toned furniture. As all moved to obey the matriarch, he noticed that she snagged his sister's arm so they sat side by side on a couch positioned against a rustic stone wall under two framed yet tattered flags: Old Glory and the California Bear.

Photographed, it would make a damn fine campaign image. *Senator Lois Platt and her daughter-in-law, member of the Ardenian royal family, Princess Roxanne.*

Call him cynical.

The senator turned toward his sister. "Roxanne, while I applaud your instinct to divert attention from unpleasant subjects . . ."

He was an unpleasant subject now! Charming.

". . . as a politician's wife, there are times when you'll have to own up to a relative's unsavory—"

"Wait." Jack looked from the senator to his sister. "Politician's wife?"

Clearing his throat, Emerson moved to perch on the arm of the sofa, close enough to place a light hand on Roxy's shoulder. "We're still in the exploratory stages," he said. "But there's a congressional seat opening up and I'm considering it."

Jesus. Jack glanced at his future brother-in-law's handsome face, then back to Roxy, who was staring into the distance. Her gaze unfocused, she was toying with something in her left hand, turning a narrow, shiny thing over and over.

He stared at it. "Hey, Rox. Did you find my lighter?"

She started, and her fingers squeezed over the metallic item as if to hide it. Then her fist popped open and the object lay in the curve of her palm. "Oh. Oh, yes. I've been meaning to return it."

Leaning down, he scooped up the cheap gadget. "Thanks," he said, pocketing it. "I didn't know you were heading for life in the political spotlight, sis."

"Emerson has considered following in my footsteps for several years," his mother answered.

"I'm curious to hear what Roxy thinks about it." Though her opinion was clear without the words. The tense lines of her face spoke volumes and spread a sick feeling in his gut. "There's a world of difference between supporting a husband in his commercial real estate business and surviving the rigors of a federal campaign and what comes after," he said.

Karen, one of Emerson's sisters, waved around her glass of wine. "We all agree that in some ways Roxanne is an unconventional—even inconvenient—choice, for reasons I shouldn't have to enumerate for you."

Meaning, exactly, him.

Roxy straightened her spine. "Wait a minute. For your information, my brother has spent the last years as a respected investment banker."

Emerson's father, bald and spare, shook his head. "Yes, but there was that little matter of embezzlement."

Spots of red showed up on his sister's cheeks. "In the Atlanta office where he worked, true, but in an entirely different department, and the culprit—"

"Was my squash partner on Tuesdays," Jack inserted smoothly. Somehow that had come out and then the tabloids had tried making more of it, adding yet another layer of tarnish to his character. He supposed sterling was highly overrated, but sometimes he got so damn tired of dirt.

"We all know," Emerson's mother said, "that the truth isn't as important as the image. As a matter of fact, image becomes truth. This will be a problem for Emerson and Roxy because of you, Jack. It's just a fact that to us in the U.S., your European lifestyle seems foreign—"

"So I'm Euro trash." Jack felt his ire rise again, though he knew he shouldn't let it. "That's what you're saying, since image is truth."

"Jack . . ." Roxy started.

He ignored her. "And because the gossip rags and the tabloid sites on two continents regularly say so, reality is that I cause ruckuses in nightclubs, commit fraud at my place of work, treat shabbily the most beautiful women on the planet, not to mention that I was complicit in my and my sister's—"

"Loss of good manners," a cheery voice interrupted. Stevie Baci breezed in, her arms embracing a half-dozen bottles of chilled wine. "Though the Platts aren't innocent this time, either. Is not one of you going to say 'hello' to the newest guest?"

The tense atmosphere in the room broke. People rose from their seats to greet Stevie, to freshen their drinks, to move as far from Jack as possible. Brooding, he retreated to a corner of the room and watched the interaction. Despite the fact that Emerson and Stevie had been over months before, the Platts appeared friendly enough with her. The small town of Edenville meant they'd probably known the Baci family all their lives.

Once Stevie had divested herself of the bottles she'd brought, he could only stare at what she was wearing. Some pale, slippery material slid over her slender body. The top of her breasts just peeped over the draped neckline. Her shoulders were bare except for skinny straps. If he brushed them down, Jack figured the whole damn dress would fall off, revealing her long torso and even longer legs.

His hand tightened on his highball as he thought about doing just that . . . and then it was her lips he remembered—those kisses in her office the other day. Her tempestuous mouth, the flagrant grind of her hips against his cock, the flush on her face that said she was as aroused as he.

Hell! Shifting on his feet, he stared into his drink, working on drowning those thoughts in the melting ice. If he didn't get a handle on himself, his reaction to her would be evident to everyone, including the Platts. Though, why should he care? They already considered him some sort of reprobate—sexual and otherwise. And hadn't he given up worrying what others thought of him a decade ago?

His gaze was drawn Stevie's way again. He replayed her entrance a few minutes before, just as he was cataloging the sins the world had assigned to him. *I cause ruckuses in nightclubs, commit fraud at my place of work, treat shabbily the most beautiful women on the planet, not to mention that I was complicit in my and my sister's—*

It bothered him that he was glad he'd left the last sentence unfinished. It bothered him more that despite his avowed indifference to others' opinions of him, he cared that she'd heard any of it at all.

6

Stevie had anticipated an awkward evening, but awkward turned out to be an understatement. As the meal wound down, she clung to the thought that the Emerson breakup meant any ties she had to the Platts had been severed as well. The clan was as sanctimonious and snobby as they'd ever been and she had to bite her tongue time and again. She'd never been at ease in their world.

Though as she applied herself to a cake layered with white- and dark-chocolate mousse, she blamed Jack for adding to the unpleasant atmosphere of the meal. He either said too little, just sipping his wine and smiling when Duane, Emerson's brother-in-law, asked him about the time Jack "borrowed" a Swiss police car and crashed it into a St. Moritz fire station. Or he said too much, as when Erik referenced an incident in which a suite of rooms was trashed at a famous Paris hotel. "Swear to God," Jack told the table-at-large, his hand making a lazy cross over his heart, "I was passed out cold in the bar downstairs that night. Someone stole my key."

When Roxanne tried protesting that both events had occurred over nine years before, the senator pointed out that in the age of the Internet, nothing seamy or salacious was ever completely laid to rest.

"Lois, baby," Jack said, addressing a standing U.S. senator with a salute of his goblet, "before now, I didn't imagine we'd agree on anything."

The tiny distressed gulp his sister made, perhaps audible only to Stevie, who was seated beside her—yes, Emerson wasn't the only obtuse Platt, his mother had directed their side-by-side placement—had Stevie scraping back her chair. "It's time for my contribution to the dinner," she said. "I've brought some bottles of Tanti Baci *blanc de blancs* for you to sample. Jack will help me pop the corks and pour."

"Debra will be happy to do it," the senator's husband said, referring to the housekeeper who had served the meal.

"I'd like to handle it, if you don't mind. This is our winery's special sparkling wedding wine," she told the guests at the table. "I do hope you're considering serving it at the wedding reception."

The senator frowned. "I suggested to Roxanne a wonderful French champagne—"

"But this is our special vintage, reserved exclusively for a bride and groom's big day," Stevie said, turning her gaze on the princess. If she was forced into this damn wedding detail, then she was going to eke out every dollar possible for Tanti Baci's near-empty coffers. "For nearly fifty years, we've kept a record of every couple that has served the wine at their wedding, and not one has ever divorced."

A choking sound drew her eyes to the most annoying, cynical man at the table. "I take that to mean you can't wait to help me, Jack," she said, glaring at him. "This way."

He followed her into the butler's pantry off the dining room, letting the door swing shut behind him. "You're kidding about that no-divorce thing, right?"

She was already pulling champagne flutes from a shelf

and placing them on a large tray. "Not kidding. It's written in all our brochures and on the website."

"But you can't believe it."

She'd always wanted to. Like the rumored treasure and the Anne and Alonzo love story, the *blanc de blancs* legend was part of her childhood. During those slumber parties in the old cottage, she and her friends had poured sparkling cider into juice glasses and pretended it was wedding wine and they were marrying the loves of their lives—usually some silly tween idol who in real life had likely been as shallow and sinful as Jack.

"Hurry and help me with these glasses," she said. "I just want this evening to be over."

"I'm a charter member of that club," he grumbled. "Christ, I thought my sister was smarter than this. Emerson and his—"

"I'll remind you I was once involved with 'Emerson and his' myself," she put in, shooting him a look over her shoulder. Even annoyed he looked unforgivably handsome. "And it's not like you're Mr. Perfect."

His jaw tightening, he crossed his arms over his chest. "I've never pretended I was."

Still, he irritated her. "Well, Liam said you were a devoted brother, and you're sure not living up to that, either."

"Whoa." His arms dropped. "What do you mean?"

"Never mind."

She moved toward the wine cooler, but he caught her bare arms before she could step past him. His grip didn't bite, but it didn't give her any wiggle room, either. "I'd never do anything to hurt Roxy again," he said.

Again? But she let that go, because she didn't want to prolong the conversation any more than she wanted to extend the evening. "Let go of me, Jack. I need to pour the wine."

His gaze trained on her face, he shook his head. "Fly in your champagne."

"Yeah, yeah, thorn on my rose, I get it." She hauled in a

breath that was warm with the tension smoldering between them. "But you should realize you're a thorn on Roxy's rose right now, too."

He frowned.

Damn. She had no obligation to smooth the princess's path. But his hold didn't loosen, and she sighed. "You're only making it worse out there, Jack."

"I don't care—"

"Your sister does. And every smartass remark you make and every cynical smile you give only winds her tighter."

He released Stevie so abruptly she stumbled a little on her heels. Regaining her balance, she took a hard look at him, but it was impossible to guess what was going on beneath the expressionless set of his face and the cooled silver of his eyes.

Unwilling to take any more time to figure it out, she moved around him, but he caught her hand, halting her again. "Thank you," he said quietly.

She tried to make light of it as he released her. "What wouldn't a woman do for her new best friend?" Bending, she reached for the handle on the under-cabinet cooler to retrieve the chilled bottles she'd brought.

"I thought I took back that friends thing," he said, his voice filled with familiar dry amusement. "I should, anyway, because Liam's my buddy and he doesn't tempt me in this way at all." Something cupped the globes of her behind. Some*one*.

Stevie jerked straight, hands going to the back of her dress as she whirled to face him. "Stop that."

"Hey, it's not my fault. You were bent over. You're in that dress."

Her sister Giuliana's dress. A simple, satiny, slip of a thing. It had looked innocuous enough on the padded hanger, and Jules had assured her that the oyster-shell color would be fine with her own black sandals and matching clutch bag. So Stevie had showered, then straightened her hair so it held a sheen as dark as her patent shoes. Still wrapped in her robe, she'd put on lengthening mascara, a raspberry lip gloss, and an extra-long pair of gold drop earrings that peeked from the bottom edge of her bobbed hair.

Then had come the dress. It had been too late for another selection when she'd realized that what was a decent hemline on Jules's five-foot-three was borderline *va-va-va-voom* on a woman who had nearly six more inches of leg.

And to be honest, she'd hoped Emerson would eat his heart out.

And that Jack would notice.

Now she edged the spaghetti strap up the slope of her shoulder, feeling like Little Red Riding Hood trekking through the forest, sans cape. The wolf wore European prince's clothing.

"I couldn't eat a bite tonight," he said, his voice soft.

Her feet shuffled back. "Not hungry?"

"Starving for something else."

She was in his arms again.

She was burning up again.

But he didn't touch her lips. Instead, his mouth went straight to the side of her throat, sliding down all the bare flesh revealed by the low neckline. Her fingers slid into his hair as his mouth traced her collarbone. She shivered, and the slender strap fell off her shoulder.

His hot mouth explored new territory and she clutched his head, shivering again. The satin fabric fell farther, revealing one sheer cup of her nude-colored strapless bra. He pulled that low and then his head dipped. Wet heat surrounded her nipple.

She bowed into the delicious suction as he plumped her breast into his hand and sucked harder.

Air moved, light shifted, a voice said, "What's taking—"

Stevie's head whipped toward the now-open pantry door. Emerson stood in the opening, and beyond him she could see the stunned faces of the rest of the party gathered at the table.

Oh, hell. It was a different kind of heat that rose along her neck as Jack straightened, his hand casually drawing up her bra and dress at the same time. He clasped her shoulder over the strap so it wouldn't slide again.

Barn door, horse.

Oh, wasn't she full of animal metaphors tonight? But clearly everyone had already seen Jack getting up close and personal with her . . . person. Damn it! What must they be thinking of her? Jack's reputation was already in smoking tatters, apparently, but now she knew her own approval rating would plunge further in their eyes. The Platts had never considered her good enough for their golden boy, but now they'd doubly bless his escape from her.

Red-faced, she started to shuffle away from Jack, but he moved along with her until they were both at the pantry threshold. Emerson fell back as they reentered the dining room.

The best thing about this, she thought, as her gaze ran around the appalled expressions at the table, was that no one would protest now if she cut the evening short. After being caught canoodling with the shady Jack, that wasn't too much to hope for.

The Platts would likely never look her in the eye again.

Clearing her throat, she fumbled for the right sort of good-bye. "Uh, I . . ."

Jack's hand squeezed her shoulder. "Let me handle this, *mon ange*."

Some instinct caused her to shoot him a look. His gaze was trained on his sister. "You can be the first to congratulate me," he said, a charming smile breaking over his face.

"Stevie's just agreed to be my wife."

~

To Stevie, turtle wax smelled like trouble. Likely because she uncapped her tub of the stuff every time she had a problem. Her little sister, Allie, turned to the stove and Giuliana buried herself in paperwork, but nothing calmed the middle

Baci sister more than rubbing a gleaming finish on one of the three limos in her stable.

But today, she wasn't convinced a morning of wax-on, wax-off would put her in a Zen state of mind.

Still, she had to occupy her hands with something, because strangling a certain someone wouldn't unravel the current tangle she found herself in. Though it was tempting to try.

Her arm aching, she paused to glare at Jack as he worked in the pocket-sized vineyard across the highway. He'd shown up in a ratty T-shirt and jeans early in the day and had been toiling among the neglected vines for hours, raking dead leaves and withered fruit into piles at the end of each row.

She could cave and approach him herself, but this damn problem was his fault and she figured it was his responsibility to find a dignified way out of it. At the Platts the night before, she'd blown her moment. Appalled by his statement, she'd been too flabbergasted to speak up and refute his claim right away. It was just a big joke, she should have said. So—ha ha—funny.

A mix of frustration and gloom rose inside her and she placed her wrist on the limo's hood and rested her forehead on her throbbing arm.

"You have any aspirin and water?" a voice asked.

Her head lifted. "You," she said, glaring at the Ardenian prince. He didn't look very aristocratic at the moment, though, with his hair wet with the sweat that stuck his shirt to his torso. He blotted more from his brow with his forearm, leaving a muddy streak that made him appear more valley farmer than royal foreigner.

It also made him appear more accessible, she mused, and then her mind wandered off, imagining her access to the hard chest muscles she could see rippling from nipple line to his waist thanks to the shirt plastered to his skin. It was a shame they didn't inhabit the same league, because his body—

"Aspirin?" he asked again.

She shook herself, emerging out of the sexual fog he cast over her much too easily. "Does something hurt?"

"For you," he said. "You look like *you* hurt."

Better than looking like he turned her on, she supposed. "Yeah? Well, guess the source of my pain."

He grinned, his teeth white against the reddish Edenville dust darkening his skin. "*Mon ange*, is that any way to talk to your fiancé?"

The angel thing put her over the edge. "Fiancé! What the hell were you thinking?" she demanded.

"It was your idea—"

"Mine?" Outrage made her voice rise.

He winced at the volume. "Calm down. I was trying to salvage a little bit of my rep—you know, make us out to be a pair of romantic, impetuous lovers instead of lust-crazed dinner guests. For Roxy's sake, I didn't want the Platts thinking I'm the kind of man who would seduce a near-stranger in their butler's pantry."

"Jack." Temper tightened her throat. "You *are* the kind of man who would seduce a near-stranger in their butler's pantry."

He shrugged, apparently unashamed.

"No one will believe it."

"Sure they will," he replied. "Ask around. People fall for other people and get engaged—and even married—in haste all the time. Took my father three days to get his ring on my mother's hand."

"Yes, but people discuss these things first. Together."

"Sorry." He said it with another of his careless smiles. "It was an impulse. Don't you ever do anything impulsive?"

Kissing him in the Tanti Baci winery offices had been an impulse. Letting him kiss her in the Platts' butler's pantry had been madness. She shook her head, disgusted with the both of them. There was no pride in being a slave to desire.

"I really could use some water," he said. "You have any?"

She gestured with her thumb toward the shed a few yards away that held her cleaning supplies and other equipment. "Red cooler inside. Help yourself."

As he walked away, she leaned against the limo in order to be comfortable as she contemplated her disordered life as well as the view inside her closed eyelids. The sound of tires on asphalt had her lifting her lashes again. She groaned, watching Giuliana brake behind the Caddie and get out of her car.

No way was Stevie going to introduce Jack as the man she was going to marry, but she was afraid he might do just that if he emerged from the shed before Jules left. Wouldn't that just tighten the tangle? Hurrying toward her sister, Stevie plastered on an innocent smile. "What are you doing here?"

"Just a brief stop on my way to meet Kohl at the hardware store. The lights in the wine caves keep shorting out and we're going to—" She broke off. "What's wrong? Why do you look so guilty? Did you get something on my dress?"

Oh, if only it was a stain. "No, no."

"Good," Jules said. "I take it you survived the dinner last night, then?"

"You could call it survival," she muttered.

Jules frowned. "I know it's hard, all of this, since you still have that thing for Emerson."

"I *do not* have a thing for Emerson," she said through clenched teeth.

"I know you, and—"

"You don't know me!" Stevie was aware her frustration was due to lack of sleep, not to mention irritation with Jack and the screwed-up circumstances, but that didn't stop her from flinging the words at her sister.

Unflappable Jules didn't blink. "I know you didn't want

to get involved in the winery business, so I'm even more grateful that you're doing this."

Guilt gave her a hefty pinch. "I don't need your gratitude. I said I'd do it."

"Yes, but before now you've always done your own thing."

Stevie swallowed, more agitated than she wanted to reveal. "We're still the Three Mouseketeers, though." As little girls, they'd been a triumvirate of sisterhood in Disneyland Minnie ears and capes they fashioned from their mother's aprons tied around their necks.

"More like two mice and a shadow," Jules corrected. "Admit it, after Mom died, you distanced yourself, always going off with Zinnia and Mari Friday or that pack of boys you ran around with."

With her two girlfriends, she'd only gone as far as Alonzo and Anne's cottage, where they'd read books and spun fantasies to escape what they didn't like in their real worlds. The boys had served their own purpose. As long as she could shag a ball or skateboard down the school steps, they accepted her without questions. Not one asked her about her feelings. They didn't probe to discover if she missed her mother.

But she had. Desperately.

"Once Mom was gone . . ." She shook her head, loathe even now to reveal how lonely she'd been. What did it matter? "We all found a way to cope. Allie had you. You had Liam."

"Liam." Jules looked down. "I suppose grief explains what happened. I was in a low place and he took advantage—"

"Bullshit," an angry voice said.

The sisters both started. *Uh-oh*, Stevie thought, catching sight of the oldest Bennett brother skirting the back of Giuliana's car. *Incoming!*

"Are you spying on us?" Jules demanded.

"Christ, you're paranoid," Liam remarked. "I have something for Stevie."

Her older sister slammed her arms across her chest. "Where's your car?"

"Across the street. At a property I recently acquired."

The property Jack had been clearing all morning. Craning her neck, Stevie saw he was back at it. Sometime during her conversation with her sister, he must have decamped from her side of the road. Good.

" 'At a property I recently acquired,' " Jules repeated, her tone mocking. "Good God, could you get more pompous?"

Steam appeared to come out of Liam's ears and his hands fisted at his sides. "I won't say what I think you are."

Stevie shot another look in Jack's direction. He'd decamped from her side of the road, leaving her alone with two enemy combatants. Bad.

"Go ahead," Jules urged her childhood sweetheart, tapping her toe. "Be honest."

"Honest is . . ." He halted to take in a deep breath, then relaxed his fingers and shook out his arms. The air he'd held chuffed out. "Jules, after your mother passed away . . . nothing that happened between us when we were kids . . ."

Stevie averted her eyes, because the moment seemed private. Painful.

"I never took advantage of you and your sorrow," he said. "You *turned* to me. We . . . Tell me you understand that."

At Jules's long silence, Stevie squirmed. Then her sister squared her shoulders and marched toward the driver's door of her car. Which took her right by Liam.

"Giuliana." He caught her elbow.

"Don't touch me."

Stevie winced, reading the flash of pain on the man's face and the abject fury on her sister's. Like the fires of hell, Jules's temper burned deep and hot, and Liam had to know that the woman could carry a grudge into eternity.

But the secret to understanding her big sister was that she only became very angry when she was very afraid.

Liam terrified Giuliana.

He dropped her arm and turned to Stevie. "I've got something for you," he said, his voice calm, his expression cold and remote. All hallmarks of his personality that her fiery Italian sister claimed to despise the most. Renewed fury radiated off Jules as she continued to stand by her car.

The chicken, the egg. The dog, the tail. Jules and Liam seemed locked in an unbreakable circle.

He dug in his pocket and withdrew a key that was attached by wire to a small circle of cardboard. "Seth told you about this, right?"

"Oh, yeah." But in all the craziness of the past few days, she'd forgotten completely. "The treasure."

"Treasure?" Jules stepped forward.

Stevie summarized. "The key—that attached tag says 'Baci' on it—was found among Liam's dad's things. It doesn't seem to fit anything in the Bennett household, so Seth's hypothesizing that maybe it's the key to the treasure." Was it wrong of her to feel a little thrill at the idea? She'd only been daydreaming about it since she was too small to tie her own shoes.

"There's no treasure," Jules scoffed.

"Well, probably not," Stevie conceded. "But it could be fun to poke around—"

"We don't have time to waste on pipe dreams, and why Seth would suggest . . ." She turned her gaze on Liam, her eyes narrowed.

Stevie resisted the urge to duck.

"Is this some Bennett plot to put Tanti Baci out of business?"

It really was an unfair accusation, Stevie thought, wincing again. The Bennetts were silent partners in the winery, meaning they all had something to lose if it went under. Of course, unlike the Baci family, the Bennetts did have other stable and solid financial ventures.

Liam appeared to be carved from ice and he regarded his first love as if she was an ant crawling across his shoe. "Tanti Baci is going down all by itself," he said, "unless you get things straightened out, little girl."

Tears of . . . rage sparked in Giuliana's eyes and she spun around to the car door.

Liam's cool façade shattered and he reached for it, too. "Jules. Sweetheart . . ."

Stupefied, Stevie watched them fight for control of the handle. Should she help her sister escape or insist that she stay and finally have it out with Liam? Still undecided, she drew back as a truck jolted into the driveway.

Kohl Friday jumped out and, in the space of a breath, yanked Liam away from Giuliana's side. They faced each other, two men, one dark-haired and massive, the other tall, lean, and blond. Both angry.

"What are *you* doing here?" they demanded of each other at the same time.

Stevie sent a longing glance across the street. Her royal fiancé confused her—what compelled a spoiled man accustomed to the wild life to attend to such backbreaking work?—but suddenly he seemed a whole lot less complicated than the trouble on her side of the road.

7

Jack was surprised by how popular this little corner of Edenville had become when his sister pulled up in her Mercedes sedan. He straightened as she approached, thinking she hadn't changed from the little blond pest she'd been since the day she was born. Always following him.

Always following his lead. His smile died.

A frown puckered Roxy's forehead as she leaned in to kiss him on the cheek and he pulled away. "Believe me," he told her, "you don't want to get that close to a man who's been sweating all morning."

Her gaze ran over him. "I see that." She stepped back to take in the two-acre plot. "Liam's making you work for your keep? There's an open room near mine at the Valley Ridge Resort. I hear they take credit cards instead of manual labor in payment."

He shook his head. "This is my own idea. Just something to pass the time until I see you safely married."

Roxy turned her head, her gaze focusing on the business across the highway and the knot of people congregated there. Stevie stood apart from the others, wearing another pair of tissue-thin jeans and a loose thermal shirt, an outfit miles apart from the shiny scrap of fabric she'd worn the night before.

"Maybe now I see the attraction," Jack's sister said, her face breaking into a smile. "Engaged! I was right, after all. You really do like her, huh?"

"Yeah." He couldn't bear to bring down her bright mood by telling the truth. "I guess Stevie and I surprised the dinner party last night."

She laughed. "It was better than double desserts, at least from my point of view."

"Well, your future in-laws seemed to see me in a somewhat kinder light after the announcement."

Her fingers toyed with a button on her pale blue parka, as if she couldn't keep them still. "They've known Stevie forever, it seems. I'm not sure they thought she'd make a good political wife, but—"

"About that, Rox," Jack said, watching his sister's nervous movements. "Is that what *you* want to be? A good political wife?"

"I want to be married to Emerson." Her chin lifted. "I'm in love with Emerson."

"I know that, *ma belle*." He hesitated. "But you never mentioned Emerson's aspirations before. You must realize a political life is a lot of pressure. Things you can't control . . ."

He hated having to mention it and would rather cut off his own arm than issue the warning. His sister's vulnerabilities were his fault, his own damn fault, and it tore at him that they had limited her for so long. Less than a year ago she'd turned a corner and he'd do what he had to— anything, everything—in order to ensure she'd achieve her heart's desire.

He shoved his hand through his hair and tried again. "Roxy—"

"I'm thrilled with the idea that you're engaged to Stevie.

I confess I was a little goosed by the idea of my fiancé's ex handling our wedding. But now that she's going to be marrying you—well, that takes the pressure off. I think we were all feeling bad—me, Emerson, even his parents—that she might have been hurt by their breakup. Clearly she's moved on."

"Clearly." Stevie'd moved on? Who knew? But if his little impromptu engagement announcement eased Roxy, then he was going to keep the middle Baci affianced for as long as necessary.

To mask his worry, he gave his sister another smile. "Can I take you on a tour of My Aching Back vineyard?"

"Is that what it's called?"

"That's what *I* call it," he said. "C'mon, this way."

They strolled through the two acres, steering around the piles of debris he'd accumulated. "The vines seem to be surviving despite the neglect of this past season. The old guy who owned the place had an idea to make an artisan wine from the grapes grown on just these two acres."

He walked her up to the small winery building, the one built on feudal lines. Roxy turned to him, wide-eyed. "It comes with a castle?"

"Guess the old guy had a fanciful imagination. Apparently plenty tried to talk him out of the whole idea. The acres are zoned for commercial, too, and he received plenty of offers to sell out, but the man was stubborn."

Roxy grinned. "Sounds like Grandpa Crawford. Remember when he was offered a fortune by the gas station people for the peach orchard at the crossroads? He greeted them at the door with his shotgun."

"You can still pick the sweetest fruit there in the summer. When I was living in Atlanta, I'd drive out and eat them warm off the tree."

His sister tilted her head. "I never noticed before how much you remind me of Grandpa."

"Oh, thanks. When he went to meet his maker at eighty-eight years old he had a bum knee, dentures that didn't fit, and a crotchety attitude."

"But a full head of hair," Roxy pointed out. "What I mean, though, is that right now, with dirt on your hands and that satisfied light in your eye . . . you're a dead ringer for him."

"Yeah?"

"Yeah." She pointed a finger at his chest. "You know what I think? I think you should buy this from Liam. It could really be My Aching Back vineyard."

"That's ridiculous," he scoffed.

"I'm not joking. Think about it. It's a little gray and gloomy today, but at other times of the year . . ."

He knew exactly what it would look like at other times of the year. The colors would be spectacular: the spring green of early foliage and fruit; that unique, bubbly quality of summer's golden light; fall's rust and purple as leaves turned and Napa's famous cabernet berries darkened. The soft grays and browns of winter were the rest before the rainbow.

The idea of seeing all those shades held some appeal, he had to admit.

Roxy must have sensed his thoughts. "You could settle in the Napa Valley, Jack. In Edenville. Then we'd both be here. We could really be family again."

He tried to imagine "settling." It didn't take a genius to figure out that half of the reason he kept moving from city to city and job to job was in an effort to escape himself. New people, new places; they worked for a short period of time to distract him from the weight of the past. Settling would mean forgoing even that temporary relief. As for family—he was accustomed to doing without that.

"You'd even have your very own castle, Jack," his sister added, wiggling her brows.

"Oh, now there's a draw," he said drily.

She laughed again. "Those redneck genes we inherited from Mom bred stronger than that blue blood coming down from Papa's side, I guess. We're more Georgia scrappers than effete aristocrats."

"Mixed breeds are always best, they say."

The good humor on her face made way for seriousness. "And we *are* strong, Jack. You know that."

But she should never have been tested. He shoved a hand through his sticky, dusty hair. "Roxy—"

"Survivors," she insisted.

"Then I guess you don't need these bottled waters," another woman remarked. Stevie.

He whirled around. There she was. His fiancée—unless and until she denied it, of course.

"Hi!" Roxy's face broke into another of her happy smiles. He could only hope Stevie wasn't about to crush his little sister. Or maybe it would go the other way around, because Roxy enveloped the taller woman in a brief, but tight, hug. Yep, this "engagement" had definitely eased his sister's anxiety.

"I have to say congratulations again," she said. "My brother is a fast worker, isn't he?"

Stevie handed him a water. "Hard worker today."

He accepted the bottle and tried thinking like an engaged man. "I'd kiss you, but then I'd really put the phrase 'lady killer' into practice. I need a hot shower and one wet . . ."

Her look told him not to finish that thought.

". . . bar of soap," he finished, biting back his laugh. Then the laugh was on him, because he could see it in his mind's eye. Those long legs, sleek with soap bubbles, her generous breasts cradled in his hands—he cleared his throat. "What brings you across the blacktop?"

Her head turned over her shoulder and he followed her gaze. With a burn of rubber, Liam's car was pulling into the road, leaving Stevie's sister and a dark-haired man staring after him. "I'm tired of complications," she said.

His eyebrows rose. So she came over here? Where her

fake fiancé was talking to his sister who was planning to marry her ex? Interesting. This could either mean her family situation was more complex than he'd managed to glean from his brief moments of eavesdropping earlier, or she was here to burst his little sister's blissful mood. He could hear Stevie now: *You've got it wrong, Roxy. Jack's the last man I'd wed.* And who would blame her?

"I'm so glad you did cross the street," Roxy was saying. "There's something I've been thinking about since last night. I don't know how . . . that is . . . maybe . . . Oh, I'll just spit it out. Our parents are going to be in town. Some other family members, too. So it might be ideal . . ." She laughed. "I'm dithering again. Stevie, would you and Jack consider a double wedding?"

The long-legged brunette's gaze snapped to his. Shock registered.

He knew exactly how she felt. Christ! Married in less than a month?

If she'd been inclined to let the engagement story lie, this would likely push her to the truth.

"A double wedding," she mused, her eyes still on Jack. "Hmm . . ." One finger tapped her full bottom lip in speculation.

Though ice trickled down his spine, he kept his stance relaxed. Damned if he'd crumble and claim it was all a big mistake, not when he'd put his little sister into such a giddy mood—but a double wedding! Hell, what if Stevie agreed?

Then her hand dropped, her mouth curved into a smile, her gaze shifted to Roxy. "It's an appealing idea, of course, but no. I think I'll milk this engagement thing for all it's worth for a while longer than that."

"I understand." Roxy hugged her again.

Jack took a swallow of his water to lubricate his dry mouth. "I'm devastated."

Stevie laughed at him over his sister's shoulder. "I'll make it up to you."

He could breathe and smile again after all. "Starting when?"

Roxy shook her head as she pulled away from Jack's fiancée. "I think that's my cue to leave."

"I'll walk you to your car," he said. "You'll wait?" he asked Stevie.

"I've got to get back," she answered, brushing past him as she started off in the opposite direction.

"Thanks," he murmured.

"It's so everyone will know I'm over Emerson," she said under her breath. "I've got to do something to quell that ridiculous rumor."

Ridiculous? That couldn't be relief he felt—except that he was relieved and glad they each had their own agenda that was satisfied by this new move. It made the situation win-win.

Roxy practically skipped at his side as they made their way back to her car. A year ago, he'd wondered if she'd ever be this carefree. Though it gave pause to his ever-present guilt, the hovering black cloud wasn't completely dissolved by her sunny mood.

As she slipped into the car, his gaze snagged on her engagement ring. God. He'd asked someone to marry him—even if it wasn't a real proposal. "What are we doing, Rox?"

She seemed to understand what he meant. She patted his hand. "Going for normal."

Normal. His gaze traveled over the small vineyard, to his dirty hands, then to the woman back at work polishing the car across the street. He'd known there'd never be normal again, not since he'd been locked in the dark ten years before. Neither he nor Roxy had fully walked in the light ever since.

~

Roxy rushed to meet Emerson in the restaurant's bar at the Valley Ridge Resort where she was staying until the wedding. The heels of her new boots clattered on the pavement as she wrestled to open the heavy carved door. It was dim inside the foyer after the well-lit exterior. She paused, blinking, willing away her temporary blindness as well as that familiar frisson of fear that always breathed across her skin when she experienced temporary blindness.

Hands bit into her shoulders and she was yanked against a hard body.

Though her vision was still not up to par, she relaxed. Emerson. He was solid and warm, not lean and cold-fingered. She snuggled her cheek against his chest and wrapped her arms around his waist as he pulled her close. "It's you," she murmured, the exact thing her heart had said almost from the first moment they'd met. Silly, maybe, but she was convinced that something inside her had recognized him as the man she was destined to love. Fated, just like a fairy tale.

She'd comforted herself with stories like that when she was fourteen and so alone.

His hold on her tightened. "You scared the hell out of me," he said, ducking his head to place his cheek against hers. "Where were you?"

Pulling a little away, she frowned up at him. "I had some things to take care of before we met up. I'm only a few minutes late."

"I know." He grimaced. "I promise I'm not turning into a psycho boyfriend."

"Psycho *fiancé*," she corrected, her voice a little sharp. Then she took a harder look at him. "What's wrong?"

"I thought *I* was going to be late. I tried calling and your cell didn't pick up and then my mind—" He abruptly released her. "I *am* psycho. Forget I said anything."

He smiled down at her now, his expression bland, his demeanor courteous. Passionless?

Was it bad of her to have enjoyed—just a little—his momentary panic? And to be resenting how easily he could redon his affable exterior? He'd make an excellent politician, she thought.

Frowning at that, she moved back farther to rummage through her purse. "Ah!" She held up her cell. "Sorry, it's not charged."

"No problem." He was still smiling that benign smile as he patted her shoulder.

She felt another spurt of resentment at the gentle touch. Shouldn't he have been annoyed, just the tiniest bit, about the phone? "I'm sorry," she said again. "Forgetting to plug it in every once in a while is an irritating habit of mine."

"Not an issue," he replied with a wave of his hand. "Nothing you do irritates me, Roxanne."

Well, shouldn't *something* about her stir him up? Wasn't he just too easygoing for a fated fiancé?

His hand went to the small of her back as he urged her in the direction of the bar. "Ready?"

Yes. She was ready for something more than shoulder pats and cheek kisses, and to that end she'd made her own plans for the evening. "I thought we'd go to my room instead."

He froze. "Uh, your room?"

What man resisted getting his intended alone? She nearly stomped her new boot into the plush carpeting. "We have the seating arrangements to go over for the rehearsal dinner, remember?"

"My mom called me about it," he admitted. "Though she's as concerned about the press conference beforehand as where the king and queen will be sitting at the table."

Roxy linked her arm in his and drew him to the exit. "I have my ideas on the latter laid out in my suite." Along with a few other things. "Right this way."

During the short walk to her suite, he went from pleasant to preoccupied, she noticed. As the door swung open, he didn't seem to register the wine she had chilling in an ice bucket on the small table, the tray of appetizers, the fire kindling in the hearth. With a little sigh, she slipped his suit jacket from his shoulders and folded it over the back of an armchair.

Tonight she wanted his mind on her, his mood passionate, and she was going to get it!

When her hands went to the knot of his tie, though, he pushed them away and worked on it himself as he strolled over to inspect the seating chart she had planned them never getting to . . . unless it was much, much later.

"I see you filled some names in already," he said.

"Ours." She joined him, standing close enough that her breast pressed against his arm. To go along with her brand-new cowboy boots—in turquoise and fuchsia!—she wore a paisley wrap dress featuring the same colors. It was almost like a robe—one little tug and the tie would fall free. Underneath she wore a matching panties and bra set that she'd been saving for the honeymoon. "I think the bride and groom should be side by side, don't you?"

Rotating her body just a fraction, she managed to press her nipple against his bicep. It was already hard, and the bra and jersey knit of her dress were both so thin that he had to be aware of her response. She could smell her perfume in the air, the scent releasing as her skin warmed.

But he seemed to notice none of that as he picked up the seating chart. The movement separated their bodies. "I see Jack on here. Where are you going to put Stevie?"

In a locked closet. But that was more than unkind, given the circumstances. Roxy yanked the dripping bottle of sauvignon blanc out of the ice and poured herself a hefty glass. Jack deserved his happiness, too, and she didn't have an objective objection to the woman he wanted. She'd been genuinely happy that the two had found each other. Relieved that she no longer needed to feel guilty for things she'd done or continually worry over Stevie still coveting Emerson. But then why did he have to bring up his ex?

He was frowning, his gaze unseeing. "Do you really think they could have fallen in love so fast? I mean, I just don't get it."

Her chest went tight. "We fell in love quickly. Unless

you're implying there's something wrong with my brother? Or"—that paragon—"Stevie?"

"There's nothing wrong with Stevie."

Roxy looked away. Long legs, sleek dark hair, and a cat face that was wide at the eyes, pointed at the chin, and full at the lips. Nothing wrong with Stevie at all. No reason to feel short and washed out at the mention of her. "Of course not."

He pulled out a chair for her. "I guess we might as well get this chart done."

Roxy glanced back, gaze falling on the open bedroom door, the fire in the second fireplace, the blankets and sheets turned back. "I guess."

When he sat on the other side of the table, even their knees didn't touch. Roxy took another swig of her wine and cursed her lingering diffidence. As much as she wanted Emerson, her inner vixen was as imprisoned as she'd once been.

And if she didn't have his touch, how could she trust in his love? It almost seemed as if the closer they came to marriage, the more he withdrew. At this rate, he'd be a complete stranger by their wedding day.

She couldn't have that.

Inhaling a breath, she leaned forward. "Look, Emerson—"

"Hell," he suddenly said. "I can't cover this up anymore."

Her heart knocked once against her chest, stilled. "Wh—"

"I'm irrationally worried when I can't reach you," he continued, running his hands through his hair, tossing the normally smooth locks. "It makes me nuts."

"Oh." Blood started moving through her body again. "I—"

"You've got to keep your phone charged, okay? You've got to humor me on this."

A smile bloomed on her face. He looked intense, upset, passionate even. A buzz of happiness fizzed in her veins.

She was so right about that fate thing. "I will. I promise I will."

But her words didn't calm him. He threw back his chair and then crossed to where she'd left her purse on the small chair by the door. "Where's your phone? Is your charger by your bed?" Without waiting for her answer, he was digging through her bag.

She sat back in her chair, smiling at him. Emerson, impatient, was at his most endearing. The show got only better when he rushed toward the bedroom, her slouchy leather bag between his big hands.

That got her to her feet, and she leaned one shoulder against the doorjamb as he dumped the contents of her purse onto the mattress. His fingers pawed clumsily through the tissues, makeup, and mints. "Hah!" he said, his voice triumphant as he held up the small device he'd been seeking.

Grinning at him, she applauded.

He didn't take a break for the accolades. Instead he located the charger on the bedside table and mated it to her phone. Wow. Her inner vixen squirmed a little at the image and she closed her eyes, savoring it. She thought of him mating with her, of his weight and strength surrounding her. The vixen squirmed again.

"You know, Emerson," she murmured. "I could use a little jolt of juice myself."

Silence was the only response. Surely he'd heard her. Half embarrassed—had she shocked him?—and half concerned—would he *never* take the hint?—she opened her eyes.

He was sitting on the mattress, obviously paused in the middle of putting her things back in her purse. How considerate! Then she noticed that he was staring at something in his hand, a puzzled expression on her face.

Her stomach folded onto itself like origami. Her palms went damp and her voice sounded unnaturally high in her ears. "What, uh—" She stopped to lick her lips. "What do you have there?"

He held it up. A pen, with a garish orange cap. It was one of those tacky things that revealed a naked woman when you positioned it right. It advertised some "ranch" that Roxy suspected was actually a brothel in Nevada.

"This is my brother-in-law Erik's," Emerson said. "He calls it his lucky pen. He's had it since he was fifteen years old. Carries it everywhere and rarely lets it out of his sight."

"Oh." The whites of her eyes were drying out, due to the innocent look she was working so hard to perfect. "You'll have to give it back to him then."

"I will." With a small shake of his head, he slipped it into his pocket. Then he scooped the rest of the loose items into her purse.

She managed to make her legs move so that she could reach for the handbag, though chills tumbled down her spine. "I'll take that."

Emerson stood as he handed it over. He frowned. "Roxy? What's wrong?"

"Nothing. Not a thing. But . . ." She swallowed hard.

"But?" he prompted. He tilted her chin to study her face.

"I have a sudden headache," she said, putting her hand to her forehead. It was true. Her temples were pounding and nausea was threatening. That stupid pen. "Could we reschedule? I think right now I'd just like to go to bed."

It was supposed to have been with him. She remembered she'd thought that unless they spent some intimate time together, they'd marry as strangers.

But maybe that was better than him learning any of her secrets.

Jack found the front door of the Baci farmhouse ajar and he widened the opening to peer inside. The foyer was empty and there was no one on the stairs leading up to the second floor. "Stevie?" he called out.

A thump and a muffled voice responded, and he followed the sounds across the threshold to a deep closet built under the staircase. Boxes and boots littered the floor outside of it. The interior was stuffed with more items—apparently this was catch-all storage—but it was the vision of a shapely rear end in worn jeans that caught his attention.

On hands and knees, Stevie was burrowing at the rear of the shadowy space. She glanced over her shoulder at him.

"Don't bother moving on my account," he said, even as she backed up. "The view from here is spectacular."

Her disgruntled expression as she rose to her feet only made him laugh. It seemed the easiest way to unsettle her was to issue a compliment. And her unsteadiness only seemed fair since just looking at her could rock the floor under his feet.

"You're beautiful when you're embarrassed." His gaze took in the flush on her cheeks. It had darkened the natural rose of her mouth, and as he watched, she moistened her lower lip with her tongue. "Do that again," he whispered.

She ignored the comment. "What are you doing here?"

He answered as simply as possible. "They told me in the winery's offices that this is where I could find you."

Her hand waved in a vague gesture. "I had Christmas decorations I still needed to put away."

He looked around at the scattered items that had obviously been pulled from the closet and then at something glinting in her hand. One step, and he held her wrist in the circle of his fingers.

She resisted his hold, of course.

"You're so prickly," he murmured, looking down at the old-fashioned key she held. "I'm not going to steal your treasure."

"I don't know what you're talking about." She yanked free of him, shoved the key she held in her pocket, then turned to toss an old umbrella back in the closet.

"The Bennett-Baci silver. I remember Seth talking about it at the poker party."

"Who would believe in such a thing?" she scoffed, using her foot to propel a crate of tattered LPs.

Jack hefted the wooden box into his arms and placed it into the storage area beside a half-dozen ancient tennis rackets, their heads bound in wooden vices. "Though I doubt you'll find anything of value in here."

"Yeah," Stevie said, her voice a little sullen. "I don't know what I was thinking."

Grinning, he turned to face her. "Ah-ha! So you admit to being a covert romantic."

Her cheeks flushed again. "I had to stash that Christmas wreath somewhere. While I was here, I thought I'd look around for something that key would fit."

"Don't worry. Your secret's safe with me," Jack said.

"It only makes you more interesting, though. You're so no-nonsense on the outside, but inside . . ."

She narrowed her eyes. "What? Sappy? Sentimental?"

"Sweet," he said, stepping close enough to trail the backs of his fingers from her temple to her chin. "I've tasted you, and inside, Stephania, you are so, so sweet."

Tension had her skin thrumming beneath his touch. But she held her ground, her chocolate eyes not looking away from his. "What's this all about, Jack? Why are you here?"

He let his arm drop. "I thought we should get our stories straight. We're engaged people now. If anyone's going to buy that, we have to know something about each other."

With a shove, she managed to close the closet door. "Like what? You want to know my favorite television show? The name of my first pet?"

"Sure." He shrugged. "Things like that. What you were good at in school. Your favorite books. The boy you dreamed about."

"I don't have that kind of time, Jack."

The problem was, he had all kinds of time. He was here until the wedding, and while he was enjoying the work at the vineyard, the physical activity allowed his mind to wander. It kept wandering Stevie's way.

He glanced around. "You grew up in this house, right?"

"Sure."

"Show me your room, then. I'll bet I can learn a lot about you from seeing that."

With a shrug, she led him toward the staircase. Her foot on the bottom step, she paused. "Are you going to share your secrets, too?"

He smiled at her. "You can find all those in the archives of *The Global Enquirer*—they're posted on the Internet. And do you know there's a magazine titled *Royalty*? I heard they devoted a centerfold spread to me once."

"I don't keep up with the tabloids," she said, turning.

As she mounted the steps, he followed close behind. "The latest stories say my father's finally disowned me."

His tone was light. "That I'm broke and in desperate need of cash, which is why my supposed friendship with the Atlanta embezzler is suspect."

He couldn't read her expression as she glanced at him over her shoulder. "Remind me to keep an eye on my piggy bank, then."

There was actually one in the room, positioned on a windowsill. Ceramic, fat, and painted like a pirate. Really, if Jack had been a criminal, he would have stolen it, because it was silly and charming and made him grin. Stevie patted its thrusting snout as she turned to gaze out the glass. "My sister Giuliana and I shared this room. We had a standing bet about who could guess the day the first cabernet grapes turned from green to purple."

Jack joined her at the window. It overlooked countless rows of vines spreading in all directions. "And you always won."

Her eyes turned to him. "You're right. How did you know?"

"You pay attention and that would pay off." He thought of how she'd read the situation at the Platts' dinner party and he was grateful for it. "Someone's mood. Another's reaction. I suppose it would work for the grapes, too."

A sly smile dug a tiny dimple at the corner of her mouth. "Our old vineyard manager was much better at paying attention than I. He gave me the date, I gave him cookies . . . that Allie had baked."

Jack laughed. "You're tricky."

"With two sisters, I had to be."

They both turned toward the vista again. He glanced at her face, glanced back. "Interesting that you're the only one who doesn't work at Tanti Baci."

Her body stiffened. "I . . . That's true."

"Yet you're doing it now."

"It's been in our family for a hundred years. I suppose I don't like the idea of our generation being the one to lose it." She made a face. "Uh-oh. That *does* make me sound sentimental."

"No. Maybe. But it also explains something to me. Liam told me the wedding sideline is easing the winery's cash-flow problems. Now I understand better why you're willing to handle Roxy and Emerson's wedding."

Her personal pride wasn't the only thing at stake. It was Tanti Baci, and Stevie was stepping up to keep it in the family. Some might call it sentimental, but he wouldn't fault her for that.

She studied his face. "What would you hate to lose, Jack? Is there something you care so much about you'd do just about anything to keep it?"

"Good God," he answered, stepping back. "No."

"No?"

"*Mon ange*, everyone will tell you my life has been an endless exercise in care*less*ness."

"I told you I don't keep up with the tabloids, Jack." But then she turned toward the room's interior and gestured with a slender hand. "Guess which half is mine?"

Appreciating the change in subject, he surveyed the space in front of him. One side of it was painted a cool, orderly green. The single bed made with tight hospital corners. The books on the shelf above the small desk looked serious. A lacrosse stick was propped in a corner.

He pivoted.

The other half of the room had walls of a delicate shell pink. The ruffled bedspread and matching pillow sham were cream, edged with more pink embroidery. Volumes of girly fiction titles were jammed in the bookshelf.

On one corner of the desk sat a paperweight shaped like a glass slipper.

Jack glanced at Stevie and the little smile turning up the corners of her mouth. "Pink," he decided.

Her eyes rolled, even as her smile turned more delighted. "You're delusional. That's Giuliana's half. So much for my inner sweet side, huh? That must mean you're not as smart as you thought."

"No, *mon ange*," he said, grinning at her. "It only means you're more repressed than *I* thought."

"Oh, please." Her smile hadn't faded. "I'm not going to take that bait."

He pretended offense instead of showing his disappointment. "I have no idea what you mean."

"Right. You weren't just hoping that I'd feel all insulted and then throw myself at you in order to prove I have needs that I refuse to bury."

"Kind of worked that way for me before." *Now* who was smug? "Remember? After that meeting in your office?"

"I remember."

She looked deliciously awkward and adorably annoyed. Not that he'd take his life in his hands and tell her. Fact was, he liked her tough exterior. It was her hidden streak of romanticism that would make a man love her.

He froze. Love her? Where the hell had that come from?

"Jack . . ." She put her hand on his left arm.

The touch seared his skin through his shirt. He looked over; their eyes met. It was like that first night in the limo; it was like every time since. Sexual chemistry bubbled. He felt himself relax.

This, he understood.

"Well?" He cocked an eyebrow at her.

She made a frustrated sound in her throat. Obviously whatever she'd had to say had been lost in the heat of their sexual connection. Fire raced down the left side of his body and then rose up the right. His shaft began to harden.

Stevie looked like she could spit nails even as her face flushed.

Laughing softly, he cupped her cheek in his palm. It burned under his hand. "Stop fighting so hard. Won't do a bit of good."

Another frustrated noise. Her body hummed beneath his touch. "Doesn't this bother you?" she asked.

"Why should it?"

"Because I—because *we* don't want it."

His thumb tickled her lips, brushing back and forth against their soft surface. "Not everything can be controlled," he answered. "That bothers some people—Roxy despises the feeling."

"But you?" When she said the words, her mouth moved against the pad of his thumb. The sensation shuddered down his spine.

"I admit under almost every circumstance I don't find the sensation pleasant, either. But I can accept and appreciate it, I guess you'd say, when it leads to something pleasurable." He leaned closer. "I keep telling you we could have fun with it."

She didn't back away. "And if I agreed to that . . . ?"

His mouth answered her. The kiss blazed, the taste of her the only thing he needed to be set on fire. "Think how entertaining it could be, *mon ange*," he whispered as he moved his lips toward her ear. "It's not something we should pass by."

This was why he'd really come to visit her today, he admitted to himself. To taste her again, and while he was here, it didn't hurt to share the personal philosophy he'd developed over the last decade. Don't get too serious about anything or anyone. Take your amusement when and where you can.

A cell phone warbled. She broke the embrace, her gaze on him as her hand crept to her pocket and pulled out her cell phone. "It's a reminder. I have a meeting with your sister and Emerson's mother in the wine caves."

He pretended that breathing was coming easy to him, despite that scorching kiss.

Her finger flicked off the alarm. "You're welcome to attend."

A meeting in shadowy, confining caves. "No, thanks. I'll catch up with you later and we'll . . . continue our discussion."

"Jack," she cautioned, that tough-girl glint in her eye. "I haven't said I'll go to bed with you."

He smiled. *But you will.*

~

Stevie made a phone call on the way to meeting Jack's sister and Senator Platt. With the cool winter air on her face and the crunch of gravel beneath the soles of her boots, she felt more grounded. All she needed now was to clear her head of this carnal confusion.

"Allie?" She frowned as she heard her sister's voice. "I thought I called Mari." Her finger must have hit the wrong speed-dial number.

"Talk to me anyway," her sister implored. "I'm bored but Penn has a fit when I start hopping around trying to find something to do. Whatever you were going to discuss with Mari is fine by me."

Stevie hesitated, torn between talking to the first person she reached and talking about it with Allie, who had never met Jack. But she had to figure out how far she was willing to take her involvement with her "fiancé."

"It's about a man," she admitted. "A . . . uh . . . beautiful man." Oh, Lord, it was going to have to come out, though, wasn't it? "Jack Parini, the brother of Emerson's fiancée. I'm sort of engaged to him."

"You're *engaged* to him?" There was a garbled noise in the background, then Allie's voice again, complete with laughing undertone. "Penn overheard and he wants to know if you asked him yourself."

"I left that to you," she said, because Allie had proposed to her husband. Twice.

A shocked silence came over the line. "You're not kidding?"

"No." She quickly outlined the situation, though she didn't go into detail about the exact circumstances in the Platt butler's pantry. "He's, uh . . . quite, um, physically appealing. And the feeling is, uh, mutual, I guess."

"Oh my God! Stevie, queen of the understatement, is talking about a mutual physical appeal." Clearly she was sharing this news with Penn, too.

Stevie groaned. "Alessandra—"

"Penn wants to know if that's how this Jack guy refers to it. Because he says 'mutual physical appeal' sounds a little limp and—"

"Nothing about Jack is limp."

Allie crowed. "Not limp, Penn, she swears the man's not limp!"

"I should never have called you," Stevie groused, shaking her head. "That's right, I didn't call you. I was phoning Mari."

"Okay, okay. I'm sorry. But I can only watch so much TV and—"

"He wants me to go to bed with him."

"Well, of course he does," said Allie, obviously unimpressed. "You have a mutual physical appeal, you've assured me he's not limp, and—"

"I'm tempted."

"Of course you are. You said he was handsome?"

"Very handsome." And so sexy, when he whispered hot promises in her ear.

"And after the way Emerson treated you," Allie continued, "it must be lovely for a man to make you feel desirable again."

Was that all there was to it? Stevie stopped walking to mull this over. Was it so mundane as that? Emerson had banged up her ego and Jack was like one of those do-it-yourself dent-pulling tools that snapped a car body back into place?

Hmm.

After considering a moment longer, she decided the image pleased her. It was simple, straightforward, and only affected the exterior—nothing deeper.

"It can't hurt at all," she murmured, starting to walk again. "It'll be a way to get back into shape."

"Huh?" Allie said, sounding puzzled. "Wait a minute, I said it was nice to feel desired. I didn't say you had to jump into anything—"

"Why not?" Stevie asked, lengthening her stride. What was lovely was feeling like herself again. Decisive. Resilient. No-nonsense. "We're both adults. We have needs. It doesn't have to be, to mean, anything more than that."

"Of course not, speaking in a purely philosophical and hypothetical sense, I agree. But, um . . . this is you, and, well, though I know you pride yourself on—" She broke off. Sighed. "You realize you're talking about sex like a man?"

Stevie smiled, happier than she'd been in days, weeks, months. "Exactly."

~

Outside the entrance to the wine caves, Roxy remained silent as Stevie Baci apologized to her and her mother-in-law-to-be, Senator Platt, for her casual dress. "I meant to change out of jeans for our meeting," she said, "but I got waylaid."

Since Roxy had recognized the car her brother was driving in the parking lot, she wondered if Jack was the "way" who'd "laid" the other woman. She snorted, then turned it into a cough as Lois Platt turned to look at her.

"Are you all right, Roxanne?"

"Of course." Her voice sounded unnaturally high to her own ears. The verge of hysteria could do that to a person. "I'm fine."

Stevie looked over her shoulder as she unlocked the heavy doors leading into the caves. As they opened, chilled air and a sourish, though not unpleasant, smell washed over them. "We have a couple of hours before the tasting room opens," she said. "That's just one part of the caves, though. Wine is stored in another area, and then there's the dining room where you'll have your dinner."

Her hand found a switch at the entrance and wrought iron chandeliers lit along the underground hall. Stevie let out an audible sigh. "We've had an ongoing electrical problem, but it looks as if we've solved it."

"Are you sure?" the senator asked. "I don't want any difficulties that night. We have the press conference first, of course, but then—"

"It will be fine," Stevie promised, smiling over her shoulder. Then her glance sharpened. "Roxy? Are you all right?"

That was the second time in five minutes the question had been put to her. "Don't I look fine?"

Stevie's gaze cut to the senator and then back to Roxy. "I would imagine anyone would be feeling nervous as their wedding approached—especially if the event will be launched by a press conference."

"Nonsense," Emerson's mother said as they followed in Stevie's wake. "Roxanne is a princess. She's accustomed to attention. She's made for public life."

Roxanne was glad the relative dimness of the caves hid her reaction to *that*. Instead, she pretended an interest in her surroundings as Stevie explained their construction. Almost five years old, the space had been carved out of the hillside, then reinforced with rebar and finished with sprayed cement. "Like a swimming pool," Stevie explained, "only upside-down."

She showed them into the cavernous space that would be used for the rehearsal dinner. It was finished with a beautiful long table and matching chairs. More chandeliers hung overhead, though it was probably shadowy enough to make those who disliked darkness a little twitchy.

That wasn't Roxy's weakness. She took a seat with the two other women at the table and pulled out the seating chart she'd filled out alone. Taking a breath, she pushed it toward the senator. "This is just a draft, of course. Feel free to make any changes you like."

The older woman's fingertips drummed as she peered at the paper through her businesslike reading glasses. Roxy forced herself to sit still during this examination, only looking up to send Stevie a half smile when she placed a platter of fruit and cheese on the table, along with small plates, forks, and napkins with the Tanti Baci logo.

As Emerson's mother continued to peruse the chart, Roxy focused on the food. There was a small silver knife for the cheese, pocket-sized, and the handle was shaped like a rabbit. Her fingers itched to touch it. She reached forward—

"Stop!" a male voice said.

She jumped, looking toward the sound with a guilty start. It was *him*! Had he driven here from San Francisco? How did he know how badly she needed him?

But then he came closer and she realized—with part relief, part disappointment—that it was a stranger standing there, a man carrying a covered tray. He was not too tall, but broad-shouldered and muscular. Though his face was youthful, silver threaded the dark hair at his temples. Smiling, he came toward her. "I don't want you to ruin your appetite for the desserts you're supposed to be sampling."

Her gaze sought Stevie's, and the other woman performed the introductions. "Roxanne, this is Charlie Howard. Emerson's mom chose him to cater your rehearsal dinner. We'll all gain weight just looking at his desserts."

Senator Platt looked up from the chart and gestured the chef into a chair. "I have several things to go over. Let me get my briefcase." As she bent to retrieve it, she glanced at Stevie. "Where should we start . . . ?"

"Charlie, you should know that before the actual dinner there's going to be a press conference—"

"You're going to announce you found the treasure!"

Stevie blinked. "What?"

The man looked smug. "I heard about it from Bud, who was told by J.D. that Seth found the key to the treasure, gave it to you, and now you've found the treasure itself. Right?"

"Wrong." Stevie was shaking her head. "It doesn't surprise me that in this town rumors are running like wildfire, but Charlie, you're jumping to conclusions."

"No treasure?"

"No treasure."

He flopped against the back of his chair. "I don't know whether I'm sad or glad to hear that. We used to hunt for it with shovels and flashlights when we were kids."

"You and everyone else in Edenville." Stevie slanted a glance at Roxy. "Short version: legend says there's some kind of treasure somewhere on the Baci land. It's a kind of rite of passage to go out looking for it. Our version of a snipe hunt."

"Then there's the ghost story," Charlie added. "If you go to Anne and Alonzo's cottage with your one true love, their ghosts will appear in approval."

"So that's why you were caught out there with a succession of girls, Charlie. You were just looking for your one true love—not trying to find a private make-out place."

He laughed. "You got me."

Senator Platt's briefcase thumped against the tabletop. "Charles," she said. "The real news is that we'll be announcing my son's candidacy for the U.S. Congress that night."

"Uh, maybe you should swear him to secrecy, Senator," Stevie suggested. "You just saw how gossip—"

"I don't care who hears about it ahead of time," the older woman declared. "It will only get people accustomed to the idea. Emerson is going to be their next U.S. representative, just as Princess Roxanne Parini will be his wife."

And there it was. Out loud. Fait accompli. Removed from Roxy's control. The princess and the politician.

She closed her eyes, her hands cradling the little rabbit-handled knife in her lap. *I have to get away*, she thought.

To the one person, besides Emerson, who had ever made her feel safe. But she couldn't go back to that other man. He didn't want to see her any longer. She didn't want to see *him* any longer.

Yet she knew she was going to anyway.

9

It was closing in on six P.M., and Stevie moved around the PR office at Tanti Baci, pretending she was doing something besides anticipating the evening ahead. Tonight she had a date with a prince—and her personal dent-puller. Jack had called her this morning and she'd agreed.

Her stomach gave a little nervous spasm, so she rushed to the full-length mirror installed on the back of the office door. Did she look okay?

She looked okay. Jack had said the evening would be casual. To that end she'd worn her bad-girl black boots with dark denim jeans, and a tight-fitting, button-up blue sweater over a matching lacy camisole. She'd fastened the sweater to just below her breasts and the lace peeked through the gap.

Her earrings were long, a handcrafted pair she'd picked up at a boutique in Edenville. They were slender rods of polished abalone shell that tickled her neck when she moved. And she couldn't keep still, driven to dance just like the butterflies in her belly.

She smiled at herself, because even nervous, she was in a great mood.

Sex like a man.

No strings. And no inhibitions, she decided. She rubbed her cold hands together and smiled again. Why not? Why hold back when she hadn't had sex in many, many, many months, not since—

"Emerson?" She leapt back, gaping, as he came barging in. "What are you doing here?"

Ignoring her, he surveyed the room, even going so far as to peer behind the door he'd opened. His hands pushed through his hair, mussing his usually precise good looks.

"Emerson?"

Now he glanced at her, but clearly she wasn't at the forefront of his thoughts. It was an expression she was accustomed to, of course, because he'd worn it often before he'd dumped her. "What's going on?" she asked him.

"Roxanne," he said.

"Roxanne . . . ?"

"Do you know where she is?" Emerson demanded.

That caused her to blink. Emerson, as a rule, wasn't a demander. He was easygoing, calm, the kind of man who rode the waves of life by staying on top of them. He surfed trouble.

He ran his hands through his hair, mussing it again, and she noticed that it and his clothes were nearly soaked through.

It looked as if trouble had swamped him.

She edged away, concerned his agitation might infect her. She was happy! Excited! Full of smiles!

"Sorry," she told him. "But I have no idea where your bride might be. I haven't seen her since we met in the wine caves yesterday."

"She didn't tell me what she was doing today. Her cell phone isn't picking up."

Out the window, she could see darkness and sheets of rain. "It's pouring out there. Maybe she's stuck in traffic."

"You don't understand—"

"Roxanne's a big girl."

He shook his head. "She's not like you, Stevie. She's . . . so . . . I don't know. Soft. Feminine."

That was it. Unfeminine, unsoft Stevie advanced on him, herding him toward the exit. "I don't have time for this." She had a good mood to nurture. "So I'll have to say good—"

"What if she's been kidnapped again?"

Her feet stuttered to a stop. "What are you talking about? Kidnapped?" *Again?*

"You know." Emerson made a rough gesture. "Jack must have said."

"His sister was kidnapped?" A trickle of ice traced down her spine, but then she remembered that Roxanne was currently hale and hearty—and planning on marrying Stevie's ex. "Look, Emerson, maybe we can have this chat some other time."

The last thing she wanted was for Jack to arrive and Emerson to be on-site. They had a special evening ahead and it would mar the mood if it began with Emerson's paranoia.

Instead of taking direction, Emerson moved only as far as one of the visitor's chairs. He pulled his cell phone from his pocket and then dropped into the seat to stare at the device, as if willing it to ring.

It was all hard to fathom, except the fact that unless she could carry him out of the room—even her unfeminine self wasn't that strong—the quickest way to get rid of him and the headache threatening to spoil her happy frame of mind was to humor him.

For five minutes.

She checked her watch. "Okay, now. What's this about a kidnapping?" A little chuckle escaped her. "Don't tell me you've found a ransom note."

He shook his head. "That's how they caught the bastard ten years ago."

The ice avalanched down her back this time and she

shivered. "You're—you're not kidding? This really happened?"

Emerson looked up. "You didn't know? It was ten years ago, but the gossip rags followed it for months . . ."

"I've never paid attention to the tabloids." And she'd been . . . what? Seventeen? Still recovering from the death of her mother and trying to escape her feelings about it by running cross-country and track and playing all-season softball.

"A friend of Jack's hatched the idea. Well, the man was actually the brother of a girl he was seeing. Sister and brother were both implicated, and both went to jail."

A friend of Jack's? "That must have been horrible."

"They were at a house in the mountains of Ardenia. Separated. Roxanne was locked in a bedroom. Fourteen years old and locked in a bedroom all by herself for five days!"

Stevie's hand crept up to her throat and she sank into another chair. "My God." Her gaze found the window and she stared unseeing into the darkness—*locked in a bedroom all by herself for five days!*

"Jack was kept in a closet."

Her head jerked toward Emerson. *"Jack?"*

The other man was shaking his head. "He really didn't tell you? You're engaged and you didn't know this about him? I'm concerned about the kind of relationship you and he have, Stevie."

A casual relationship. A convenient one. "Sex like a man," she whispered.

"What?"

Then a flurry of movement and rain-scented air redirected her attention. Jack strode into the office, stopped short. "What the hell are you doing here, Platt?" he asked, frowning.

Emerson jumped to his feet. "Where's your sister?"

Jack's eyes narrowed in suspicion. "Why? Are you afraid she'll find you here?"

Confused by his tone and everything she'd just learned, Stevie waved her hands. "Emerson's misplaced Roxanne. Have you spoken with her?"

His gaze flicked to her. She felt it run from her eyes to the lacy inset over her breasts, then back to her mouth.

Her skin prickled in that odd, maddening way it did around him. Her lips tingled. "Jack!" she said, to bring him back to the subject. "Roxanne?"

He turned his head toward Emerson. "She's in her room at the resort. I just spoke with her there. She'd just gotten in."

The other man didn't relax. "She doesn't pick up her cell."

"I talked with her on the room's landline. Maybe you can't reach her on the cell because of the rain, but most likely it's because—"

"She forgot to keep it charged," Emerson finished. He was already rushing for the door. "I'll take care of that."

Stevie waved to his retreating back. "Great talking with you, too."

"I've noticed sarcasm doesn't work with him," Jack said, moving closer.

She moved back, suddenly, acutely aware that the man coming toward her was a stranger. *Jack was kept in a closet.* Ten years ago, he and his sister were kidnapped. Rescued, obviously, but *kidnapped.*

Should she bring that up?

He tilted his head. "Did I get the day wrong? The time?"

"What?" She bit her lip, still mulling her options.

"You don't look very happy to see me."

Happy! That's right. She was supposed to be in a good mood. Fifteen minutes ago, she'd been looking forward to spending time with him. "Of course I'm pleased to see you," she said.

He took her shoulders in his hands. "Happy, *mon ange.* There's a difference."

Jack Parini had been kidnapped once upon a time, but he'd decided not to share that information with her.

"Smile, darlin'."

She glanced up at him, surprised by the Southern drawl he'd affected. "What's that?"

"Just my Georgia charm oozing out." This accent was as flawless as his French. "Do you like it?"

She laughed despite herself. "You're impossible."

"There's my girl."

He bent his head and kissed her. It was a stranger's mouth on her; a stranger's hands drawing her close to his hard chest. But then her brain stopped working and her body responded. *This is Jack, the man who makes me feel like I want to crawl out of my skin and find my way into his.*

Her arms went around his neck, her mouth opened, and she slid her tongue against his in warm, wet welcome. The kiss turned more desperate, then he pushed her a little away, breathing hard, his expression bemused.

"Sweet thing." Still Southern Man. "You've got me all riled up and the evening hasn't even begun."

Desire made her dizzy, but not enough that she could forget how little she knew about him. But what did that matter? This . . . this thing between them was for the present. Sex like a man.

She wasn't expecting a future, so why would the past matter?

It shouldn't, she told herself. It didn't.

~

Emerson Platt paused outside the door to his fiancée's suite. There were lights on inside, he'd spotted her car in the parking lot, her brother had assured him she was fine and dandy. He could take a few moments to compose himself.

He was a composed kind of man. Steady. Some might

call him a little too middle-of-the-road, but the fact was, he liked treading that secure center ground. No highs, no lows to trip a guy up.

Blowing out a breath of air, he slid his palms over his hair to smooth it. Since puberty, the stuff growing there had become a weak point. The strands were straight and thick but somehow, when he turned thirteen, they turned unruly. Even with the most expensive of stylists wielding their scissors, the haystack atop his head refused to lie quietly against his skull without the application of industrial-strength agents.

The product he used now was called Glop. Seriously. Emerson Platt, successful businessman, son of a U.S. senator, had to hold his hair down with Glop.

His mother would shudder and suggest using something with a more dignified name. So he didn't tell her. He liked his Glop.

Not that his mother's opinions weren't valuable. He considered her a very astute woman and an excellent senator—he'd been voting for her since he'd turned eighteen, even though no one would know if he didn't, would they? Her judgment was something he found he could rely on and he usually did. So he'd heard and heeded her opinion about him turning to politics.

It was a fact that he enjoyed working in the commercial real estate business, but he could see how his best talents could be put to use doing something else. Modesty aside, he had a true facility for getting people to trust him and for discovering their particular needs. Negotiation came easily to him.

All qualities that would prove useful in DC, and when he had at his side a beautiful wife—

Wife. Panic clutched at him again. Thoughts of hair, his mother, his career vanished.

He had to see Roxanne and make certain she was safe. His fist pounded the door in a most uncomposed manner. No problem, he assured himself. As soon as he saw her, his heartbeat would calm; his stomach-churning anxiety would quiet.

Light poured out as the door swung open. It framed Roxanne's petite figure and added a golden glow to her honey-colored hair. "Emerson?"

He yanked her against him. She fluttered a bit in his hold—he wasn't prone to yanking and likely surprised her—but settled once he buried his face in the perfumed warmth of her hair. After a moment, her arms circled his waist.

"Are you okay?" she said against his shoulder.

"Yeah." He lied, because his heart still slammed unevenly against his chest. But he didn't want her to notice that, so he managed to put some inches between them. "I'm, uh, just glad to see you."

She raised an eyebrow. "You haven't been that glad to see me in a while."

Without responding, he walked around her in order to get inside. As she shut the door behind him, he peered into the suite's bedroom. Her phone was connected to the charger. He shot her a glance over his shoulder.

"Guilty," she said, looking even more so. "But I plugged it in as soon as I got back."

"Where were you today?"

"I drove into San Francisco to see . . . to see a friend." Her gaze cut away from him. "Someone I haven't seen in a while."

"Oh." He didn't look at her, either, afraid she might make out the dregs of his earlier alarm on his face. Now that she was here, looking cozy and pretty in a fuzzy sweater and jeans, his reaction at not being able to reach her seemed like an overreaction.

Not the least bit level-headed.

He found his way to the sofa in the sitting area and lowered himself onto the cushions. Stretching his arms along the top, he took a few more deep breaths. There. Almost normal.

His fiancée walked toward him, her delicate perfume reaching him first, and his pulse scrambled again. Crap! He was Mr. Imperturbable. It was one of his favorite things about himself, something he wouldn't trade even for hair that didn't need Glop.

Roxanne sat beside him, such a featherweight that the cushion didn't jiggle. "Where have you been?" she asked, reaching up to stroke his cheek.

At her touch, his pulse jolted, started thrumming again. "I went to see Stevie," he said.

Roxanne's hand dropped.

Emerson cursed himself. Why had he mentioned her? But maybe Stevie had something to do with this roiling tension in his belly. He'd always been a decent guy. No slapping his buddies on the back when they stepped out on their girlfriends. Casual hook ups or booty calls had never been his style. Still weren't, of course, but how things ended with Stevie had left him with the bitter aftertaste of shame in his mouth. He'd actually thought getting back on a normal footing with her through this wedding process would dissipate that.

"Sometimes I'm an ass," he murmured, tucking a tendril of hair behind Roxanne's shell-like ear. It was pink, and in the light from the lamp, he could almost see through it. "You're so delicate," he said.

It was the first thing to strike him at that planetarium party. He'd been dragged there by an old frat brother who'd immediately gone off with some scary-looking woman dressed like the character Ripley from *Alien*. At Emerson's elbow stood a shy-looking Princess Leia.

Shy enough that he would have normally kept his distance—his instincts were good when it came to that kind of thing, too—but something about her had upset his normal process. He'd approached her. Bought her this terrible glass of wine. Wandered around beside her while taking in all the bizarre outfits and interesting astronomical displays.

When she'd mentioned he wasn't in costume and bemoaned her own humiliating hairstyle, he'd promptly bought a pair of green antennae fastened to a band. Then he'd put the damn thing on, knowing perfectly well it would mar the Glop-induced order of his hair.

That was the first time his gut had tightened in worry around Roxanne. He was pretty picky about his hair.

"Sweet girl," he whispered now, recalling how helpless he'd been against the softness of her voice, the clean lines of her face, the graceful moves of her petite limbs. Yet despite her small size, she'd knocked him over with the speed and surprise of a boulder tumbling downhill. He hadn't known he could feel like this.

Swallowing past the lump in his throat, he attempted acting like his normal, stalwart self. "What were you doing before I showed up at your door?" he asked.

Her mouth primmed in a clear refusal to answer the question, but her gaze gave her away as it jumped to the open notebook on the narrow coffee table in front of them. He recognized her precise handwriting and straightened to peer at the lined paper. "What do we have here?"

She swiped the notebook from the table and closed it. "I was working on my wedding vows . . . that is, if you still want to get married."

"Of course I do," he replied, though apprehension squeezed him again. Marriage!

"Good," she said with a little nod. "Then I'd recommend you start working on yours as well."

"Wedding vows, you mean? Doesn't the minister read them and I just, uh, repeat?"

A line appeared between her downy golden brows. "Emerson," she chided. "You agreed that we would write our own."

"I did?" He had? Good God, this marriage business was unbalancing him. Truly, he couldn't recall any such agreement.

Panic washed through him. At least he figured the

cold-sweat feeling was panic, though it felt much worse. It wasn't his memory lapse that made him feel so anxious, however. He could understand that, what with all the wedding details that had been thrown at him lately, not to mention his mother urging him into fast-forward with the political plans.

It definitely wasn't forgetting the promise that unnerved him, but that he'd agreed to it in the first place. For God's sake, writing original wedding vows sounded so damn . . . was *geeky* the word? No. Besotted.

Emerson Platt wasn't a man capable of that kind of emotion, was he? Infatuation like that struck him as just too extreme.

Out of character.

Uncomfortable with the thought, he jumped to his feet and started pacing the small room. He sifted his hands through his hair, trying to get a handle on everything that was running through his head.

"What's wrong?" Roxanne asked.

He paused, arrested by the reflection he saw in the ornate mirror hanging over the fireplace. The Glop had lost its power and his hair was on end and every which way—precisely how he felt in general. "I don't recognize myself," he muttered. *I don't feel like myself.*

She came to his side. "What?"

"I was worried about you today," he admitted. *I worry about you every day.*

Every damn thing about her scared him.

How can I live like this? he wanted to say. She put her hand on his arm and he jumped. Jumped!

"Emerson," she said in that soft, gentle voice of hers. "Your muscles are tight. Why don't you come into the bedroom and lie down?" Her hand petted him as if that could soothe his frayed nerves.

It didn't.

"I know a way to work off your tension," she said, a sexy little suggestion in her voice.

Oh, no. Oh, hell no. She'd been after him to make love to her, but so far he'd resisted. At first, because he knew she was a virgin and he thought that waiting for their wedding night would be something she valued. Now, it was because getting even this close to her made his lungs expand and his head spin.

Any closer and he could die of a heart attack.

"I've got to go," he said, and he meant it. He'd come by to ensure Roxanne was safe . . . only to realize that *he* might never feel safe once he married her.

10

What are we doing, Rox?

Going for normal.

For days, Jack hadn't been able to get that exchange with his sister out of his head. Though he was convinced that "normal" didn't exist for a man with his past, he had a temporary opportunity to experience it with Stevie. By asking the beautiful woman out on a date tonight, he had hopes the evening would end in a normal and very satisfying manner.

Except, despite yet another scorcher of a kiss, at the moment the beautiful woman was looking at him with an odd light in her eyes. Just as he tightened his fingers to draw her near again, she stumbled back.

He closed the distance between them, wanting to reassure without letting her get away. His knuckle traced the clean edge of her jaw with a slow stroke. "Hungry?"

She let out a short laugh that didn't release the tension radiating from her. "Jack," she admonished. A flush flagged her cheekbones.

He chucked her chin. "Get those dirty thoughts out of your head. I meant for dinner."

"Sure." She retreated again, her feet tripping over a cardboard carton. "I knew that."

This time he let her have her space. "Our reservations aren't for an hour, but it's raining like hell out there."

She seemed to relax at the notion that he didn't consider having her as the appetizer on tonight's menu. "I'm ready to go," she said, "I just have to bring these boxes of stemware into the caves. Can you help?"

"Bring them into the caves?"

Already she was lifting one. "It will only take a couple of minutes if you can grab the other two."

He could do this. Of course he could do this.

With the stacked cartons in his arms, Stevie's tension dissipated by half. Her stride was confident as they exited the winery offices, though she let out a whistle at the heavy downpour. So heavy, he could hardly hear their footsteps over the sound of striking drops on the gravel parking lot.

The two of them remained dry, however, as the pathway to the caves was covered and brightly lit. More lights flanked either side of the entry.

He stared at their yellow glow, then eyed the heavy wooden door. Stevie set down her box and fumbled with a key ring. "So, uh, how extensive are these?" he ventured.

She glanced back. "There's approximately five thousand square feet of working area, including barrel storage. We have another fifteen hundred feet of entertainment space, which includes the tasting room, the dining room, and kitchen."

As she pushed open the door, more light flooded the first corridor from wrought iron chandeliers hanging every eight feet. With a gesture, she welcomed him inside.

He eyed the passage ahead. "What about earthquakes?"

"We're safe," she answered, scooping up her box. "The excavation into the hillside is only about five years old, and though the caves were expensive to build, they're a great place to store and age wine. No AC units, no need for heaters."

"Yeah. Caves keep the humidity and temps fairly constant," he said, approaching the threshold.

"That's right, you know this stuff." She preceded him into the passageway. "Humidity hovers around fifty-five percent. Which means less evaporation from the barrels. The temperature average is about sixty degrees."

A shiver tracked from the back of his neck to the base of his spine as he followed. Sixty chilly degrees. He cleared his throat. "Where are we taking these things?"

"Just follow me."

The entry door closed, shutting out the sound of the rain. It was quiet inside. Tomblike. Anyone might find the atmosphere confining, he told himself, though the ceiling height was fifteen feet and the passage they traveled down was another twenty wide. With a shrug, he tried dislodging the uneasiness pressing against him. "How much farther?"

At a juncture, she turned left. "Just into the dining room where we'll hold the rehearsal dinner."

It was gloomy ahead. She paused.

He froze. "Lights?"

They came on as the word left his mouth. These chandeliers matched the others, though he thought the wattage of the bulbs might be less. Eyeing them, Jack blew out a breath. "I'm starved. How about you? Let's get out of here, down a beer, grab some grub."

" 'Down a beer?' " She tossed him a smile over her shoulder. " 'Grab some grub?' Prince Jack, you'll have me thinking you're just some ordinary American boy."

"That's me," he muttered. "Ordinary." Normal. That's what he was doing tonight, remember? Going for normal.

"And here I thought you might be different," she teased, disappearing into another doorway.

He followed her into a spacious room with lit sconces and a long slab of a table. She slid her carton of stemware onto its surface and crossed her arms over her breasts.

"Different how?" he asked, putting down his own boxes.

"I thought perhaps the state of your stomach might come second to finding yourself alone with a woman in a romantic setting like this one. That you might—"

"Good idea," he said, drawing her arms from across her body to loop them around his neck. She wriggled as their bellies met and their mouths fused. "Best idea."

The cold fled. She was warm in his arms, then hot, as the kiss deepened. He stroked into her mouth, this cave sweet and wet, and his hands slid down to cup her ass. Her hips tilted into his and she rubbed against his stiffening erection.

He groaned at the goodness of it: the pressure, her taste, the rightness of her slender and strong body. His hands rushed to find bare skin, and there it was, that sweet dip above the waistband of her jeans and under the soft give of her sweater and the stretchy thing she was wearing beneath it. Goose bumps broke out on her silky skin and he chased them up the sides of her ribs.

She made a needy, feminine noise, and when he boosted her onto the table, she widened her thighs to keep him close. His cock pushed against their juncture as his hands yanked her double layer of top clothing upward. In the light, her nipples showed a dark pink against her nearly transparent bra. He put his mouth on the closest one, sucking strongly and tonguing it through the thin fabric. He knew she liked that.

Stevie bowed into his arms. He glanced up at her face and saw her dark lashes fall to her flushed cheeks. Her hands cupped his head, and then her nails bit into his scalp as he lifted his mouth. "I like your claws, *mon petit chat*."

Her hold immediately eased. Her top teeth seized her pillowy bottom lip.

"No, *mon chat*," he said, his voice soft. "I *like* the sting."

She shook her head, sucking her lip harder. He kissed her chin, her cheek, trying to distract her. Then he sighed. "No," he said again, touching his forefinger to the corner of her mouth, gently releasing the clasp of her teeth. Taking moisture from her tongue, he painted the abused bottom lip. "Mine to kiss," he scolded her. "Mine to bite."

Her eyes flew open as he did just that, a tender warning that he soothed immediately with another pass of his wet fingertip.

"Jack . . ." There was a note of alarm in her voice. "I don't . . . I feel . . ." She was panting a little, small hot exhalations against his cheek that only raised his internal temperature.

"Shh . . ." he said, trying to soothe again.

"Seriously, Jack." She tried scooting back on the table, but his splayed hand at her back kept her close. "This, uh, can't be normal."

He smiled. "You don't like my kisses? My touch?"

"Sure, but it's so much, so fast . . ." She shivered as he ran his hand up the silky skin covering her spine. "What the hell," she murmured, and her arm curled around his neck and brought his mouth to hers again.

She kissed him even as he felt her slender hand slide beneath his jeans and boxers. Her fingers were hot against his hip.

His body jerked, his cock twitched as desire surged, hardening his flesh, tightening his balls. It burned in his blood, and as she circled his stiff flesh, he thought he might come.

Damn! It was so much, so fast. She was right, it wasn't normal. She squeezed.

Okay, it was better than normal.

He cupped her breast in one hand and scooped her closer with his other arm. The table would be a fine surface for what his body was clamoring to accomplish. Tilting his head, he changed the slant of the kiss.

His tongue surged into her mouth. She sucked on him and—

They were plunged into darkness.

No. No! His head jerked from hers.

She squeaked in protest, then pulled in a sharp breath. "Oh. The lights went out."

"Yeah." He was clutching her, he knew that, but she was the only solid thing in the profound blackness. Disoriented, he only tightened his grip. "What now?"

"We should wait here. Maybe the electricity will come back on—"

"*No!*" He modulated his voice, even though anxiety was rising within him with every passing millisecond. "No. I think we should get outside." He had to get outside.

In the gloom he could feel her fumbling with her clothes. He kept one hand on her forearm and helped her ease down the hem of her sweater.

Sweat pricked his belly and back. His pulse continued rising until he could feel it pounding at his temples. When she moved to get off the table, it took him a moment to unlock his muscles and give her room.

He kept his hand curled around her bicep.

"I'm pretty sure I can find our way out."

Pretty sure. *Bordel de merde.* She was merely pretty sure she could find their way out. With his heart slamming in his chest and his breath only reaching as far as his collarbone, the single thing *he* could locate in the dark was an overwhelming state of panic. Nausea churned in his gut.

He struggled to keep the bile down. "You lead then."

They held hands. He knew he was crowding her, but God, he needed to feel another human's heat. They shuffled forward, then turned right.

Left! Shouldn't it be left?

He didn't think he screamed it aloud, but she spoke to him in a quiet voice. "Right here, then another right at the next junction."

Who could fucking *see* the junction?

Bile rose again. More sweat popped. He felt it trickling down his face.

He wished he could run the hell out of here, and would have tried, but even in panic he thought she was his only

chance at escaping these catacombs of hell. Maybe he tightened his grip on her hand, because she squeaked again.

"I have this friend," she said, moving steadily—but
slowly, oh, so damn slowly!—forward. "Her mom never
carries a purse. But she has everything you could ever need
regardless."

He couldn't acknowledge her talk, afraid if he opened
his mouth, it would only issue a primal scream.

"One time we were searching for our car in the north
forty of a parking lot and I wished aloud that I had a flashlight. Pat—my mom's friend—pipes up, 'Oh, I do,' and out
of her bra she pulls a flashlight."

She laughed. "No lie."

As if he'd answered her. As if words could be pushed
past his dry throat.

"Not much farther," she said now, taking another turn.

They'd already baby-stepped a marathon.

Then, in the space of one short breath and the next, Stevie crumpled, yanking free of his hand.

He froze. So this was cardiac arrest, he thought. His
chest tightened, his head pounded, he thought he saw the
River Styx in the near distance.

But the little whimper at his feet wasn't from a vicious
three-headed dog. "Stevie?" He squatted, his outstretched
hands encountering her soft hair, her shoulder. If she felt
his trembling, she didn't mention it.

"Stupid bad-girl boots," she muttered instead.

He heard himself make a sound—was it a laugh?

"Their oh-so-fashionable needle noses caught on something." She shifted and he heard a second stifled whimper.

"You're hurt."

"I twisted my ankle." Her voice sounded strained. "I
don't think it's broken or anything, but—okay, it really
hurts."

He was drowning in physical responses. Sweat, nausea,
cold, shortness of breath. But he had to do something. Help
Stevie. Get out of the effing damn dark.

Just run, the primitive core of him urged. *Find your way out. Find a way to get her later.*

He jolted to his feet. Hunkered down to touch her. Jack-in-the-boxed up again.

LaLanne? Stevie had questioned him on New Year's Eve. *O'Lantern? In the Box?*

He remembered how she'd amused him. Intrigued him. Aroused him from his first glimpse of that sweet full mouth.

She was hurt. Stevie was hurt.

He squatted again, battling panic. "Let me pick you up," he said, his breath soughing out in rough gasps. "We'll get out together."

She might have protested, but frankly, he couldn't hear anything very well, not over the death knell that was his heartbeat. Her weight felt light in his arms. Against his chest, it seemed to slow the organ inside a fraction.

"I'll put my hand against the wall," she said in his ear. "Walk slowly and we should be out in a few short minutes."

A week or two passed. Then his toe bumped one of the wooden doors at the entrance to the caves. Another day went by and then they were outside.

The lights at the entrance were out and the pathway from the winery administrative offices was no longer lit. But compared to the stygian atmosphere of the caves it seemed as bright as dawn. With Stevie still in his arms, he basked in the feeling of freedom.

"Jack." Her hand trailed down his face and surely she could feel his cold sweat.

"Yeah." He gulped more breaths of chilly, damp air.

"In there . . . you . . . the dark . . ."

Yeah. Though if he talked about it, she'd know . . . But shit, normal wasn't in his sights now, not even temporary normal, he thought, resigned. It had always been an off chance anyhow.

He stared out at the rain. "As I'm sure you've guessed,

I'm terrified of it," he admitted, his voice thick. "Prince Jack Parini, terrified of the fucking dark."

~

Stevie and Jack arrived at the Baci farmhouse like the victims of a natural disaster. From outside the caves, she'd noticed the light illuminating her old home's front porch, and they'd agreed to head there.

Jack had sprinted to the parking lot for his car, but there was no human speed fast enough to avoid a thorough soaking in the driving rain. By the time they made it to the front door of the farmhouse, Jack carrying Stevie in his arms, they both looked like half-drowned swamp rats. "Are you sure I shouldn't be taking you to the emergency room?" he asked.

She shook her head, her own arms linked around his neck. Already her ankle was better. It had been one of those severe-but-short-term wrenches. The only reason she'd allowed him carry her was because that way she could hold him, too.

Once inside, she gave directions. Lights were flipped on, the heater activated, and she was deposited in the bathroom attached to the downstairs guest room. Though she offered him the first shower, he refused.

She didn't make a protest. A few minutes under the hot spray gave her time to think about her next move. Wrapped in a terry cloth robe, she opened the bathroom door to find him waiting. He had a bag of ice bundled in a dish towel and an elastic bandage he'd scrounged from someplace.

"I hate ice," she complained as he set her up on the guest bed, first winding the bandage in figure eights around her sore joint and then arranging the bag on top of it.

"Jock like you? Suck it up." But he pressed his lips to the top of her damp head. "I'd be on my way, *mon ange*, but I don't trust you to stay off that leg. Now be a good girl and rest while I get cleaned up."

He shut the bathroom door and she hurriedly abandoned the ice bag. Her injury was just a minor twinge as she limped about to collect some of her brother-in-law's clothes from the master bedroom. After leaving them on a chair outside the guest bath, she made her way into the small living area where she managed to put a match to the logs laid in the fireplace.

When Jack arrived on scene—wearing Penn's battered jeans and a *Build Me Up!* T-shirt—the room was warming, despite the rain drumming on the roof. Atop the small trunk that served as a coffee table, she'd set a platter of cheese and crackers. A bottle of a neighbor's cabernet sauvignon was breathing beside two wineglasses.

She busied herself by pouring the liquid into the stemware. "Tell me what you think. Last time I had this, I found it a little too jammy for my taste, but a fruity red sounds perfect for the moment."

He lingered in the doorway, shaking his head. *"Mon chat . . ."*

Cat. *I like your claws, little cat*, he'd said. *I like the sting.*

Underneath the long, thick robe, she was naked, and her skin bloomed with heat, as if she was already imbibing intoxicants. Her hand trembled as she poured the second glass. Good God, the French thing was going to kill her.

"You should have that foot propped up, Stevie."

"I will, once you sit down," she bargained and held out one of the wines.

Still, he didn't move. "You're probably wondering . . ."

"Nope," she said, shaking her head.

He narrowed his eyes at her as he crossed the room to take the glass and sit on the sofa. One considering swallow, then he set the wine aside in order to lift her injured leg and rest her heel on his thigh.

She grasped the edges of the robe together to maintain her modesty as he stuffed a throw pillow beneath her calf. "There," he said. His hand squeezed her bare toes.

She was insanely glad that Mari had recently dragged

her in for a pedicure. Her nails were painted a very feminine pink. A tiny red heart adorned her big toe.

His forefinger traced the lines of the elastic bandage at
her ankle and goose bumps crawled up her inner thigh. Her
leg twitched. It seemed to fascinate him as he took another
sip from his glass. "About earlier—"

"Forget about earlier." She leaned over to pick up her
own wine. "All I want now is a glass or two of this stuff
followed by . . ." Her nerve petered out.

His eyebrows rose. "Followed by?"

Stephania Baci was the brash sister. The bold one. The
bad one.

Keep your voice down, Stevie.

Do you have to clatter like that up the stairs?

Ladies wait to be asked.

She took another swallow of her wine and gazed at him
over the rim of her glass. Brash cat. Bold. "I want to do it."

His eyebrows shot toward his hairline.

She'd thought it through in the shower and decided that
her original intention for the evening was the best course.
"I want to have sex like a man."

"Uh." He took a hefty swallow of wine. "I think you're
scaring me. What exactly is 'sex like a man'?"

Her arm gesture rolled a wave across the surface of
the liquid in her glass. She pretended she wasn't flushing
again. "You know. We do it. We do it once. And we don't
have to get all touchy-feely about it."

"Problem." He rubbed his jaw with his free hand.
Slowly. "When I have sex, I find that touchy-feely is of the
utmost importance."

She glared at him, frustrated, until she saw the spark of
amusement in his eyes. Settling back on the cushions, she
ran her fingertip around the rim of her glass and then set it
aside. "You get what I mean, Jack."

Clearly he was fighting a smile. "Are you sure I do? I
may be unfamiliar with your American idioms."

"Right. This from the guy who not long ago told me he

was ready to 'down a beer' and 'grab some grub.'" She swung her leg to the floor to scoot closer to him on the sofa. His wineglass went back to its post on the trunk beside hers. "But just in case I haven't been clear, Jack," she continued, taking handfuls of his T-shirt to draw him nearer, "I want to fu—"

His mouth slammed against hers. She smiled inside, where she'd been aching since realizing what their adventure in the darkness had done to him. Sex would dissipate the awkwardness that lingered.

She opened her mouth for his tongue. The taste of him—that jammy fruity taste of the cab that was winter-night sweet—rushed to her head. Her fingers tightened on his shirt, and then she raced them to its hem to yank the fabric away from his skin.

He groaned, broke their kiss, threw off the shirt.

Heat poured from his flesh. She closed her eyes and laid her head on his chest, rubbing her cheek against his heartbeat.

"*Mon chat,*" he whispered and caught her chin to still her for another kiss.

She wanted to purr.

That feline sensation he created inside her curled in her belly and then unfurled throughout her body. It lengthened her muscles, warmed her blood, clamored for her to crawl over him, marking him with her scent and her heat.

Her nails scraped down his torso, his hard ab muscles shuddering at her touch. He ended the kiss to draw in raspy breaths, then he tucked his face against her neck and she trembled herself as his exhalations teased over her skin.

"Stevie." His mouth moved against her throat. "Listen. I owe you an explanation about . . . about earlier. Let me tell you . . ."

She couldn't hear it. She didn't want to. Right now the only kind of intimacy she could handle was his touch. His body against hers. Anything more was too dangerous.

Sex like a man.

"Talk later," she said, shifting back to put room between them. Her hands curled around the lapels of the robe. "This now."

She jerked the material to her waist.

His cheekbones flushed. His gaze focused on her breasts, and as if he was touching her, her nipples tightened into berries the same shade as that color flagging his face.

She swallowed, then crawled toward him.

He held her off, his hands on her bare shoulders. "More space," he said. "A bed."

And for the third time, he swung her up in his arms. The robe was left behind as he found her mouth and strode to the guest room.

The sheets were cool against her heated nakedness. Jack came down on her, his jeans abrading the skin between her legs. His big hands framed her face and he kissed her eyebrows, eyelids, her nose, her chin. Sweet, for-girls-only kisses that made her heart capsize—and made her anxious all over again.

Sex like a man!

"Hurry," she urged, fingers tugging at the fastenings at his fly. His own big hand took over, even as he still cupped one palm around her cheek and plied her with more of those gentle busses that threatened to drown her single-minded intent.

"Hurry, hurry," she urged again.

He laughed but didn't protest as she helped him shove the denim down his hips. Then he was there—*there*—solid cylindrical heat against her wet soft folds. She wiggled, the emptiness where she needed him aching. Insisting.

"Condom," he said against her mouth.

Oh, *God*! She didn't have one!

But he did, it was in his hand, and he lifted his hips in order to don the protection. Then he was back in place, sliding against that special spot, prodding her, teasing her, acting as if he meant to prolong this when she *burned* for them to be joined.

She tilted her pelvis, wriggled to get the parts lined up, then pressed down on his hips. Even as wet as she was, as ready and willing, the fit wasn't easy. Impatient with half measures, she whimpered.

"Sh, sh, sh," he said against her temple. "Relax, let me work it in. Slow, *mon chat*. Slower, *mon ange*."

But all the French endearments in the world couldn't douse the need driving her. Whimpering more, she lifted her knees to his flanks, jerked her body high, pushed his hips low. He sank deep.

She reeled at the full, stretched sensation. "Oh, God."

"Too-eager angel," he chided, his voice rough. "Now take it eas—"

But she was already moving again, afraid to unhurry the pace, afraid that something, something frightening, would catch up with her if she did. She closed her eyes against the brightness in the room and went into the darkness that so disturbed him.

No, no. Don't think about that! Feel—no, don't do that, either!

He surged with each undulation of her body, surrendering to her tempo. She worked herself on him, worked herself against him, as the pressure rose, driving her up, and up, and . . .

It burst.

She cried out as Jack drove into her once more, a second time, and then he spasmed, his mouth latching on to hers.

Moments later, he flopped to the mattress, his head on the other pillow. His chest moved up and down with heavy breaths. "Jesus, Stevie."

Her palms went to her head, feeling around to make sure it was still on top of her shoulders. Assured, she let her hands drop back to her sides. *Wow*, she thought, more than a little smug. She'd had sex just like she'd wanted. Wham, bam, thank you, man.

Then Jack moved an arm closer. His pinkie linked with hers.

She froze, no longer satisfied, now almost . . . scared. No. Surely not. Surely she was fine because she'd just had sex like a man! His littlest finger curled more tightly around hers.

Inside her chest, her heart lurched again, and she knew what had to be done. Immediately. She commanded her own hand, and after a few misfires, it finally slid away from his.

She breathed a little easier with that connection severed. But it worried her still, it did, that with just the slightest touch . . .

Jack could make her feel so much like a woman.

Jack woke up in a strange bed.

He wasn't alarmed. In the last decade, he'd changed cities and domiciles often enough that a momentary disorientation upon opening his eyes was a familiar sensation. It was waking up in sheets that smelled like a woman that was peculiar.

Because in that same last decade, he hadn't slept, actually *slumbered*, with a bed partner. His nightly quota of REM was substandard at best, but his SAS—snooze after sex—was nil.

Without exception, after the deed was done he always made his excuses and headed back to his own place.

Still fuzzy from an atypically deep sleep, he slowly took in his surroundings. The room's lights were blazing and the window shades were open. Outside, it was full day. He was alone in the bed. A sheet of notebook paper lay on the adjoining pillow. He reached for it.

Stevie's handwriting was angled and distinctively unembellished. No plumpness in the round vowels, no stylized consonants. She hadn't even signed the note. It read:

Had an airport pickup.

That's it. No "call me" or "see you soon" or even an "I'll phone you." He should feel relieved.

Instead, he felt . . .

Queasy, maybe. Not like last night in the wine caves when panic had scooped out the insides of his belly and heaved them toward his throat. This was more like a mild seasickness, as if the ground beneath him was shaking.

Damn woman unsettled him.

Last night, she'd refused to hear his explanation about what happened to him in the dark. Not that he'd wanted to talk about his experience, but he'd steeled himself to follow through with it. No way had he expected her to derail the discussion.

It had struck him as compassionate.

Kind-hearted.

But now . . . now he wondered if she'd had her own agenda.

Hmm . . . He'd started out that evening wanting some hot and sweaty sex and—

Hell. That's exactly what she'd given him. Crazy woman. Sex like a man!

Frowning, he looked at the damn note again. She'd walked away from him, no strings, no sweet talk, no nothing.

He decided it was annoying not to know how she looked as her eyes first opened. How she'd looked at *him*. Had her expression softened? And what about her physical self? Was her ankle fully operational now, or had she limped out of bed?

He crumpled the page in his hand. She'd done it on purpose, he thought. It was a diabolical move on her part, but it had worked like a wicked spell.

Instead of being satisfied with what had happened last night and relieved at avoiding all the potential after-orgasm complications, her actions had left him frustrated.

His appetite was whetted. He wanted to see her. He was hungry to see her and disappointed that she'd left him like this.

Like the way a man leaves a one-night stand.

Damn it!

He swung his legs out of bed, cursing her, him, the combustible chemistry that was the two of them together. Yesterday he'd anticipated a lighthearted little fling, a way to scratch an itch and get a craving out of his system, and now he knew—despite her pithy, pitiful note—that he wasn't done with Stevie.

If he'd followed his usual MO, he would have enjoyed a mutually pleasurable event in her bed and gone off alone. But because of that panic attack or some special Stevie-power or other odd unnamable, after coming he'd fallen asleep in her bed and then she'd turned the tables, leaving him.

His fingers uncurled from the balled paper and he smoothed it out, compelled to make sure he hadn't missed some subtle signal. He studied the page, turning it over, turning it upside-down, but there was nothing new.

Had an airport pickup.

Oh, hell! he thought, a new thought piercing his rattled brain. He had an airport pickup to make today, too. Scrambling around for his clothes, he tried figuring out how it had come to this. For a man who liked his relationships casual and his women at arm's distance, female complications appeared ready to take over his life.

~

After back-to-back airport passenger pickups and deliveries, it was late afternoon by the time Stevie dropped off her last party. Now she didn't know what to do with herself and so she settled on wandering downtown Edenville. Browsing the shops that bordered the city square was safer than either returning to the winery or hanging out at her limo service headquarters. At either place, it was possible she'd encounter Jack. She didn't want to encounter Jack.

Because what she didn't know was how to do post-sex like a man.

Men never agonized about an awkward morning-after, did they? You never heard them confess to a self-conscious heat rising to their faces when they happened upon the previous night's object-of-lust.

It was entirely possible that men didn't blush, damn them.

The scents in the organic bath-works shop made her sneeze, so she ducked into the small cookware place next door. Its narrow aisles were crammed with everything from ladles to latté machines, knife sets to nutpicks, aprons to asparagus steamers.

She was flipping through a stack of blank recipe cards when she heard a man call her name. Her stomach flipped as heat bloomed on her skin. She turned.

"Emerson," she said, keeping her groan to herself. He was a close second in her Persons-I'd-Rather-Not-Run-Into contest. But this was Edenville and there were busybodies everywhere. It wouldn't do to be seen running away from the man. Glancing out the store's plate-glass window to see who might be passing by, she sketched him a small wave. "Uh, I've got to go."

But he already had a hand on her elbow. "Not until you help me pick out a gift," he said, tugging her into the next aisle that put them even more on display to those traversing the wide sidewalk. "What do you think? There's these designer spatulas or this extra small-sized silicone oven mitt."

She blinked. "Are you choosing a gift for the family housekeeper?"

"No, no. For Roxanne." His expression turned sheepish. "I do realize it's not the most romantic kind of present, but I thought I'd select something that would show my commitment to our new life together. I don't think I've been communicating that clearly enough lately."

Put like that, she supposed he didn't seem quite so doltish. "Still . . ." Wouldn't lingerie or jewelry or even a box of hand-dipped chocolates be more appreciated?

But hey, it wasn't up to Stevie to promote relationship health between her ex and his princess. She reached for a mesh tube filled with sink scrubbies in rainbow colors and handed it over to him. "Nothing says 'I can't wait to marry you' more than a tool designed to remove stains from your porcelain."

Emerson gave the purple scrubbie a testing squeeze. "Really?"

Hell, she couldn't go through with it. "No," she said, snatching the item out of his hand and rolling her eyes. "I must say that I didn't know love could make a man quite so stupid."

Instead of taking offense, Emerson sighed. "You think that's it? You think I'm in love?"

She stared at him. "What?"

"You know me, Steve. Maybe better than anyone. Do I seem like myself?"

"Not now you don't." Without thinking, she reached up to smooth a funky cowlick springing up at the crown of his head. Emerson was usually so well-groomed. "What's wrong with your hair?"

His hand tried smoothing it himself. "The Glop isn't working," he said, his voice morose. "I don't know what's next. Kindergarten paste?"

She glanced out the shop window again, wondering if men in little white coats were hovering nearby, waiting for their latest patient to emerge from his shopping excursion. "Emerson, maybe you need a cup of coffee or a candy bar. Something."

"I need answers." Reaching out, he gripped her shoulders and pulled her close. "Stevie, you gotta tell me."

"Tell you what?"

His fingers tightened and his eyes bored into hers. "Can it be real? I had this instant alertness, you know? A sense of . . . well, under other circumstances you might call it doom." He let out a raw laugh. "Because it was as if I recognized her somehow and I knew that from then on my life was never going to be the same."

Stevie recalled New Year's Eve. Her immediate interest in the dark figure exiting the resort. The way she'd studied the man she now knew was Jack, the shiver she'd felt tracking down her spine when she was sure he was studying her in return.

How she worried he might wound her.

"I know what you mean," she murmured absently, looking over Emerson's shoulder and out the plate-glass window without really seeing any of the passersby. Her mind remained fixed on that very first night. She remembered Jack sliding along the front seat of the limo. His scent. His leg nudging hers and the way that simple touch shot through her system, causing that weird hiccup in her breathing. "Though I haven't a clue what to call it."

"Love," Emerson supplied.

"What?" Her gaze jumped to his.

"That's what I'm talking about," he continued. "I'm actually looking for a little reassurance here. I've been doubting myself. You know, wondering if it could be real, when it happened so hard, so fast."

Ice invaded her veins. "That's not love!" It couldn't be. It wasn't.

Emerson frowned, his hands still gripping her shoulders. "Yes, it sounds like a storybook, but it happened to you, too, Steve. You knew Jack for . . . what . . . five days? And then—"

"I happen upon my brother-in-law-to-be," a silky male voice said from behind her, "manhandling my—"

"Darling!" A woman's voice gushed.

Emerson turned, his hands dropping to his sides. He was immediately enveloped in the embrace of a tall, platinum-haired woman while Jack looked on, wearing a bemused expression. The trio stood between Stevie and the shop's exit, leaving her no choice but to scurry in retreat to the rear aisle.

From between a stack of Julia Child's *The Way to Cook* and cork coasters shaped like grape leaves, she played Peeping Thomasina. The blonde's back was turned to Stevie, but even so, she clearly had the figure of a stunner. She was chattering away, one hand on Emerson's forearm, while her other was tucked in the crook of Jack's elbow. A lover?

As if he heard her question, he glanced around and she ducked her head, grabbing a copy of Child's title. On page twelve it described how to prepare cream of corn soup. For a few moments, she pretended to purée Jack instead of the yellow kernels.

A mouth touched her temple. A voice murmured in her ear. "You left me to make the walk of shame alone."

She whirled, then caught his amused smile.

"Yeah, as if men do the walk of shame," she retorted, putting space between them. They didn't blush, they didn't shame, and while that all seemed like a fine example to her, she could feel embarrassment creeping over her skin anyway.

Last night she'd ground herself against him in wild abandon. He probably thought she was desperate.

"I wanted to take my time with you, *mon ange*," he murmured now. "It was over so quickly . . ."

Yes, desperate.

She moved a little farther from him, even as she shot a look at the woman he'd accompanied into the shop. "You can thank me, as it looks as if you're a pretty busy guy."

He followed her gaze, grimacing. "That's exactly why I need a do-over for last night's missed dinner. Without some other distraction, being at her beck and call will send me straight over the edge."

She glared at him. "I'm not something you use to avoid your . . . your . . ."

"Mother." Jack turned her to face him fully, a smile hovering on his lips. "You realize that's who that is, don't you?"

"I don't care who it is." His *mother*? She peered at the other woman and now had a better view. Tall, buxom, blond, but definitely not a young woman. Her outfit was chic: dark jeans, boots, a navy blue blazer over a silk shirt. There were tasteful diamond-edged hoops in her ears and . . .

"Is that a crown on her head?" she asked Jack, her eyes wide.

"I wish I could deny it," he said. "Roxy and I have tried for years, but . . ."

It wasn't ostentatious, not really, but holding back her platinum hair like a headband was a simple, diamond-edged tiara. "Wow," Stevie said. "I guess she takes the Queen of Ardenia thing seriously."

"If only it were that," Jack replied. "This affectation is actually a throwback to her pageant days."

A squeal came from the woman in question and she tented both hands over her mouth, as if she'd just been announced Miss Universe. "Jack?" she called out. "Jackie-boy?"

"Oh, God."

Stevie slanted him a look, not bothering to suppress her little grin. " 'Jackie-boy'?"

"Just wait," he murmured.

Glancing around her, his mother raised her voice. "Where are you, darling? Emerson says you're *engaged*?"

"Oh, God." It was Stevie who prayed this time. "*Oh, God*, I hadn't really thought . . . I never took it this far in my head . . ." Though she'd told Allie and then Jules the truth, she'd not refuted the lie in front of the Platts and had even counted on the news making the rounds of Edenville, depending upon it to squelch the persistent rumor that she was pining over Emerson.

But beyond that, she'd not fully considered the ramifications.

"I'm an idiot." She turned to him. "What the hell are we going to do?"

"What we were going to do from the first. Keep the fantasy going and then later, after Roxy's safely married, break it off."

"I'm really looking forward to that," she said, with feeling.

He grinned. "No doubt. But for now . . ." Taking her hand, he tried towing her forward.

She dug in her heels. "No! Not now! I can't—"

And then her body was enveloped in a warm, scented embrace. Jack's mother was slightly taller than Stevie and she had to bend a little to kiss her once on each cheek. She laughed, then said, "That's enough of the European bullshit," and swept her in for another lavish hug.

Once released, Stevie felt a little dazed. "Uh . . . nice to meet you, uh, ma'am." Was she supposed to curtsy or something? She glanced at Jack, who looked much too attractive with a glitter of laughter in his eyes.

"This is Stephania Baci, Mom," he said. "Stevie, this is my mother, Her—"

"Oh, stuff it, Jack. Don't try that crap on my pretty American friend." She grabbed Stevie's hand and squeezed. "I'm Rayette—after my daddy, Ray, of course—and my favorite title is my very first—Junior Miss Vidalia Onion. I was named that at eleven. Later, I went on to be Miss Georgia Peaches & Pralines, and after being crowned in Atlanta, I traveled to Ardenia and met Jack's father. He was a stubborn, handsome son of a bitch—still is—and the ass wouldn't let me leave the borders unless I married him."

It was really too much to take in. Rayette was stunning, gregarious, and talked like a truck driver. "Uh . . ."

Jack was openly laughing now. "Mom, I think you're shocking poor Stevie."

His mother rounded on him. "Now why would that be? Shocked that I called your father stubborn? You're exactly like him in that way, as I'm sure she's already found out for herself." Then she gazed back at Stevie. "Now, when can I meet your parents?"

"I . . ." Shaking her head, Stevie just went with the truth. "Unfortunately, you can't. My father passed away last year and my mother . . . a long time ago."

"Then *I* will stand in for her, starting today," Rayette declared.

Jack cleared his throat. "Mom . . ."

She ignored him as she studied Stevie. "You are such a pretty girl. Strong cheekbones, long eyelashes, that cute pointed chin. In the pageant circuit we called those lips you have a 'blow-job mouth.' Automatically doubled your points in the appearance category from the male judges. Those dirty old men got all riled up around girls with mouths like that."

"Mom." Jack had his hand over his eyes.

"Well, it's true."

Stevie found herself laughing despite the awkward situation. For a second, she supposed that the queen might be the kind of woman who wouldn't mind a little girl wandering the house with grape-stained clothes and a collection of rocks.

Rayette beamed at her. "This is going to be wonderful. We'll all have dinner together tonight. You'll tell me about your wedding dreams, we'll think about dresses and trains . . . I always like a dramatic cathedral length, don't you? Roxanne has insisted I'm completely hands-off when it comes to her big day—both my damn children can be so hellishly stubborn like their father—but you don't have a mother, so maybe you'll let me do for you what she . . ."

Stevie's laughter had died several sentences ago and

she moved closer to Jack, clutching his wrist. *Save me*, she telegraphed.

"Mom. Mom."

She broke off, frowned at Jack. "What?"

"I'm sure Roxy and Emerson expect your full attention tonight. Why don't you focus on their wedding first?"

She waved a beringed hand. Her manicure was perfect. Maybe, Stevie thought, she wouldn't overlook grape stains after all.

"Jack, I can focus on both! I can focus on many things at once!" She smiled at Stevie. "My husband says I'm like a spider, I have eight eyes and they're looking everywhere. I like spiders, but I tell him he's damn lucky I'm not some black widow. So about tonight—"

"I can't make it tonight," Stevie said quickly. "I'm sorry."

"No?" The older woman frowned, but then her gaze caught on Jack's. "Ah. Oh. Well."

Stevie shot him a warning glance, but he ignored her to slide an arm around her shoulders. He nuzzled her temple again. "You read my mind, Mom."

"It wasn't that hard," his mother responded drily. "In my experience, men's thoughts rarely stray from a single track."

"Well, you guessed right. Stevie and I have special plans of our own this evening."

No, they didn't. Her jaw dropping, she half turned under the tight grip of his hand. Hadn't she made clear they would be together like that one time only? One sex-like-a-man time.

His mother had wandered away to look for Emerson when Stevie rediscovered her voice. "Listen, Jack—"

"You wouldn't want to make a liar out of me, darlin'." The Southern Man had reemerged, likely due to his mother's own impossible-to-ignore accent.

Stevie bristled. "Oh, I certainly—"

His hand clamped over her lips, muffling her protest. "Mom's only half right about that blow-job mouth. I'd quadruple your points in the appearance category."

The comment left her speechless. And allowed him—the man she'd meant to avoid—to hustle her out of the shop.

It was raining again, the sky so low that the clouds seemed to hover at head level. With Jack at her heels, Stevie ran across the parking lot that served both Edenville Motor Repair and Napa Princess Limousine. At the rear of the lot was a stucco two-story duplex, half of which she owned. Her bedroom was on the second level and she operated her business from the kitchen table.

Unlocking the front door, she glanced behind her. "I still don't know why you're here."

"We're going for a second try at that dinner we missed." Jack shrugged. "You said you wanted to change clothes, and—"

"My clothes." She'd wanted to change because before that dinner she also had an after-five meeting at the winery, but now it registered that she'd met Jack's mother in her black-and-white driver wear. "Do you think Emerson told your mom what I do for a living?" *That her son is engaged to a chauffeur?*

He shrugged again as he followed her over the threshold.

"Why does it matter? My mother spent her formative years working in a business that had her spreading Vaseline on her teeth and supergluing her bathing suit to her butt. She's not one to judge. My father, on the other hand . . ."

She didn't insist he elaborate. "Stay here," she said, pointing to the kitchen. "I'll be right back."

With a man downstairs, her closet turned into a fabric jungle—hot, tangled, and dangerous. "Why did I agree to go out with him again?" she mumbled to a leather belt coiled like a python around a hanger.

Because they'd missed their dinner the night before, he'd reasoned.

She knew it was because what they had done the night before made it that much harder to resist him. Add in his French accent, his Southern drawl, and his amazing body and her willpower was toast. Ten minutes, four outfits, and a pile of discards later, she descended the stairs in clothes she'd never worn before.

"Nice," said Jack, lounging against the newel at the bottom step.

She plucked at the thin black sweater. It was tucked into a red skirt that Allie had decided was too tight for her. It was red, full, and buttoned up the front, the high waistline tight to her ribs. She wore black tights, slouchy boots with low heels, and a black and red scarf wound around her neck.

Also red lip gloss.

She never wore red lip gloss.

And his gaze was focused there. *Mom's only half right about that blow-job mouth. I'd quadruple your points in the appearance category.*

"Ack!" she said, squeezing her eyes shut. "This is all your fault. Every bit of it."

His grin was lazy. "Haven't we gone over this before? It's just a chemical thing, *mon chat*. Nothing to get your fur ruffled about."

She let that be the last word on it, because there was a

He turned to her with a little smile. Just a year older than Stevie, Seth had the golden Bennett good looks. After law school, he'd gone to work for his family, keeping all their various businesses on track. She'd always had a soft spot for him and smiled back.

Jack must have noticed. His hand tightened on her leg and he whispered in her ear again. "Remember you're an engaged woman."

"I still have my memories," she whispered back. "I can't look at Seth without remembering our kiss."

"What?"

At the outburst, those circling the table turned to Jack. "Is there a problem?" Seth asked.

"I, uh . . ."

"I think he's jealous, Seth," Stevie put in, taking the opportunity to needle the man whose palm was hot and hard on her knee. "I told him about our big smooch."

"Is that right?" Seth's smile grew and his eyes warmed. "That *was* pretty memorable. Why your lips—"

"Don't talk about her lips." To Stevie's shock, Jack's chair legs screeched against the floor and he half rose. "Don't say another word about her mouth."

"Good God," Jules said, rolling her eyes. "Seth was ten, Stevie less than that, and she pushed him into a pile of manure right after the fact."

"Then we tussled in the stuff," Seth reminisced, as if they'd been rolling in sweet-smelling clover. "First and last time I let a girl get the best of me."

"Oh, please," Stevie said. "You cried like the little baby you were until I took pity on you." Then she turned to Jack. "I was sitting on his chest and he claimed he couldn't catch his breath. Do you believe that?"

All the earlier temper was gone from his face and he was smiling that amused smile again. He cupped her cheek with his hand. "Absolutely, *mademoiselle*. You take away my breath on a regular basis."

Flustered and hot, Stevie jerked free from his touch and

primly folded her hands on the table. His seductive manner was unlike the way any man had ever been with her, and she kept running into corners trying to escape it. "The meeting . . . ?"

"As long as you're finished teasing your guy," Seth said, "we'll go right ahead."

At her embarrassed nod, he began. A few minutes of routine matters followed. Then he tapped his pen on his pad. "We started these monthly meetings so that there's more communication between the two families. Everyone here—with the exception of you, perhaps, Jack—knows that Tanti Baci is teetering on the brink. Allie's weddings bought us time with some much needed cash flow, but with her laid up, we might need to rethink the viability of keeping that side of the business going."

"I'm doing my part," Stevie said, leaning forward in her chair.

"For the moment," Jules said. "But facts are facts, and you've never been keenly committed to the winery."

"But . . ." But it was true. She'd been the first to divorce herself from the winemaking tradition; the one who always felt she was watching the family business from the outside. Six months ago, when they'd faced up to the disaster that was the Tanti Baci finances, she'd been an advocate for cutting their losses and selling out.

"Stevie's stepped up now, though," Jack said. His hand stroked from her nape to her waist in a soothing caress. "While your sister's out, she's handling the weddings."

"We still have to consider that the weddings may not be enough," Seth said.

"Maybe . . ." Stevie didn't know where this sudden desperation had come from, but she didn't want to hear him say the winery had fallen so far it would never get back up again. "Maybe I can find the treasure," she blurted.

She must have grown a second head, the way the assembled company stared at her. "You know . . . Seth gave me the key. It could . . . I don't know . . ."

Giuliana shot Liam a hard look. "I blame you and your brother for this. Feeding her silliness—"

"I don't have a silly bone in my body," Stevie protested.

"Until it comes to ghost stories and treasure hunts. How many times did you read *Robinson Crusoe*?"

"Hey!" she complained.

Jack found Stevie's hand, squeezed. "My sister says that wedding venues aren't easy to come across. Can you charge more?"

Liam was shaking his head. "Maybe, but we're pretty competitive on that score, according to Allie. Our new issue is that due to her marriage, she's not in northern California full-time. We run her ragged when she's in Edenville, but there are still gaps, which means to keep this end going we should hire someone we can't afford."

"But if we can't keep the weddings going," Stevie said, "then we can't afford—"

"The winery," Jules finished. She sighed. "It keeps coming back to that."

Stevie clutched Jack's hand. It wasn't supposed to be like this. Her sisters and the Bennetts had agreed to keep the place on life support for at least a year, but now they were giving up? Except she couldn't complain about that, could she, when she was the one who'd walked away.

"I'm back in," she said suddenly. "Full-on. Full-time."

"Back in what?" Jules asked.

"Back in the winery. We said we'd give it twelve months and for these remaining six I'm committed to Tanti Baci." Her stomach felt sick at the promise and she had to repress the sudden urge to leave the table and run away. Jack seemed to sense it, and he gripped her hand that much tighter.

She turned panicked eyes on him and found herself glad he'd followed her home and then to the winery. She needed a strong hand to hold on to. Because what had she just done? Why had she made such a perilous promise? Everybody knew that the more you cared about something the harder it would be to lose.

~

Some instinct told Jack he should take off following the meeting at the winery. Make excuses and then plan a date for a different night, because now he needed some breathing room. Seeing Stevie interact with family and friends had peeled back yet another layer of her and the resultant glimpse of her emotional inner self compromised the casual approach he'd been working on with her.

Her sister called her silly, yet she'd just made a serious six-month-long commitment.

She still mooned over a legendary treasure, probably just as much as when she'd slapped down Seth Bennett for stealing a kiss.

As tough as she always tried to sound, she'd clung to his hand when they'd discussed the loss of the winery.

Until this moment, he'd never known what a sucker he was for strength paired with vulnerability. That was Stephania Baci: tough as nails, sweet as fiery candy.

And, Christ, in that skirt the color of the cinnamon Red Hots in a dish on the desk in her office, she looked the part, too.

They'd moved from the conference room to that smaller space where Stevie would conduct her appointment with an upcoming bride. He hovered at the doorway, studying her as she moved around the room, tidying papers and files.

"How about if I catch up with you later," she said, sliding a look at him as she bent toward a box on the floor. "We can meet somewhere in an hour or so."

That would work well enough, he decided. He'd go off, busy himself with something. An hour should give him time to screw his head back on straight.

"Yeah—" The word choked off as she bent lower. He stared at the glimpse of creamy skin rising above the band of her thigh-high stockings as her hemline rose. "What the hell are you wearing on your legs?"

She jerked straight, her hands going to the back of her skirt as a blush bloomed on her face. "I don't know what you're talking about."

"You're wearing those to deliberately provoke me, aren't you?" he asked, thoughts of leaving flying from his head. "You let me get a glimpse of them just to torture me."

She glared at him. "I let you get a glimpse of them because I hardly ever wear skirts. My mother used to forbid me from playing in dresses in case boys would get a glimpse of my underwear. So I'm a jeans and pants person, which means I forget how easily these ridiculous hemlines rise up. And I'm wearing thigh-high tights because I won't be caught dead in panty hose until the President of the United States is wearing them at a State of the Union address. Though I'm sure that will never happen because once we have a woman in the White House, the damn things will be outlawed."

He would have laughed if lust hadn't given him such a single-minded focus. He stalked toward her, his hands itching to slide back under the skirt and touch that silky, creamy skin. Maybe he'd even get her to bend over again, so he could see all the way to her contraband panties.

His intent was likely etched on his face, because her breathing quickened and she took a step back for every one of his forward strides. "Jack . . ."

"Now, Stephania," he said. "You know you set out to tease me."

"I did no such thing!" But her face flushed and it had to be guilt that caused her to bite her bottom lip. "Everybody knows I'm not a teasing kind of girl."

He trapped her behind her desk. "*I* don't know that. Or is it that I'm the only one you like to tease?"

She shook her head. "Straightforward Stevie. That's me. Shoots from the hip."

He had her nervous now, and he liked it, because damn if he hadn't been nervous with those weird tender feelings for her welling up in his chest during that meeting. Turnabout made the play more fair. "I shoot, too, remember? Also from the hip."

Color blazed across her face. "Jack!" Her gaze darted to the door. "I'm expecting a bride."

Oh, yeah. That. Though it was after five and he'd noted the rest of the office had cleared out—including the Bennetts and Giuliana—the doors were open in expectation of her appointment. He assured himself he wasn't sulking as he allowed her to push past him. Grabbing a handful of that cinnamon candy from the dish, he considered leaving again.

But hell, one hour wasn't going to cool him down now.

There was a commotion in the hall outside her office and Stevie crossed to the doorway. Dual squeals had his hands slamming over his ears and he saw her leap into the reception area. More slumber party–styled shrieks. Then Stevie was reentering her office, dragging a young woman behind her.

"The appointment log only said 'Bride G,'" she explained. "I had no idea it was you, Gertie."

Gertie, a buxom blonde who had wide blue eyes, giggled. "I had them write it in that way on purpose. I wanted to surprise you."

Clearly delighted, Stevie turned toward Jack. "I babysat Gertie and her little sister, Gretel, for years." Her gaze went back to the younger woman. "You can't be old enough to get married."

"I'm twenty," she said. "And you're getting married, too." Curiosity filled the gaze she turned on Jack.

He smiled at her. "Was my fiancée a good sitter?"

"The best." Gertie clasped her hands together. "We always asked for her because she'd actually play with us. The others would watch TV or talk to their boyfriends on the phone, but Stevie would take us outside and play catch or teach us to turn cartwheels."

"Cartwheels? Now that I'd like to see." He raised a brow

at Stevie, and from the widening of her eyes, he knew she realized he was imagining her playing acrobat in that full little skirt. Bad Jack. He hid his smile by stuffing his mouth with another handful of Red Hots.

The two women chattered after that and he only half listened to the talk of attendants, floral arrangements, and justices of the peace. He'd heard enough about that kind of thing from his sister to last a lifetime. He didn't tune back in until Gertie returned to reminiscing.

"Remember all those fairy tales you used to read us?"

"Oh. Sure." Stevie darted a glance his way, an embarrassed smile turning up the corners of her mouth.

"Stories of knights and maidens and princes and castles. And now you're going to be a princess yourself. Imagine that."

"Imagine that."

Gertie grinned at Jack and then at Stevie. "A fantasy come true."

"Exactly right," Stevie agreed, her face going pinker. "A fantasy come true."

Jack smiled and fed himself another fistful of Red Hots, then waved a good-bye to the bride as she exited the office, still babbling on about how she wanted Stevie to meet the guy she'd marry. Sweet as she was, Jack was still happy to see the last of her.

Because then he was alone with his cartwheel-twirling, fairy tale–loving, temporary princess-to-be. She came back into the office, smiling. "That was such a . . ." Her voice drifted off as she caught the look on his face.

"Surprise?" he supplied in a soft voice. "Bolt from the blue? Don't say pleasure, *mon ange*, because I assure you, that's about to happen right now. Lock the door behind you."

"Jack . . ."

"I can't wait, I don't think." He was leaning against the front of the desk, having pushed the visitors' chairs out of the way. "And it doesn't seem like I should have to. You just said I'm your fantasy come true, so now I think it's time you make one of mine come true, too."

One of the best things about Stevie was that her moments of indecision didn't last long. She flushed at his words, looked poised between running off and giving him a tongue lashing, and then she squared her shoulders. Reached behind her to turn the lock. Swaggered in his direction.

He was going to enjoy kissing that smirk off her face. Their mouths met and she jerked away. "Hot," she said.

The candy. "Mmm," he agreed and reached behind him to grab a couple more. He tossed them in his mouth and then slid his hand around Stevie's neck to pull her to him again.

He tucked one cinnamon sweet between his cheek and his back teeth and pushed the other in her mouth with his tongue. Maybe it was the extra source of heat, but something had her melting against him. With a hand on the small of her back, he used the other to unwind the scarf at her throat. He let it drift to the floor as he peppered her neck with kisses.

When he widened his stance, she cradled closer to his groin. The rub of her lower body shot another spike of lust into his bloodstream. He bent lower, taking her breast into his mouth over sweater and bra. She made a sound and he bit down, trying to reach her nipple through the thick layers of fabric.

It wasn't enough. He spun around to boost her to the desk and then yank her sweater free of that high-waisted skirt. Her breasts heaved over the top of her bra as he whipped her upper garment over her head and let it fly. Then he tucked her bra cups beneath her breasts, too impatient to remove that, and applied himself to her hard, tight nipples. She jerked into his mouth, making him wonder if she felt the extra heat of the candy there, too.

He popped more of them into his mouth, rolling the Red

Hots against the tight furls of her flesh. Stevie slammed her hands against the desktop to maintain position. It thrust her breasts forward.

He sucked on them harder.

His heart was slamming against his chest. There was a matching throb in his groin, a driving need to have more of her, to make it last. He wanted to suck her like he savored those cinnamon candies.

Talk about a fantasy.

He hooked his foot around one of the visitors' chairs and dragged it forward. Then he shoved Stevie's skirt high, taking in those thigh-high tights, then the tiny black panties that had a little frill around each leg opening. The lights were on, he didn't feel any panic, but he might still be having some sort of attack.

She didn't resist when he drew up her legs so the soles of her boots also rested on the top of the desk. "Jack. God, Jack."

"My turn," he reminded her. "My fantasy."

Putting another handful of candy in his mouth, he sank onto the chair, putting him right at the level of those cute little panties.

He teased the little ruffles around one leg. "See? It's not so terrible to let a boy see this."

Her voice was faint. "Jack. I . . . What are you doing?"

Payback. Lust abatement. Keeping the focus strictly on the physical. He didn't know which was the right answer, only that he was in control this way. Like this, he could take her up, make her fly, make it less . . . less . . .

Less something.

He rolled the candies around with his tongue. Glancing up, he saw that she was looking at him, her eyes sleepy, that blow-job mouth pouting. Pretty, she was so damn pretty. He felt his chest make that weird, tender twinge again, so he let his gaze drop to the apex of her thighs.

Oh, sweet Georgia corn in the morning, there was a wet spot on her panties. His angel was a bad girl, too, just as he wanted her to be. This little fantasy of his was kind of raunchy, he knew that, and not every woman could let herself go with it. Go with him.

"Jack," she whispered in entreaty, a tremor passing through her erotically posed body.

"Shh. We'll get there," he said.

Then he curled his finger under one of the elastic edges between her thighs and pulled it to one side, revealing deep pink petals, glistening like fruit dripping with dew. He groaned. He was going to get his fill of this, of her, he decided, tonight. He was going to make it last long enough for a lifetime.

The last Red Hot melted on his tongue. Then he leaned closer to Stevie, pulling at her panties to reveal more of her soft, pretty parts. More of her *chatte*. He blew a stream of warm air across her clitoris.

She moaned.

He smiled, settling in for a long banquet of her needy sounds. The flat of his tongue stroked her hardened nub.

And she came.

Just like that. Hard, fast, and then it was over.

Shocked, he stared up at her.

She looked back, wearing that tiny self-satisfied smile again.

"Damn it," he muttered. Damn her. While he was happy to have pleased her, he knew *she* was happier because it had been accomplished with such speed. With such a lack of intimacy.

She'd done it again! Sex like a man.

And damn *him*. Because really, for a careless, casual man like himself, shouldn't that be enough?

Stevie gazed down on the files she'd spread upon the desk in Allie's—their—office. The desktop computer was up and running, the monitor displaying the master calendar for the next six months. The time she'd committed to Tanti Baci.

Of course that didn't mean she'd given up Napa Princess Limousine, but she was going to have to find a way to make a go of both. Allie had been ecstatic at the news that Stevie was going to job-share with her and was already full of ideas about how they could divide the duties.

Stevie hadn't confessed to her sister that she wasn't nearly as excited about the arrangement. As she'd realized at the end of the meeting with the Bennetts, by making the commitment to Tanti Baci, she was putting her heart into it. And if things went south . . . that's where her heart would go, too.

Sliding into the desk chair, she blew out a sigh and then spun away from the paperwork. She didn't know why she felt unsettled, but her stomach was in knots and her temples pounded. Taking in another long breath, she let it out slowly, willing the sense of disquiet to dissipate.

Brash, bold, *strong* Stephania Baci had never felt so shaky.

A knock on her door spun her back. "Come in," she called, eager for the distraction.

Roxy Parini popped into the room.

"Oh," Stevie said. "Hi."

"You have to hide me," the blonde announced. "I promise not to be a bother, but I'm desperate to get away from my mother."

Stevie cocked an eyebrow.

"You've met her, right? We were taking a tour of the wine caves, but now she's determined to whisk me back to the resort so she can experiment with pageant updos for the wedding."

"Uh . . ."

"Beehives, Stevie. She wields a mean ratting comb. You might think I'm kidding, but from there it's just a small step to wearing a crown for the ceremony. Let me hide in here and I won't be any trouble, I promise."

"Uh . . ."

Roxy made a face. "Okay, I know I interrupted your plans with Jack last night and I apologize for that. But she's relentless! Merciless! When she started talking about me wearing elbow-length gloves and my paternal grandmother's diamond-and-emerald choker, I had to make the emergency call for reinforcements. Forgive me? I'm so sorry."

Stevie wasn't sorry, not so much. It had been within moments of that incredible episode on the desk—her belly tightened just thinking of it—and if Jack hadn't received his sister's phone call and then taken off, she would probably have escaped alone to a dark corner of the nearest utility closet.

It was one thing to confidently strut toward him when he was talking about fulfilling his fantasies, and an entirely different one to face him down in the trembling afterglow of sizzling physical intimacy—in her office! On the desk! Maybe a man could handle it with aplomb, but she was still working on her skills in that department.

"You're forgiven, Roxy," she said. "Don't give it another thought."

"I'm afraid Jack won't let it go so easily. He growled and snarled and was generally bad-tempered all night long."

Stevie shrugged a shoulder. Deciphering Jack and his moods wasn't something she planned on adding to her agenda, which was full enough. As if to prove that fact, the desk phone rang.

Roxy snagged a bridal magazine from a stack by the door and dropped into one of the visitors' chairs. "Pretend I'm not in the room. I'll just sit here and quietly read."

The call didn't take long and even after it was over, Roxy kept silent as promised. For about forty seconds. When Stevie stood to rummage through the top drawer of the file cabinet, she looked up.

"Oh, pretty," she said, nodding at Stevie's outfit.

She flushed, and rubbed her hand over her hip. The stretchy black skirt was fitted to the knees. She'd paired it with black-and-white flats. On top was a slinky violet camisole that she'd covered with an amethyst cardigan that had silky ruffles around the buttons. Amethyst drops hung from her ears.

As a representative of Tanti Baci, now that she was actually working at the winery, she'd turned to her meager supply of skirts. She'd thought it best to accentuate her feminine side when she met with brides.

"Jack's tongue will fall out," his sister said.

"I didn't dress for him," Stevie said quickly. "I have no plans to see him today."

Roxy smiled. "As if he'd stay away."

The promise only served to add to Stevie's general uneasiness as she flipped through the files, absorbing virtually nothing of the information they contained. Her life had been tumbling out of control since the day Jack had stepped into her life. From the smoldering attraction to the impromptu engagement, he'd unsettled her at every turn. She was aware she needed to refind her center, but so far it was eluding her.

Maybe her restlessness telegraphed itself to Roxy, because she started fidgeting, too. Her knee jiggled as she flipped through the glossy pages of a half-dozen magazines. Then she checked her cell phone, dug through her purse for a lipstick, and finally got to her feet to pace the small area.

At the shelving with the wedding cake toppers, she halted. With her hands behind her back, she gave them each a serious inspection. Then she reached out to touch one miniature bride with a fingertip.

"Is something the matter?" Stevie asked. When the other woman didn't respond, she tried again. "Uh, Roxy?"

Roxanne started, her hand jerking down. "I wasn't—" She blew out a breath. "Sorry, just a little jumpy."

"A little?"

She gave a rueful smile over her shoulder. "I *am* being disruptive, aren't I? Sorry for that, too."

"You don't have to apologize . . ." Stevie started.

"Yes, I do." Roxy whirled to face her. "That's exactly what I have to do. I'm thinking that's what's wrong. Maybe that's why I've been, so, um, uh . . . impulsive lately."

Stevie blinked. "Huh?"

"I haven't been honest and I need to get this all off my chest."

The pretty young woman did not have cankles or a wart, as Stevie had originally imagined, but she was starting to feel very sorry for her anyway. Her face was pale, and she looked as if she'd lost some weight in the last couple of weeks. Imagining the disaster if the wedding gown didn't fit, Stevie supposed it was in her best interests to soothe the bride in any way possible.

She indicated the chair across the desk. "Feel free to say whatever you'd like."

Roxy spun back to the wedding cake toppers instead of taking a seat. Her fingertip stroked the bouquet held by the tiny bride. Then she played with the nuptial couple line-up, moving the ones from the rear to the front and vice versa.

"Roxy?" Stevie asked, knowing there'd be no peace with all this anxiety crowding the room. "What's the matter?"

She mumbled something about Emerson.

"What?"

"I stole Emerson from you."

Cold rushed over Stevie's skin, then heat prickled at the back of her neck. "You did what?"

"I stole him." She glanced over her shoulder, went back to perusing the cake toppers. "I knew he had a girlfriend. He mentioned it the first night we met—which was totally by accident, by the way. But I knew about you from the very first and I went after him anyway. He hadn't broken up with you when we began dating."

The burn on Stevie's neck didn't abate. She'd wondered about the timing between Emerson's breakup with her and then the appearance of a new woman in his life so shortly afterward. But men were like that, weren't they? They didn't see the need for a decent interval between one woman and the next.

Everything was casual with them.

Jack was like that—he made no secret of it.

But she hadn't wanted to believe that Emerson had actually valued her so little that he'd cheated on her. Betrayed her.

With Roxy, who'd been a partner in the crime.

What he'd said when ending things with her had, if she was honest with herself, hurt, but now . . . Now humiliation curdled in her belly and she wished to be anywhere but in a small room with the woman who had thought nothing of robbing Stevie.

She didn't want to know this! She didn't want to be here! She didn't want to care about anything: not what Emerson had done, not whether the winery would survive, not . . .

Not anything.

"I think . . ." She had to swallow. "I think you'd better leave."

Roxy whirled again, her hands in fists at her sides. "I wish you wouldn't make me. I wish you'd let me explain."

"Don't bother," Stevie said, forcing out the words. "Obviously it's not all your fault. Obviously Emerson wasn't taken from me against his will. But I'd prefer not to discuss it."

"We have to," Roxy insisted. "Don't you see? Because we're going to be family."

Oh, God. Stevie put the heel of her hand to her head. Would it be better or worse if she confessed the truth to the princess? What a tangled web . . .

"We're going to be sisters," Roxy continued.

"Even if we are . . ." Stevie's head hurt so bad she had to stop again.

Roxanne pressed the flat of her hand to her chest. "I want you to understand that when I met Emerson, I'd just decided to change my life."

Stevie stood. "Well, good for you, but—"

"The man who'd kidnapped us had just died in a shoot-out." Roxy's mouth trembled. "As well as his latest victim."

Stevie's knees gave out. Her butt hit the seat of the chair and she again put her hand to her head. "God."

"Emerson said he told you about the kidnapping," Roxy said, with her big eyes and pale face looking not a day older than the fourteen she'd been at the time of her abduction. "They caught the guy, and his accomplice—his sister. He spent nine years in prison and was out only two days before he kidnapped another child. There was a standoff and ultimately the two were killed."

"God."

"For ten years I'd been in a kind of prison, too. Neither Jack nor I lived in Ardenia again. We found different ways to cope with our memories. I hunkered down. Didn't ever go out, didn't date. And then, after those two deaths, I realized I might as well be dead, too, if I continued living like that. So I went to my first party in forever and I . . . I fell in love."

Stevie didn't know what to say. She stared at Roxy, cold and hot rushing over her again.

The younger woman gave a little smile. "Nothing would have stopped me from grabbing what I wanted. Who I wanted—Emerson. Nothing. Not after finally waking up to how easy it was to lose everything. Could you . . . could you possibly understand that?"

Could Stevie understand? She'd lost her mother and her father. Her sister Allie's fiancé had died on the morning of their wedding day. People went away, things, too, even things like the land and the winery that had been in the family for over one hundred years.

But she'd been trying to distance herself from all of that understanding by walking away from the wine business and opening her limousine service. She'd put space between herself and everyone and everything she had lost . . . and was terrified of losing.

Yet here she was, back in the heart of her family and in the heart of the family business.

Stevie found herself on her feet again, despite the continued pounding in her head and the turbulence in her stomach. "Don't worry, Roxanne," she said, brushing past the other woman to exit the office. "I do understand."

Only too well.

~

Stevie retreated to Anne and Alonzo's cottage to nurse her new wounds. It wasn't the tumbled-down-yet-picturesque adobe it had been when she was a child. Now getting through the front doors required a key. The renovated interior boasted gleaming wood floors and freshly painted walls. The massive rock fireplace was original, though, and she drifted toward it, remembering how she'd set up camp beside it as a girl.

In a flash of memory, she saw her father standing there, too, with her little sister on his hip as he told yet another story from the Baci past. Allie had always been Papa's little girl, while Jules was their mother's shadow. Stevie had orbited outside the planet-moon relationships of the two pairs. The outsider.

The one without tight attachments to other people.

That should work for her now. It wasn't as if she'd been so certain her relationship with Emerson was destined for marriage. His dishonesty should be easy to shrug away.

After her buddy Jeff's ugly breakup with a girlfriend, she'd once accompanied him to the local tavern prepared to commiserate over beers. But Jeff had been all smiles that night, and when she'd questioned his happy mood, he'd claimed it was a man's natural aptitude. "We just cut the blood flow to the part that hurts. Goes numb in no time."

That's what she was going to do, she decided, starting right this instant. Freeze the part in pain.

She crossed her arms over her chest and wandered to the windows overlooking the vineyard. A large group of visitors was gathered beside the vines as one of the interns played guide. Stevie ran her gaze over the people on tour and found herself wondering how many had cheated, how many had been cheated upon.

Emotion tried to lift its head, but she ruthlessly wack-a-moled it back into its icy burrow. *Freeze the pain.*

Footsteps sounded on the floor behind her. Damn, she'd left the door ajar! All she wanted was to be alone in that separate orbit of hers, to work on her anesthetization process. To send the newcomer on their way, she turned.

From the doorway, a stranger gave her a polite smile.

It was a man—late fifties, maybe? Trim and with short silver-shot hair and a thin mustache. "I'm sorry," he said, his voice threaded with an accent. German? "I let my curiosity lead me."

A refugee from the tour, Stevie supposed. She pasted

on a polite smile and told herself that two minutes of effort on her part could lead to profit if he bought a case of wine or—better yet—joined the wine club. She'd made that promise to pitch in, after all, so she tried to widen her smile.

"Your curiosity brought you straight to the root of the winery, actually," she said. "This is the home of Anne and Alonzo Baci, the founders of Tanti Baci. It's nearly one hundred years old."

He strolled farther into the room. "We should all look so well at such a great age."

Her second smile felt more natural. "It went through a big renovation a few months back. In this central space, we hold weddings and the two adjacent rooms are where the bridal parties prepare for the ceremony."

Her stranger paced about, his hands clasped behind his back. He wore wool slacks, a sweater, and a houndstooth check sports jacket. Expensive-looking shoes.

Definitely a candidate for the wine club, she thought.

He ran a long-fingered hand over the stones of the fireplace. "Beautiful workmanship."

"Original," she said. "Alonzo Baci, my great-great-grandfather, built it." Before she knew it, she was sharing with him the story of the partnership with that other Liam, the romantic triangle, the treasure, and the long-standing feud.

"I heard some of this from the young person leading the tour," he commented, nodding out the window. "Do people really explore your property looking for the rumored silver?"

"As recent as six months ago. When we were restoring the cottage, someone pulled away the new wallboard looking for a hidden cache."

The older man ran his gaze around the room. "Then I suppose one must surrender the idea that it's hidden here at your cottage. It would have been found during the modernization."

"I suppose you're right." She sighed. "But old legends don't die easy."

"Like old habits," he mused in a quiet voice, strolling toward the doorway to the bride's boudoir. "And old disagreements."

He disappeared into the other room, leaving behind an odd sense of . . . something she couldn't put her finger on. Melancholy, maybe? Regret?

It infused her, too, then, mixing with the humiliation that had swept over her at the knowledge that Emerson had not just dumped her, he'd cared so little for her that he'd cheated on her first. Her chest ached and the chill soaking into her bones wasn't because she was "freezing the pain."

It was because she felt lonely. Unwanted, even.

If a friend had been the victim in this story, she would have told them the man wasn't worth a moment's thought. That he wasn't worthy of her experiencing the tiniest sting.

And yet, Stevie felt embarrassed. Rejected.

Closing her eyes, she let herself admit the truth. Yeah, she hurt.

Warm arms drew her against a warm chest. "*Mon ange.*"

She started, eyes opening even as she was aware it was Jack—his gentle voice, his hard body, his unreadable gaze. His lips brushed her cheek. "Hey."

Instinct drove her to step away from the circle of his arms. "Hey, yourself," she said. "What are you doing here?"

"I . . ." He looked down at his clothes. Flannel shirt, down vest, boots, and jeans. They were all dirty enough to make clear he'd been working in Liam's vineyard again. "I happened to call Roxy. She admitted to me what she admitted to you. I didn't know the details before and . . ."

Stevie crossed her arms and tucked her hands under her elbows, pretending a hot wash of humiliation wasn't climbing her neck. "Don't tell me you feel sorry for me." Just saying it aloud made her stomach pitch.

"No, that's not it." He ran a hand through his hair, looked at her, looked away, then looked at her again, his expression baffled. "I . . . Damn it, I . . . I just *feel* for you, Stevie."

She stared at him.

His gaze shifted away from hers. "It doesn't make any goddamn sense to me, either," he muttered.

"Your cursing, your attire, neither make sense to *me*," a cold voice said. "Is this how you dress now, Jack?"

They both turned toward Stevie's stranger, who had walked back into the main room. Clearly he was not unknown to Jack, though. The younger man's expression smoothed. His smile was sharp enough to draw blood. "How do you do, sir? Long time no see. I thought you weren't expected for a few more days."

"I came in early as a surprise. Which brings up something I've been wanting you to know," the older man said. "Your long absence upsets your mother."

Was this Jack's *father*? Stevie glanced between the two men, noting the similar build and facial structure. They watched each other with the same deep wariness.

"Mom always knows where I am," Jack answered, his voice mild. "She's even managed to visit me a time or two."

"She's seen you at least once every year," his father corrected.

Jack shrugged. "There you go."

The man's gaze ran over the son again. "You look like a laborer."

"Funny, because I *am* a laborer. I'm laboring in one of Liam's vineyards, trying to pay my way with work since I'm mooching off him for room and board."

The older man tensed. "You have access—"

"I wouldn't touch your money." The words were pointed, yet the tone so pleasant it made Stevie's stomach clench. "And despite what you've heard, I have my own."

Jack's father's expression went even grimmer, his accent more clipped. "I do not understand this. I do not understand you. I do not understand my son working someone else's land when—"

"I don't think we've been formally introduced," Stevie said, surprising herself by stepping between the two. This wasn't her battle, but she couldn't seem to help herself. "I'm Stephania Baci, and you must be . . ."

"Excuse our manners," Jack said. "And Dad is usually a stickler for such things."

A ruddy flush spotted the older man's cheekbones, signaling a direct hit. But he moved toward Stevie, his own hand outstretched.

Jack continued. "This is my father, as I'm sure you've guessed. Ardenia's k—"

"Wil," the older man said, cutting off his son. "Just call me Wil, or Mr. Parini, if you find me too old to refer to by my Christian name." At Jack's astonished expression, he even managed a small smile. "I'm in America. Your mother swore she won't speak to me if I put on airs."

"Mom puts on airs."

"No, Jack." Mr. Parini shook his head. "Your mother puts on *crowns*."

And then they both laughed, though the sounds were so rusty and uncomfortable, that Stevie found herself aching all over again. But this time for Jack . . . and for his father.

Mr. Parini—she would never call the king of Ardenia *Wil*—quickly excused himself as if the showdown with his son had sapped him of energy.

That left her and Jack looking at each other, and clearly he felt as exposed as she had a few minutes before. While Jack knew that Emerson's actions had wounded her, she now knew that his relationship with his father was strained to the point of pain.

Jack reached out, tugged on the ends of her hair. "How are you really doing?"

She looked away until his knuckle tickled her under the chin. His gaze was serious. "Stevie?"

What the hell. "I'm a little raw." She hesitated. "You?"

He glanced in the direction his father had exited. "That's a good word for it. I'm a little raw, too."

Then they stared at each other and it was weird, because she could tell he was, like she, coming to grips with how that brief exchange of words felt more like an event. Important. Altering.

As if they'd traded state secrets. Or rings. Or . . . trust.

And because it all felt so heavy, she was driven to lighten the moment. Desperate, even. "You're going on the wine walk tonight?" The Bacis, Parinis, Platts, and Bennetts would be taking a tour of the Edenville tasting rooms together.

"Mmm." His knuckle teased her bottom lip before he backed off. "I suppose I should leave to get ready. I'm dirty and sweaty."

"But perfect for what I have in mind," she said, yanking him close again. "I say we go back to my place and get ready for tonight in my shower. Together."

His eyes gleamed. Clearly he was as happy to divert the discussion as she. "I'm excellent with soap and shampoo."

They walked toward the door. "We have to be quick," she warned. "According to my calculations, you'll have, oh, about eleven minutes to show me what you can do with bubbles."

Jack groaned. Cursed. Muttered something about men and then swatted her on the butt to hurry her along. She counted it a victory that they were both smiling.

Emerson realized that the evening ahead was a command performance on many levels. He had parts to play: son-in-law-to-be, devoted fiancé, aspiring politician. The final role had been assigned to him at the last minute. As they stepped onto the sidewalk bordering Edenville's town square, his mother murmured into his ear, "From now on, remember that every time you're in public, it's an opportunity. Make the rounds, shake hands—"

"Kiss babies?"

The senator frowned at him. "To travel this path, you need to take it seriously."

He swallowed his sigh and then leaned down to kiss her cheek. "I will, Mom. I'll make everything just fine."

That was his intention for the night. Roxy, her parents, his parents, he was going to reassure them that he was dedicated to the path he'd decided upon. The woman, the wedding, the new career. He wanted each of them, right?

He hustled to catch up with Roxy, walking with her parents a few feet ahead. Sliding his arm around her shoulders, he felt the tension in her delicate frame. Still, he pasted on a smile as if there wasn't a lingering strain between them. "Ready for your first Edenville wine walk?"

Then he craned his neck to address her parents, who he was still trying to think of as Rayette and Wil. "This is our version of a pub crawl," he told them, filled with pride for his town. "Thursday evenings in spring, summer, and fall we hold Market Night, and everyone comes into town to sample the area wares from booths set up around the square. Winter, the tasting rooms and cafés stay open late and we do the meet-and-greet inside."

The king and queen of Ardenia nodded and allowed themselves to be ushered into It's a Grape Thing, a paneled tasting room that had a carved wooden bar at the rear and numerous tables and chairs filling the rest of the space. Along the left wall, a long buffet held platters of cheeses, crackers, and diagonal slices of crusty baguettes. The Bennett brothers had already arrived. Emerson steered the royals toward the two men and watched them welcome Roxy's parents warmly. Obviously they were previously acquainted.

When his mother beckoned him toward a group he recognized as local bigwigs, he left her parents with Liam and Seth but grabbed his fiancée's hand. "Come with me," he urged. "There are some people I want you to meet."

She hesitated. "We should talk. I haven't seen you in days, and—"

"Emerson! Roxanne!" His mother waved to catch their attention. "Over here."

He looked down at Roxy and his heart contracted in a painful ache. A warning? "Honey . . ." His hand went to his head before he remembered the haystack, the Glop, the way he shouldn't touch his hair once the two had negotiated a successful meeting at his bathroom counter. Groaning to himself, he smoothed his palm over his skull. "I don't know if now's the right time for a long discussion."

"What's going on with you?" she whispered in an urgent demand. "Are you having second thoughts?"

"About what?" he scoffed, pushing away the question. "Except, perhaps, about starting off with white wine tonight. I'm going straight for an intense red." A shot of whisky sounded even better, but it wouldn't do for a would-be politician to go straight to the hard stuff when making the rounds in wine country.

His mother called to him again, and he nodded in acknowledgment but didn't head her way until he had a glass of an intense zin in his hand, one that he knew to have a good balance of cherry and clove flavors. Roxanne didn't follow his lead, instead ordering a wine that was the delicate pink color of a young girl's blush.

"Are you sure?" he asked, watching her take a sip. "That particular rosé has a surprisingly tart kick."

She narrowed her eyes a little, their blue glittering in the tasting room's low light. The sharp point of her high-heeled boots nudged his shin. "That might be just what's needed."

What *he* needed, he realized she was saying as he took his own swallow. And, God, he would take the kick, on the shin, on the ass, right in the head, if it would clear out the misgivings that kept invading his mind. "Roxanne . . ."

She went on tiptoe and placed her mouth against his. Rosé to zin. The blended tastes should have been wrong—the delicate flavor of her wine overpowered by the brawny taste of his. But it worked somehow, he decided, as he held her close. There was enough structure in the rosé to hold its own against his more dominant zin.

"Roxanne . . ." he whispered against her mouth, a different kind of ache inside him.

She drew away from the kiss, sending him a mysterious smile. "A nice pairing, don't you think?"

He wanted to agree, but those doubts continued to plague him. As an American, he didn't stand in awe of her royal lineage, so it wasn't that. Yet still, she was a princess and he was a guy who . . .

His mother called to him again. "Emerson!"

A guy who was destined to become a politician.

Though, God, it didn't seem to make sense that he loved his part of the world enough to consider spending months away from it on the other side of the country. But pushing his personal dilemmas aside, he strode forward to reach out his hand to those grouped around his mother. They welcomed both he and Roxanne to their conversation and it only took a moment to realize wine was the topic here, too.

A couple in their small crowd was new to the area and the growing of grapes. Eager instructors were giving them a crash course in winemaking. "A particular vine isn't a good producer forever," his mother said. She slid a glance at Emerson. "There comes a time when the old must be replaced with the new."

The mayor of Edenville, a canny type who was at home with everyone in the valley, from the laborers who worked the vines to the fat-cat status seekers who paid over-the-top dollar to claim they owned a vineyard, cocked an eyebrow at Emerson. "Is this some sort of announcement, Lois?"

Not yet, his instincts wanted to shout. But he'd promised to do his best tonight, so he smiled.

His mother did, too. "We're talking about winemaking, David," she hedged, but there was a wink in her voice. "Nothing more, nothing less."

The new-to-Edenville pair seemed to take that statement at face value, because they asked for a simple explanation of a common word in the wine-country glossary: *terroir*. Glad to leave innuendo behind, Emerson relaxed and enjoyed his wine as his father took up the topic.

"In simplest terms," Ned Platt said, "*terroir* refers to the combination of soil, slope, and climate." He went on to explain how growing regions were made distinct through their terroir and given an official designation as an American Viticulture Area, or AVA, by the Bureau of Alcohol, Tobacco, and Firearms. Then he discussed how a terroir's attributes might be enhanced or reduced during the winemaking process and ended with why many considered the best wines to come, oddly enough, from the worst soil.

"As in all things," Emerson's father finished, gesturing with his glass, "the struggle to grow makes the vine work harder, extending its roots and absorbing elements that make it produce a more interesting fruit."

"Which right there explains the banality of my grandsons," a silver-haired septuagenarian groused. "Things have come too easily to them. They've never had to exert themselves or overcome anything."

"Lucky spermers," his elderly companion said, as if it was an epithet. Then he glanced at Roxanne. "No offense, young lady."

"None taken," she murmured, though her puzzled gaze flicked to Emerson.

He murmured a polite "excuse us" as the discussion continued around them and edged Roxanne away from the group. Duty done for now.

"Uh, 'lucky spermers'?" Roxy asked as he towed her toward the bar.

During a wine walk, they usually moved along to another tasting room for the next glass, but he couldn't wait that long. "Winners of the sperm lottery, he means. A reference to those who inherit their wealth and position."

A blush the color of her wine tinged Roxanne's cheeks. "I suppose that's one way to describe me."

Emerson stopped. "*No*," he exclaimed, brushing a strand of hair off Roxanne's warm face and cursing the old coot who'd unwittingly hurt her feelings. "Not you."

At fourteen the young princess of Ardenia had been kidnapped. For five days she'd surely wondered what would happen next. For five days, she'd had to have questioned whether she'd get home alive.

She'd survived all that to emerge, shy as a butterfly. Perfect. But so damn fragile.

His chest hurt again and he turned away from her. "If that described anyone, it would be me. You . . ."

God, he didn't deserve her, he thought. Maybe that's what was wrong with him lately! His subconscious was trying to catch him from making a mistake—from heading down a road that wasn't for him.

Newcomers pushed through the door of It's a Grape Thing. Roxanne's brother, Jack, and Stevie, Emerson's former girl. His gaze ran over her familiar figure, taking in her attempt to mock-slug Jack in the shoulder and how he ducked her swing and ended up with her wrist in his grip.

Laughing, the other man twisted Stevie's hand behind her back. It looked playful, but . . .

He found himself across the room, his own hand closing over Stevie's other arm. "You okay, Steve?"

Startled, she stared at him, the teasing smile on her mouth sliding away. "What?"

"You okay?"

"Of course I'm okay," she answered. Her gaze swung to Jack. "Uh . . ."

Too late, Emerson realized the other man had murder on his mind. His eyes were narrowed, his jaw was hard, he was staring at the place where Emerson touched Stevie. He wanted to be enraged right back at the arrogant asshole, but that only confused him more. Everything was jumbled in his head: intentions and regret, guilt and longing.

For who? About what?

"Get your hand off her," Jack said, his voice terse.

"Oh, cut it out," Stevie put in, her tone annoyed as she stepped away from the two men. They both released their holds. "I can take care of myself."

And there it was, Emerson realized. Her ultimate appeal. Stephania Baci was strong. Invincible, even. She wasn't perfect, but her flaws only made her more attractive. Brash and outspoken, a man wouldn't have to protect her, worry about her, strive to shield her from every slinging arrow, from even the slightest scratch that might mar her perfection.

Around her, a man could breathe.

What the hell had he done?

Fifteen minutes later, he still didn't know. But the group was moving on to the next stop on their wine walk. At the exit, he pulled open the door to hold it for the rest. As his mother and Roxanne crossed the threshold, lights flashed.

Photographers.

A gaggle of press crowded the sidewalk, and from the questions and attention, clearly they'd been alerted to the presence of the Ardenian royal family. The winter months were slow in the wine country, and news like this would liven up the local press and likely make it to San Francisco and beyond. The king and queen were a glamorous couple and one of the pair was American, so they'd always been of interest to the U.S. media. Their generation's Princess Grace and Prince Rainier.

In slow motion he saw his mother look at him over her shoulder, speculation in her eyes. Oh, hell. Did she see this as the moment to make the announcement of his candidacy? It wasn't what they'd discussed, but she always told him that part of her success was her ability to think on her feet.

He couldn't think at all, beyond trying to telegraph to her *no, not tonight*, but if she went forward, he'd have to put a good face on it. Convince even more of the world that he was dedicated to the path he'd decided upon.

At the exact same moment when he couldn't convince himself he was heading in the right direction.

~

Two days following the wine walk, Stevie was finishing breakfast while reading a book in the farmhouse kitchen when Giuliana hurried in. "It's you!" she said to her older sister and tried looking innocent as she casually drew her crumb-sprinkled napkin over the open volume.

Jules had a sheaf of papers in her hand and was frowning as she took in Stevie's attire. "Are you moving back home?"

"No." Since Allie and Penn were still in Malibu, she'd spent a night or two in her old bed, though. "But maybe I should leave some night gear around for my occasional sleepovers. I had to resort to Allie's flannel pajamas that match that god-awful fuzzy robe of hers." Both had pink flamingoes printed on a field of pale blue.

Jules's gaze was wandering toward the reading material spread on the table, so Stevie stood up and raised her voice to reclaim her sister's attention. "We did get her some pretty things for the honeymoon, didn't we? I hope she took them south when she left the last time, or else we're going to have to sit her down and discuss the facts of life."

"You've been searching for that ridiculous treasure," Jules said.

"No! I agree with you it's an absolute long shot and I really don't have time—"

"How did you find that book, then, hmm?" Her sister nudged her aside and flipped the volume shut for a moment to display the cover emblazoned with suggestively arranged fruit around the title, *Making It.*

"It was on Allie's bookshelf," Stevie lied. "Found it when I went scrounging for pajamas. Maybe we should have that 'facts of life' discussion in any case. The girl had to buy a book!"

Jules lifted an eyebrow. "One that you're now reading. And since when is Allie's bookshelf in that little basement closet?"

"Oops. Busted." Then her eyes narrowed. "Wait. Wait, wait, wait, wait. How would *you* know the sex book was in the basement closet unless it was *your* sex book?"

Her sister's face reddened. "It was from a million years ago. And beside the point."

"It's certainly a point more interesting than whether or not I'm poking around looking for legendary riches."

"Which reminds me," Jules said quickly, obviously trying to dodge the new thread of conversation. "Emerson's

mom is looking for that bracelet she always wears, you
know, the red, white, and blue one? She can't remember
when last she had it—maybe in the wine caves—but knows
it's gone now and thinks it might be here at the winery.
Keep your eye out for it?"

"Sure," Stevie replied, then smirked at her sister. "And
in doing so, who knows what dirty books and other little
secrets I might uncover?"

Jules's mouth opened, and then shut. Her gaze moved
to the papers in her hand, which Stevie saw now were a
couple of newspaper sections and some sheets off a printer.
"About little secrets . . . And about your fiancé . . ."

"I told you he's really not. He's really not anything to
me. It's just for show."

"A show his parents seem to have bought."

"Yeah, well." She waved off the issue with a hand. It
had been a little weird during their wine walk evening to
be around his parents as their son's intended. His father
hadn't blinked an eye at the news, but since Jack was the
family's black sheep, she hadn't taken it as actual approval.
The Parinis had been gracious and friendly, however, and
since she was well aware a wedding would never come to
pass, she'd managed to ignore her nervous, fish-out-of-
water feelings.

"In any case," Jules said. "I think you should see these."

Stevie took the proffered sheaf with a frown and leafed
through them. "Oh. They published the photos taken outside It's a Grape Thing."

There were two in the Napa County paper. And there
was another in the lifestyle section of the one from San
Francisco. When their group had been caught by the press
on the sidewalk, it had been almost comical to see Emerson's mother, the senator, virtually ignored in favor of the
Ardenian royals. Both papers had run photos of the king,
queen, Roxanne, and Jack. The Napa paper had included
another of Roxanne and Emerson.

She tried returning them to her sister, but Jules put

her hands behind her back. "You should read what they wrote . . . or just go straight to the printout to save time. It's today's blog posting from that social media guru that WildHart winery hired last year."

It was titled "A Prince of a Guy: Jack Parini." "Yeesh," Stevie said. "I know it's quiet in January, but don't you think a wine guy blogging about Jack is a bit of a stretch?"

"Oh, he's stretched back ten years."

Stevie glanced at her sister and then focused on the paper in her hand. It was about the kidnapping. Some of the information was known to her: that both Jack and Roxanne had been taken and held for five days. That the police had found them because of a clue in the ransom note mailed to their parents. It even noted that Jack had been dating the kidnapper's sister and she had been the bait in the trap that had caught him and Roxanne.

Most unsettling was the repeated rumor that the Ardenian police had suspected Jack was part of the plot from the beginning. The blog implied that many—including his own family—still believed in his complicity. What! Jack would never do such a thing. But his playboy ways while hopscotching through European capitals and then the various jobs he'd held over the years were pointed to as further evidence of his careless and unsavory character.

"This is disgusting," she muttered, her hands tightening on the papers. "He should sue."

"It's nothing that hasn't been written before and most of it's actually true."

Jack's voice. Her head came up. Jack, standing in the doorway to the kitchen. Jules, sketching a wave as she slipped past him and out the door. It shut behind her with a click.

The prince of Ardenia leaned a shoulder against the jamb and crossed one foot over the other, appearing elegant in black jeans and a V-neck black sweater. A man without a care in the world. Casual Jack, his best look. "Your sister beat me to the heads-up."

She wondered what it must have been like for him, rescued from one ugly situation only to be thrust into another nightmare. Had no one stood by him? Stevie couldn't imagine Miss Peaches & Pralines doubting her son for an instant, but there was that distinct coldness between Jack and his father.

God.

She tossed the papers onto the table, no longer willing to touch them. "So."

A smile ghosted over his mouth. "Stephania Baci, finally without words?"

The weird little lump in her throat made long speeches impossible. Especially when she couldn't get out of her head how it must hurt to have been so distrusted—and for that distrust to still be hounding him a decade after the fact. Her gaze cut from Jack to focus on the brewing machine on the countertop.

She cleared her throat. "Want coffee?"

He ignored the offer. "I wondered if you knew the whole sordid story—I guessed not. It appears I was right."

"Yeah, well, I don't Google my friends."

"Or your fiancés?" When she glanced at him, he gave her another cool half smile. "Don't worry. That's why I'm here, to end our engagement."

"Which is fake anyway."

"Yeah, but since so few know that, you're now unfortunately associated with me and my disreputable past. A breakup will end the embarrassment."

"So you say." That lump threatened to strangle her. "Except I'll be left manless once again."

He chuckled. "Surely it would be more humiliating to stay linked to me now that this old story has been dredged up."

"I don't know." She pretended to consider it. "It's going to be pretty mortifying to confess I've been dumped twice in twelve months."

"You can do the dumping, of course. Tell people you didn't know enough about who I am . . ."

But she did. She thought she knew him very, very well. So even a phony connection wasn't that easy to sever. "Your scenario makes me out to be a cold-hearted bitch," she mused aloud. "A woman unwilling to give a guy a second chance."

"Sorry about that, but—"

"But think of this instead." She couldn't walk away just yet, not under these circumstances. "Think of what mad props Edenville would give me for taking you on. For rehabilitating you." Crossing to the coffeepot, she peeped at him.

He'd gone still, his eyes narrowed on her. "What are you saying?"

The decision had been instantaneous, really. Simple. "I'm saying I really can't let you out of our agreement until after Emerson and Roxanne's wedding. Remember? I'm using you to escape Edenville's pity."

"*Mon ange* . . ." He nearly groaned the words.

"Later, when we do end the engagement, everybody in town will sigh. I'll say I tried my best, but . . ."

"I was beyond redemption."

She pursed her lips, as if running that through her mind, though her chest ached at the idea that he might really believe the words. "Your debauched reputation might even give me some cachet, you know? Before I've only been buddies with the bad boys, but after you leave? They might take a second look at me."

In a blink, he was beside her. "Ah, now. Be careful talking about other men, *mon chat*, since you're still my woman."

She cracked down on the shivery thrill his possessive tone sent along her spine. They were just playing a game, she reminded herself, even though his body heat made her skin prickle in yearning. Facing him, she walked her fingertips up his chest and thought maybe he shivered, too.

"Jack . . ."

He caught her hand and flattened it over his heart. "What?"

"You'll pine for me when it's over, won't you?" She looked up at him through her lashes again.

"Like no one's ever pined before," he promised.

Her chest ached again, because no one ever had. "Will you send me flowers every day for a month after we break up?"

"For two months." Smiling, he leaned down to kiss her mouth. "Three."

"You don't think that will be too much? Considering we only have another couple of weeks together?"

He slid an arm around her waist. "I plan on making each one seem like a year."

Worry cooled the little fire his nearness was kindling in her belly. Turning weeks into years sounded serious. Not casual, not a game, the way she kept describing for herself this thing with Jack. But he was kissing her again, his mouth soft and tender on her neck, sliding up to her chin, finding her mouth.

Scattering her concerns.

"I think of you every minute of every day," he said against her mouth.

She was woozy. "What?"

He brushed her nose with his. "Just practicing what I'll write on the note cards—the ones I send with the flowers. What color roses are your favorite?"

"White." She said it without thinking how . . . how bridal that sounded.

"White. Got it. I'll send you a dozen every day." He pulled her into a tighter clinch. "Now will you tell me why you're studying a book on blow jobs?"

She gasped, whirling, only to find herself caught, his arm around her belly, her back to his chest. The pages of

Giuliana's book had ruffled and on those now displayed there were diagrams. "It's Jules's. And it's not all . . . you know. That's just in chapter seven."

His hands slid up her rib cage to cover her breasts, then lightly squeezed. "I don't think I've ever goosed a flamingo."

Oh, God. Allie's stupid flannel nightwear. "You have to promise never to bring up these dumb pajamas again."

"It'll cost you." His fingertips tweaked her hardening nipples.

Her entire body flushed with heat and she sagged back against him. "Cost me what?"

"A study-buddy session on chapter eight."

She didn't remember what was in chapter eight. She didn't remember her name, not when he slid two fingers between the buttons of the pajama top and scissored them around the tip of one breast. "I have to get to work," she whispered. "I don't have a—"

"—lot of time," he finished for her. "I know. But I'm a fast learner. Every guy has had to cram a time or two."

"Jack," she complained. "Cram? That's just bad."

He grinned as he spun her toward his mouth again. "So make me over, *mon chat*. You're going to try to rehabilitate me, yes? And I so want to be good for you."

15

To Roxy, the carpeted path between the reception area of the Platts' commercial real estate headquarters and the anteroom to Emerson's own office seemed two miles of swampland littered with potential hazards. Any second now she expected an alligator to appear in the form of a simple question: *Roxanne, what are you doing here when Emerson's at a meeting in Napa?* Or it might be a trailing vine to stumble over, causing her purse to fall and its secret contents to spill.

The alligator would then speak up: *Roxanne, what are those odd little objects you're carrying around?*

In an attempt to put the torturous thoughts from her head, she inhaled a deliberate breath and then released it slowly. The key, she knew, was to cope with her anxiety in a new manner. It was the major stressor of her kidnapping that had led her into this ugly habit that she'd once conquered . . . and now fallen prey to again.

Finally, she reached the door to Emerson's secretary's office. The woman was on her lunch hour, Roxy knew, giving her a sixty-minute window to follow through with her plan. *Plenty of time*, she thought, slipping into the anteroom and closing the door behind her.

Her glance darted toward Emerson's office, but there was nothing to see, as that door was firmly shut. Alone, Roxy had only to get ahold of herself, take care of business, and then escape, order reestablished. Her honor salvaged. Her shame safely hidden.

Except the chaotic pounding of her heart made it difficult to move. *Walk to the secretary's desk*, she ordered herself. *Reach inside your purse.*

Her feet followed instruction. Her hand slid inside the slouchy bag on her shoulder. The object was cold to the touch, but as she drew it out, it wiggled, as if alive.

Startled, she emitted a bleat, and the item fell to the floor and half rolled under the desk.

The door to Emerson's office popped open. Whirling toward it, Roxy bleated again.

Emerson. He was saying something, but she could hardly hear him over the slamming sound of her heart in her ears as she kicked out with her foot, hoping to make contact with the thing on the floor. She only found air.

"Wh-what are you doing here?" she said.

"I just asked you the same thing." He came toward her, studying her face. "What's wrong?"

"Not a thing. I just dropped by to . . . to . . ." She waved a hand. "But I thought you had a meeting?"

"It was cancelled. I've spent the last half hour on a conference call with my mother and her chief of staff." Emerson found one of her cold hands and gave it a squeeze. "Have you eaten?"

"I couldn't." Food wouldn't stay down.

"You look pale," Emerson said, tugging on her fingers. "Come sit in my office and I'll get you coffee or tea. Maybe hot chocolate?"

She shook her head. "I have errands." Other places to visit, other items to replace.

"God. You can't eat. You look unwell." He watched her edge away from him and ran his free hand through his hair, making it stick up like a little boy's. "This is all my fault."

"No." This was because she was weak, because she'd relapsed, because ten years ago she'd felt so powerless for five days.

"We have to talk. We really have to talk." Emerson's fingers tightened on hers and he tugged her in the direction of his office.

What could she do? She stepped forward and then— wouldn't you know it?—her foot found the object she'd dropped. Stumbling, she might have gone down without Emerson's strong hold on her.

"You okay?" His gaze dropped from her face to the floor and his expression turned from concern to puzzlement. Leaning over, he swiped the figurine from the floor. "It's Patsy's hula girl."

The figure's body swiveled as Emerson held its legs stationary. Roxy stared, mesmerized by the way the straw of her skirt moved.

"Patsy's been looking all over for this since it disappeared a couple of weeks ago."

Thirteen days.

"It . . ." Roxy wet her lips. "It must have rolled under the desk."

Emerson frowned. "I'm sure she looked there. And of course the cleaning crew would have found it before now."

Helpless, Roxy shrugged. Then Emerson did, too. Next, he propped the little dancer against his secretary's computer monitor and tugged Roxy toward his office again. "Patsy will be happy."

That makes one of us, Roxy thought.

Emerson hesitated. "I'm sorry, Roxanne."

Had she said it out loud?

"I want you to be happy. You deserve to be happy."

She *had* said that out loud.

"I don't deserve any—"

"Roxanne." Emerson groaned. "Don't think I don't realize I've been running hot and cold these last few weeks."

"Cold and cold," she whispered.

He closed his eyes. Then he led her to the love seat positioned against one wall of his large office. She sat at his urging, though he paced about the room. Her hands clutched her purse in her lap.

"I wish I knew when this went wrong . . ." He continued to pace.

The seeds had been sown ten years before. When she'd been rescued, there'd been relief and elation . . . and then a lingering anxiety any time she felt buffeted by events. When things seemed beyond her influence, her uneasiness built and built until finally she could no longer resist the compulsion. Then . . . then she took "control" back in a small but insidious way that left her feeling ashamed and sick afterward.

Years ago she'd found the courage to address the urge and finally deal with it, which made the habit only more repulsive upon its return two months ago. No wonder Emerson had cooled. He'd sensed the hideous flaw lurking inside her.

A tear burned her cold cheek, and she wiped at it with her hand. When she was fourteen, she'd learned that crying never solved anything. Without that outlet, though, she felt the tension inside her lurking, stress in every corner, stress preparing to strike like those alligators she'd imagined before.

She cut her gaze from Emerson's restless movement and looked toward his desk. Beside a leather square full of pens and pencils was a walnut-sized green frog. It was a candle, actually, a silly token she'd found when they'd first started dating. She'd teased him that he was the frog she'd kissed to find her handsome prince.

When really, the one with the green skin and the warts was her.

Suddenly, the urge came over her. Powerful, dark, a little thrilling. Impossible to resist. She wanted the frog; if she had it, she'd feel comforted. Soothed.

No.

She slid her hands beneath her thighs, appalled and angry at the craving. To distract herself, she took a breath and held it. And then held it some more, seeking the point of discomfort to punish herself for her weakness.

It didn't help. As soon as she found herself gasping, she also found her hands free again. They wanted to feel that smooth wax and she could imagine the pleasure of rolling it against her palms, running her thumbs over the friendly googly eyes.

No!

She was breathing too hard. Closing her eyes, she attempted more deep inhalations, trying to relax and let the feelings of anxiety and impulse roll through her. They clung tenaciously.

And the little frog would make her feel so happy.

"Roxanne."

Her eyes popped open. She realized she was on her feet, and the candle was in the clutch of one fist. Emerson was staring at her.

Busted.

"You're taking back the frog?" he asked, his voice husky. There was something pained in his eyes.

Her fingers uncurled and there the amphibian sat, in the cradle of her palm, smiling like she couldn't. "I . . ."

"God, Roxanne." He dropped to the love seat and put his head in his hands. "How could I have done this to you?"

It wasn't him, though. It was that other man, those dark days, that fourteen-year-old girl who'd been so afraid. With Emerson by her side, she'd thought that girl had finally vanquished all her weaknesses, but they still breathed fire in a secret place inside her soul.

He lifted his head. "If you weren't so beautiful, maybe I could take a chance. If you weren't so perfect . . ."

Beautiful?

Perfect?

She couldn't stay to hear any more. Rushing toward the love seat, she made for her purse. In her panic and haste, she reached out with the hand that held the frog and she bumbled both. The candle fell to the carpet, the purse tipped.

The contents landed on top of the candle, an avalanche of other people's things.

Stupid things. Valueless things.

But not her things.

"What is all that stuff?" she heard Emerson ask.

As she knelt on the ground to scoop them back into her purse, the words fell from her mouth, as suddenly and quickly as the purloined items. "They're my big, bad, ugly secret."

"Roxanne?"

"I'm not perfect, Emerson. Not perfect at all." She stared down at her small, yet criminal hands. "After the kidnapping . . . I . . . I developed an impulse-control disorder. I started, um, taking, um, stealing things." Humiliation burned like cold fire over her face and down toward her churning belly.

"An impulse-control disorder," Emerson repeated and leaned from his place on the love seat to pick up the laminated card that indicated the U.S. senate's in-session dates. "This is my mother's," he said. "I bet she has a drawerful of them in Washington. She would have given it to you if you'd asked."

Her fingers curled around a thumb-sized kachina doll that she'd pocketed just yesterday. Her mother had bought it for Roxanne's half brother's small daughter. She'd stolen a child's toy from her own mother. "You don't understand."

"I know I don't. I'm so . . . so surprised."

She couldn't look at him. "I don't *want* these things. I take them when I get . . . anxious. It's how I take control of my fears."

"What do you have to be afraid of, Roxanne?" He still sounded baffled.

"You." Lifting her head, she met his beautiful blue eyes. Her prince, who'd once considered her perfect. "I'm afraid that you don't love me anymore."

Without waiting for a response, she ran out of his office, leaving the frog behind.

But taking her warts and green skin with her.

~

"Come on," Jack had said softly, as if he was offering a polished apple. "You know you want to."

"No," Stevie had protested. "It's only a fantasy."

"That doesn't mean we shouldn't give it a try." He'd kissed the side of her neck, and it was sweet until he ended it with the slightest sting, a combination sure to have her melting—and likely leaving a mark behind.

She'd shivered. "Well . . ."

He'd tipped up her face to gaze into her eyes. "*Mon petit chat*, it will be fun."

The French got to her every time. She sighed. "But you can't tell anyone, Jack. Not ever."

"It will be our secret, *mon ange*," he'd said, smiling. "Our dirty little secret."

Which, of course, dirty it was, since what he'd coaxed her into doing was going up in the dusty farmhouse attic in search of the legendary Bennett-Baci treasure. Perhaps there, he'd reasoned, they'd find the lock that fit the key that Liam had turned over to her weeks ago. She'd been carrying it around with her ever since—not that she'd let Jules know.

But Jack knew. Jack seemed to know exactly what made her smile, laugh, sigh. That was the real reason she'd agreed to the attic adventure—to give herself something to do besides moon over her fake fiancé. These last couple of days, ever since they'd decided to stay engaged, the mooning had only gotten worse.

But even with decades of detritus around them, he still made her nuts, from the provocative body brushes he managed as they moved about the space to the way his smile gleamed knowingly at the responses she tried to suppress. The bulb-and-chain lighting made brave inroads in the gloom of the cramped quarters, but the setting felt more intimate than she'd expected.

Which fed her need to break away. "I'm going to take this box downstairs," she said, hitching it onto her hip. "It's photo albums from when we were kids that Allie and Jules might like to see. Are you okay up here alone for a few minutes?"

He was restacking boxes by the narrow window that he'd cracked to allow in fresh, cool air. "Sure," he said lightly. "As long as you keep clear of the fuse box."

The darkness. She'd forgotten his fear of it. And somehow, knowing his vulnerability only increased her own sense of defenselessness. Her stomach tightened. "I'll bring us up some wine and cookies," she said and hurried back to the kitchen.

They'd made spaghetti earlier in the evening, one of her few culinary feats. There was half a bottle of a Chilean cabernet sauvignon/sirah blend left over from their meal, and as far as she was concerned, it would do. Anything went well with the chocolate-chip treats from the bakery next door to Edenville's old-time hardware store. She put a few on a platter, then set it and the bottle on a tray along with a couple of stemless wineglasses. Time to head upstairs again.

But instead, she hesitated, hearing a little voice whispering at the back of her mind. *Don't go into the attic.*

Her fingers squeezed the edges of the tray, even as she scoffed at that horror-flick phrase. Don't go into the attic? Come on. There weren't any monsters up there.

Only Jack . . . so don't go into the attic.

A chill trickled down her spine even as she scoffed again. Jack wasn't a monster! Jack would never hurt her! He wasn't dangerous—

But Jack *was* dangerous . . . to her. The knowledge of

that had been looming like Lon Chaney since New Year's Eve, when he'd been merely a shadow on the resort's portico and she'd been forced to reassure herself that no man could make her bleed.

Could Jack?

Her heart jolted, as frightened as if someone had suddenly surprised her from around a corner. It started knocking against her rib cage loud enough to hear—

No. That was *real* knocking—the sound of knuckles on the back door. She crossed the floor to pull it open.

"Emerson!" She blinked. Though he wore his usual coat and tie, his hair was standing on end.

In one stride, he was over the threshold and had her shoulders in his hands. He slammed her against his chest and planted a heavy kiss on her mouth.

How many seconds passed? Two? Three? But once her brain re-righted itself, she shoved him away. "What the hell? What are you doing?"

His breathing was labored. "Stevie. Oh, God, *Stevie*."

Jack, she corrected, casting a quick glance over her shoulder. It wouldn't be good for him to find Emerson here. "You need to go away," she told him.

Instead, he shut the kitchen door and took both her hands. "We need to talk."

"Nuh-uh." She backed away, slipping from his hold. "How'd you know I was at the farmhouse?"

"I stopped by your duplex. When you weren't home, I talked to your next-door neighbor, Gil. He said you were here."

With *Jack*. "Well, I'll be sure to thank Gil for that." Though she'd prefer to sock him in the stomach, she doubted she'd get the chance. His new wife, her friend Clare, was fiercely protective of her six-foot-five Italian stallion. "Now, Emerson, you're interrupting—"

"That's exactly what I mean to do. Interrupt the crazy train. It's time I put a stop to all that's happened since I donned a pair of fuzzy green antennae."

"Oh, jeez." Was that what had happened to his hair? Green antennae? "If it's the crazy train you want to get off, Emerson, you'll have to speak to the conductor, and he isn't here."

"I did wrong by you. I'm sorry."

"Yeah, yeah, yeah." She waved that away and then gestured toward the door. "Let's talk about this some other century, okay?"

He stubbornly stayed put. "No. Tonight. Now."

She sighed. "Emerson—"

"I've always liked you, Steve. Since we were kids. Then when we started dating . . . Well, you were easy to be with. You're so strong. Capable. Self-reliant."

"Darn," she said, sotto voce. "And they still wouldn't let me join the Boy Scouts."

"You don't know how appealing those qualities are," he said. "I never lost sleep over you. I never wondered what would make you happy. You'd speak up for yourself."

Because he'd never thought about what mattered to her on his own. Emerson had never taken the time to figure out something she might need. Jack's image popped into her head, smiling, coaxing, *understanding. Come on*, he'd said. *You know you want to.*

"It's time for you to leave, Emerson."

He appeared not to hear her. "Best of all, a man didn't have to worry if he always said the right thing around you."

She winced.

His face fell. "Steve . . ." He rubbed a hand over his eyes. "I know, I know. About that—"

"I don't want to talk about that."

"We have to talk about that if I'm going to make this right. If I'm going to get back on the right track."

She just wished Emerson and his crazy train had bypassed the winery altogether tonight. "We're definitely not having that discussion," she said, her voice fierce.

"The things I said . . ." He sifted his hands through his hair and it went even wilder. "It's just that . . . You're going to think I'm an even bigger SOB, but at the time when I broke it off, I . . . I . . ."

"Was already seeing Roxanne behind my back."

He looked sick. "You know."

"Yes. Roxanne—"

"She's not to blame! I met her at a party, and . . ." He shrugged.

Stevie leaned against the countertop. "She told me she stole you."

The starch seemed to go out of his dress shirt. "I can't talk about that."

"Fine," she said, pushing off from the tile. "We're done here."

"No!" He moved closer and grabbed her hands. "That's exactly what I don't want. I don't want to be done with you, Stevie. Not ever."

She stared at him. He looked sincere.

His fingers squeezed hers. "That must be where it all went off track. I was wrong. It's you. I want you back."

"You can't."

"I do. I was stupid. Blind. Foolish. Call me a thousand names and I'll agree with every single one. But I'm desperate. I'm desperate to have you in my life again."

This was a dream come true. The man who'd done her wrong was actually groveling. She was pretty sure she could serve him an entire humble pie and he'd sit down in the middle of the town square and eat bite after bite in front of everyone she knew.

What she'd always wanted.

But she didn't want him.

So instead of being filled with smug satisfaction, she only felt . . .

Sorry.

Her chest ached, and she realized she felt sorry for Emerson and for Roxanne. And for Jack, too, who she understood had a huge emotional stake in his little sister's happiness.

She didn't protest as Emerson drew her close. His arms wrapped around her back and she patted his shoulder, wishing she could straighten this out for all of them. "I can't believe I said those things," he murmured.

She closed her eyes. "Never mind."

"It was because I thought I was in love with Roxy. I had to—"

"I know."

He held her tighter. "You're a wonderful woman, Steve, and I hope I didn't ruin our chance to get back together. I should never have said—"

"Please, Emerson. *Don't*." Though the wound had healed over months before, deep below it still ached.

But he continued talking. "I should never have implied you weren't good enough for me. I should never have said that the mother of my children couldn't be a limo driver with a high school education and a single business course under her belt."

The pain lashed again, but before she could react to it, a new presence blasted into the kitchen. It snatched her from Emerson's embrace and then it faced Stevie's ex, a monster dark and angry.

"Emerson," Jack said through his teeth. "I am going to break your face."

As he lunged forward, Stevie leapt between the two men. The flat of her hand met Jack's chest. His furious energy surged up her arm, shocking her system, electrifying her with the piece of knowledge that had been hovering for days.

Emerson's defection hadn't made her immune to danger. Sex like a man wasn't going to save her either. Jack *was* a menace to her, because if she didn't tread carefully, very, very carefully, she could fall in love with him.

16

At Stevie's touch, the ravening beast inside Jack paused in its forward rush. "Get out of the way," he spit out.

She didn't move. "I know you're upset about your sister."

His sister? At the moment he wasn't thinking about his sister. He was thinking about that dumbass hay-head, Emerson Platt, who had told Stevie she wasn't good enough. *The mother of my children can't be a limo driver with a high school education and a single business course under her belt.* He might be a careless man, but he couldn't just let that go.

Stevie blinked at him. "Are you growling?"

"Get out of the way." His eyes on Emerson, Jack wrapped his hands around her upper arms, preparing to move her himself.

"Jack—"

"Hey, a party!" a cheery voice called out. A small woman with curly blond hair stepped into the kitchen. "Why didn't anyone call?"

Stevie's head whipped around. "Mari. What are you doing here?"

"Gil told me—"

"Gil again." Stevie frowned.

Jack took the opportunity of her distraction to steer her in the direction of the other woman. "Go to your friend. Go call Gil. Just go away."

"No." The stubborn woman dug her feet into the worn linoleum. "This is between me and Emerson."

"*I'm* between you and Emerson." Jack looked over to see that the other man had sunk into a chair at the kitchen table. His head was in his hands. "Get up, you asshole, and take what you have coming."

"Hey, Stevie," Mari said, again in that jolly tone. "Looks like a guy's fighting for you."

Stevie rolled her eyes. "This is about Roxanne."

Jack felt another spurt of anger. "This isn't about—"

"Roxanne," Emerson groaned. He yanked on his hair, then slid lower in his seat. "I've screwed up everything."

"I'm going to screw you to the wall," Jack said, surging forward again.

Stevie held him back, using all her tough-girl strength. "Jack," she said, her voice urgent. "Let me do this. Let me talk to him. I can fix this for your sister."

"This isn't about my sister!" This was about Stevie, his tough girl with the soft heart of gold who'd been willing to stay engaged to a man with a sullied reputation.

"Okay, okay. I understand," she soothed, but he was certain she didn't. Still, when she cupped his cheeks between her palms, he was forced to meet her eyes. "Give me a few minutes. If you're not satisfied when I'm done, *then* you can break his face."

"*Stevie . . .*"

"Please."

"*Merde.*" Her sloe eyes were sending out a spell. He hadn't done anything for any woman besides his sister in ten years. "Fine."

"Step outside with Mari. Just for a few minutes." Her gaze sought out her friend. "You'll keep Jack company?"

The other woman came forward to link her arm in his. "Nice to meet you. I'm Mari Friday, friend and free spirit."

Once outside, drawing cold air into his lungs didn't cool his simmering fury. He crossed his arms over his chest and cast his glance back toward the kitchen door. Stevie's voice traveled through it, into the night. "Face it, Emerson. You're a chronic second-thoughter."

Mari smothered a laugh as she sat on the bottom step. "God, she's got that right. I think it comes from his middle-of-the-road mentality."

"Yeah?"

"Yeah. Guy would make a decision, then agonize over it for weeks. The color of his tuxedo shirt for prom. His college choice. In high school, whether he should run track or play tennis in the spring. Imagine going to the ice cream store with him as a kid. Thirty-one flavors might as well be thirty thousand. I was shocked when he settled on your sister so quickly."

It didn't make Jack feel any better. "You've all known each other a long while."

"Oh, yeah." She half turned to smile up at him. For the first time, he noticed her round cheeks, her round eyes, the unabashed Kewpie doll sexiness that made a man want to smile back. Her gaze traveled from the top of his head to the toes of his shoes. "That's why we lap up fresh blood."

He might have laughed at her last remark and the flirtatiously wiggled brows that went along with it if he wasn't so wound up. He might have flirted back, asked the Kewpie doll out for a drink, and then driven away from all the drama in the Baci farmhouse.

The Jack Parini he'd looked at in the mirror the last ten years would have done just that. His hand slid into the pocket of his jeans to locate his car keys—only to encounter Stevie's "treasure" key instead. "Damn woman," he muttered.

She'd let him get dusty but wouldn't allow him the dust-up he needed. He wanted to murder Emerson.

"Huh," Mari said, still looking him over.

He frowned down at her. "Huh, what?"

"You'll do. It surprises me, given what I've heard and read, but"—she lifted her hands—"there it is."

"I'll do—what?" He frowned at her. "I have no idea what you're talking about."

She flashed him those cutie dimples again. "I gave you my best good-time smolder, and you resisted. It rarely happens, you know."

"Sorry if I insulted you." He glanced back at the kitchen. "I have other things on my mind."

She bounced on the bottom step, smiled again. "I know."

"I should be in there pounding some sense into that son of a bitch," he burst out. "The things he said to her . . ."

Mari's head tilted. "You don't think she can take care of herself?"

He stared down at that key in his hand. "She's perfected her independent act, but she shouldn't always have to take care of herself," he muttered. "Everybody needs somebody sometime."

His head jerked up. His gaze met Mari's amused eyes. "Tell me I didn't just start talking in song lyrics."

She shrugged. "Sinatra? Dean Martin? Maybe it was Ann-Margret."

He groaned. It only made it worse that he was thinking in Vegas-style song lyrics. His hand tightened on the key. "Run away with me, Mari. Let's go somewhere, have a few drinks, have a few laughs."

She was already shaking her head. "It's too late for that, pal. It's too late for you."

He wasn't listening, just as he wasn't really interested in going anywhere with Mari. He wanted back inside that house, where he could—

What?

Find Stevie's treasure? Slay her dragons?

Next you're going to imagine you're her fucking prince, a scornful voice said in his head. *And you, Prince*

Charming-but-Careless, have nothing to offer anyone but a sordid reputation and a need to leave a light on at night.

Her murmuring voice made it through the door again. He couldn't hear the exact words, only the tone. Unruffled. Calm. Strong.

But beneath all that, he knew she was vulnerable and romantic. Her mind was full of fantasies of ghosts and gold and silver. She held tight to dreams she pretended not to believe in, and the knowledge of all that was touching the heart Jack thought he'd left behind in the dark a decade ago.

The mother of my children can't be a limo driver with a high school education and a single business course under her belt.

How could Emerson have said such a thing? But the man was regretting the words now, and Jack didn't know how his remorse might work on Stevie's soft center. Jesus, might she take her old boyfriend back?

Careless Jack didn't care to stay to see that, he decided, shooting to his feet. Tossing the key to Mari, he jogged down the steps.

~

Emerson knocked and the door to Roxanne's room immediately opened. "There," he said, and his nerves were clattering against each other like cymbals. "That's part of what's wrong. Not only am I one of the 'lucky spermers,' but women are always making things too easy for me."

Her hair was pulled back in a tight ponytail and her lips were colorless. Even as still as carved marble, she was beautiful to him. "I beg your pardon?"

God, he was going about this all wrong, but with his pulse clanging in his ears and that infernal noise his nerves were making, he couldn't think worth a damn. Still, he had to try to explain himself or he'd never take a full breath again. "Can I come in?"

She hesitated. "Would that fall under the category of making things too easy for you?"

"I suppose," he admitted. "But with a wedding scheduled in ten days, we're going to have to address some salient issues."

He was talking like his mother, the senator. Emerson shoved his hands through his hair and wondered if his life and his locks would ever run smooth again. "Please, Rox," he said softly.

The door widened. Steeling himself, he stepped inside. Unlike times before, there was no evidence of wedding in the room. No seating charts, no scribbled vows, not even the box of wedding favors that had sat in one corner the last time he was there.

He went clammy with a cold sweat.

Turning away from her, he closed his eyes. "Name your favorite color."

"Teal." She hesitated. "Am I supposed to know yours?"

"Go ahead and ask me." He turned back to look at her.

Her legs folded beneath her as she took a seat at one corner of the sofa. "What's your favorite color?"

"I like beige. But then I think of gray and that's nice, too. The color of the Lexus I had before the white BMW was nice. It was a slate blue that I consider attractive without being too garish. And then there's—"

"You have a terrible time committing."

"Yes." It was a relief that she'd figured that out. "Exactly. Stevie says I'm a chronic second-thoughter."

"You've spoken to Stevie."

"She wouldn't take me back."

Roxanne jerked as if he'd slapped her. Color rose up her neck. "And I thought you just said women are always making things too easy for you."

He lifted a hand, let it drop. "You didn't just happen to run into me at that coffee place near the family house in San Francisco."

The red color on her face burned brighter. "Remember that first night we met? You said you were a creature of habit. 'Coffee at the same Peet's every morning, seven A.M.' You even mentioned which street, which corner."

"You told Stevie you stole me from her, and it was more intentional than I believed before."

Roxanne bit her bottom lip. "Fine. Though I knew you had a girlfriend, I also knew where you bought your coffee every morning. So I managed to run into you there because I wanted you."

When he didn't speak, she bit her lip again, and then continued. "Getting you was the first time I took real charge of my life and my . . . desires in a decade. Maybe I should apologize for that."

He waited.

She shook her head. "I won't apologize to you for it. I've already told Stevie I was sorry for how she was hurt. But I'm not sorry about going out on a limb for what I wanted. You could have said no. You could have brushed me off."

And he hadn't. She'd been there, acting, he realized now, surprised to find him in line waiting for his morning beverage, black, two sugars. They'd talked for two hours and both had called in late to work. He'd asked her out for dinner. She'd accepted.

Knowing that he was seeing someone else—that they had a relationship—had seemed . . . insignificant in the face of the emotion sweeping over him every time he was with the pretty, perfect princess.

Not so perfect.

He reached into his pocket and drew out the frog candle that she'd almost taken from his office. It sat in the cup of his palm for a moment, then he set it on the coffee table in front of her.

She stared at it. "I don't want—or need—it at this moment," she said. "I've gone back to the counselor in San Francisco who helped me overcome my impulses a few years ago. I think he can help me again. I hope he can help me again."

"That's good, Roxanne . . ." His voice trailed away as he saw her begin to tug at the ring on her left finger. He went clammy for a second time. "Is that what you want?"

She hesitated. "What kind of politician can have a wife who might steal a fork at the next fund-raising luncheon?"

He noticed she hadn't answered his question—and that the ring was still in place. "I wonder . . . when we decided to step up the campaign for congress—is that when things started to spin out of control for you?"

She shrugged. "What does it matter?"

It mattered because he disliked the idea of her hurting in any way—and he'd been doing that to her himself lately. "I looked at you, Rox, and I saw someone perfect—perfect, but fragile. From the beginning that scared me. I wasn't sure I deserved your perfection and I also worried I could harm you in some thoughtless way."

"I'm not a piece of china."

"No. But I was a little afraid of you—and for you, I guess."

She looked away. "Then when I confessed how flawed I am, you came to the realization you didn't want damaged goods."

"No." He strode to the coffee table and sat down, facing her. "Then I ran scared because I doubted my ability to be your strength when you needed me—selfish ass that I am."

"Emerson . . ."

"It didn't make me love you any less, Rox. You've got to believe that. I only wish you had told me sooner."

"I didn't want you to know my weakness . . ." Roxanne looked down at her lap.

"But without knowing it, Rox, I couldn't know *you*— and I couldn't know how much I never want to be without you in my life."

Her head came up. The blue of her eyes was magnified by the tears swimming in them. Last week he would have found them unnerving. Her vulnerability had made him run to Stevie earlier today. But now he stood his ground, firm in the knowledge that there was no escaping his feelings for her. He didn't want to escape them.

His hand reached into his pants pocket and he pulled out a Tiffany-blue box. He held it out to her.

As she reached for it, he noticed that both their hands were trembling. Emerson Platt, Mr. Middle-of-the-Road, did not feel the least bit centered when it came to the love of his life. He was starting to get accustomed to the idea.

Roxanne lifted from soft cotton a gold bracelet. Hanging from the eighteen-carat links was a puffy heart, encrusted in diamonds. He saw her swallow.

"I don't know what this means," she said, dropping the bracelet back into the box. "I don't know if it's right for us to be together when I have this problem that can impact your future."

"You're my future." It was the single thing he was focused on now. "From that moment when I turned to see that *Star Wars* princess beside me, somehow I knew."

"You were with Stevie then."

"Not a proud moment . . . and it only reminds me"—he blew out a breath—"that I'm flawed, too."

For a second time, her fingers closed over the bracelet. She lifted it from its satin nest as her gaze met his. Then she held it out to him, silently asking for his help in fastening it.

He scooted closer to take the piece of jewelry and then closed it in his fist. "Mine," he said.

Her eyebrows rose.

"It symbolizes my heart, Rox. And I have this idea . . . maybe it won't be this easy, but can we see if every time you feel the urge to steal something that instead you take the bracelet from me? Because I gave my heart up to you long ago, and you're most welcome to it."

She made a funny sound between a cry and a laugh and launched herself into his arms. He laughed, too, and pressed his face against the candy-floss softness of her hair. "Princess, you and me, that's more important than anything. Do you believe that?"

She nodded against his throat.

"Ah, it's so good," he said, and kissed the top of her head. "I don't have to think anymore. And rethink. My favorite color? You. My favorite flavor? You. My favorite woman?"

He took her by the shoulders and held her away so he could look into her eyes. "Always and forev—"

She pressed her hand to his mouth. "No. Don't say that. Don't make that promise."

He pulled her hand away and ran his thumb over her knuckles. "You're wearing my ring," he reminded her.

"And I want it there," she said. "But as for 'forever' and that wedding we have scheduled . . . let's just table the discussion for now."

"But . . ." The stubborn look on her face made him stop the flow of words. His sweet princess was showing that same streak of ruthlessness that had sent her to Peet's one morning months ago.

He sighed. "What do we say to our families?" Though his nerves were no longer clanging, his future was far from settled, it seemed. "When will you decide—"

"I'll let you know." She held his gaze, clearly resolute on this.

And Emerson discovered he was smiling. He didn't know why . . . unless it was the knowledge that Roxanne Parini hadn't thrown him over . . . and that she was going to be the one woman who wouldn't make it easy on him.

17

Stevie watched as Liam and Kohl faced off, the tension between them reminiscent of two elks preparing to clash antlers. One of the attractions, she decided, to hanging out with men was that their stupid testosterone antics made her feel genius by comparison. Wearing her lucky ripped jeans and her bleach-stained sweatshirt, she perched on the back of a leather couch in the Bennetts' spacious second-floor game room while the two men hashed out the terms of their upcoming game of darts.

J.D. strolled over, his eyes fixed on the same tableau. He glanced at her. "You'd think it would be enough that in their quest to vanquish the other they took one hundred and fifty of my hard-earned dollars at poker tonight."

"That's because you can never remember about straights and flushes, dumbass."

"Ouch. You've been in a mean mood since before we dealt the first hand."

Her gaze slid toward his. "Mention PMS and you die."

He raised his hands in surrender. "You're sunshine.

You're cotton candy. You're warm, wiggling puppies."
Then he took another swig of his beer and continued. "And
do you got anything going on Sunday? I could use some
company when I change my oil."

"I'm busy on Sunday."

"Okay, I can switch to Saturday afternoon, but we'll
have to be quick because I have a hot date with—"

"J.D., I'm not going to help you Sunday, Saturday, or
any day."

"But you always help me do car stuff." He sounded put
out and halfway insulted.

"Too bad." Stevie took a big swallow of the sauvignon
blanc she was drinking. Tonight had called for a beverage
with enough acidity to match her mood as well as pair well
with the fish and chips the Bennett brothers had provided as
the pre-poker meal. "I don't have a single favor left in my bag."

She'd doled out enough for a lifetime, hadn't she? Helping the guys fix their cars, helping her ex find his way back
to his fiancée, helping Jack rehabilitate his reputation by
entering into an engagement-in-name-only.

J.D. pointed a finger at her, clearly still sulking. "You're
just mad that your guy went AWOL."

"He's not my guy." Though, as she'd known it would,
the fake news of their impending marriage had spread
faster than the vineyard fire in the WWII–era flick *A Walk
in the Clouds*. Of course, Jack's sudden absence had just as
quickly made the rounds of the Edenville coffee bars and
tasting rooms.

Moments after she'd patched up the leaks in Emerson's
good sense and sent him back to his princess bride, she'd
discovered that Jack had disappeared. Mari hadn't been
any help. She'd merely shrugged her shoulders, handed
over the old key, and said the man hadn't left any message
behind for Stevie.

The dumbass was her for asking about one, she thought
with a scowl.

J.D. glanced over at her again and she could tell he was

still miffed. That's what happened when you were too nice. People kept expecting you to be that way.

"Don't give me that dirty look, Steve," he said. "It's not my fault you can't hold on to a man."

A red haze came over her vision. "I swear I'm going to—"

"Hold my coat while I punish J.D. for that remark," a smooth voice put in.

Jack.

"You won't talk me out of it this time," he added.

She shrugged. "This time, I won't bother."

"Hey!" J.D. said. "I was just razzing the girl."

Jack shoved J.D. in a way that wasn't as friendly as it might be. The other man stumbled back, grumbling, then joined the rest of the poker buddies—Seth, Chuck, and Ben—on the other side of the room. Jack took J.D.'s spot, leaning against the back of the couch beside Stevie's perch.

She didn't look at him. "My hero."

"My ass." He slipped an arm around her waist and brushed his mouth against her cheek. "Is that the word around Edenville? That you've lost another one?"

"I don't care what anyone says about me."

He didn't try to argue with her, and instead nodded in the direction of Liam and Kohl. "What's going on here?"

"They're fighting over my sister, Giuliana."

Because she still wasn't looking at him, she felt rather than saw her stare. "Looks like darts to me," he said.

"Yeah." She sighed. "But it's about Jules. She and Liam had a thing ages ago that's not completely faded. It pisses Kohl off. It pisses Liam off that Kohl's trying to move in on his old territory."

"Sounds like it makes you a little sad."

It embarrassed her that he'd picked up on it. She shrugged a shoulder. "I don't know that Kohl is right for my sister, but I'm afraid too much time or pain has passed between her and Liam for it ever to be right with them again, either."

"Maybe you could try spreading around some of your special matchmaker pixie dust," he said lightly, then went quiet a moment. "Thank you for bringing Emerson and Roxy together again—it appears she's back to happy, though I'm not convinced the idiot deserves her."

"He's all right. I think what he feels for your sister is so big it just took some getting used to."

"Yeah? Well, I still want to break his face."

She didn't answer. Liam and Kohl's voices rose as they continued hashing out their dart game. It had escalated from a simple cash bet to an exchange of insults and a call for higher stakes. "Geez," she said, shaking her head. "Why are all you men so stupid?"

"An eternal, unanswerable question in the same vein of why they bother manufacturing fat-free potato chips or how it could be illegal to marry both in a set of blond, busty twins."

Stevie slid him a quelling look.

He laughed and leaned over to brush her cheek with his lips again. She knocked him away with her elbow and he rubbed his ribs, smiling. "Damn, I missed you."

"Shut up."

Then Jack did, focusing on the opponents as the two men exchanged death grips. "Am I understanding what they just agreed upon?"

"Liam's an idiot. If Kohl wins, he gets the two-acre vineyard. If Liam wins, Kohl quits working for Tanti Baci."

"Liam's smart," Jack corrected. "If he wins, Kohl's away from Jules. If Kohl wins, he'll likely be splitting his time between the little vineyard and Tanti Baci—again, distancing him from your sister."

"You're right." An embarrassing sting pricked Stevie's eyes and an undeniable melancholy pulled on her already-low mood. "I can't watch this."

"What's wrong?"

Shaking her head didn't dislodge the despondent feeling. "I don't want Tanti Baci to lose Kohl. I don't want Jules to despise Liam any more than she already does, which she will, because once she hears about this she'll see it as sabotage instead of . . ." A stupid tear ran down her cheek and she lifted her shoulder to rub it surreptitiously away.

"Stevie?"

"Just sock me or something, okay?" She slid off the couch to land on the soles of her ragged sneakers. "Right now I despise myself for being such a soft, sentimental sap."

Jack caught her elbow and turned her to face him. The touch, his face, it was like the punch she'd asked for. She sucked in a breath. That powerful spark of attraction, those handsome features of his—both brought home to her just how much she was at the mercy of him. How could it be like this? How could her body burn and her heart pound from looking at him when she wanted to hate him so much for leaving without a word?

"Sock me," she said again, desperate now to remember how dangerous it would be to care for him. "I could use the distraction."

"You could use something that will put you in a better mood." He blew out a dramatic sigh. "And since I owe you for running out a couple of days ago like that, then I'll make the sacrifice."

Her eyebrows drew together. "What sacrifice?"

"You can use me."

Heat rushed between her breasts and up her neck. "Use you . . . how?"

"Like you always do. Quick and dirty. I keep telling the mirror that no one can make me feel slutty but myself."

She released a little laugh. "Shut up," she said again.

"I have a bedroom just down the hall. It has an iron headboard and I have a collection of silk ties. You strike me as the type who would like to tie me down."

Her skin went hot at the thought, until her brain caught up to his last words. *You strike me as the type who would like to tie me down.* "As if I would with all the guys in the house," she blustered, then flattened her hand to push at his shoulder.

He caught her wrist and yanked her against him. Hard.

Her heart pounded against his chest, her skin flushed hot again, her gaze stuck to his. "Where did you go?" she heard herself whisper.

"There wasn't any place far enough," he murmured, then took her mouth in a deep, claiming kiss.

Stevie pressed herself tighter against him, resenting any distance now, as one elbow hooked his neck and the other hand took a grip of his shirt. Jack didn't back off, but banded a forearm around her ribs while his palm slid under her extra-large sweatshirt to find the small of her back. His fingers dipped beneath the waistband of her jeans to the second knuckle, the tips flirting with the shallow, sensitive crevice of her bottom.

A shudder ran through her and she felt herself go wet. Her mouth opened wider to welcome the heavy thrust of his tongue.

Then there was clapping in the distance. Woots and whistles. Stevie jerked way, mortified to be making out in front of her poker buddies. But her hand was still fisted in Jack's shirt and it wouldn't heed her mind's command to loosen. What would the guys see in that possessive grasp?

To cover the moment, she slapped on a saucy grin and started backing out of the room, towing Jack with her. His mouth smiled but his eyes were serious as she tugged him toward the stairs.

"My room's that way," he said, pointing in the opposite direction.

"My limo's this way," she said, continuing to pull him along. "I drove the Caddie tonight."

He groaned. "No sheets, no pillows, no two of us on the mattress until morning? It's going to be like that, is it? Leather and lust?"

"I'm afraid so," she said, mustering up some sympathy to infuse her voice. "I'm taking you up on your quick and dirty offer—though I'll let you play with the dashboard dials afterward."

Afterward, he didn't seem to have the energy to climb up front. She had pushed him into the back of the vehicle, and he'd yanked her after him, where they set about a session of torturous necking like two teenagers on prom night.

Her legs straddling his lap, she'd feasted on his mouth and speared her hands through his hair. He'd shoved up her sweatshirt and found the front release of her bra. When her naked breasts met his callused palms, they'd both groaned. He'd flicked her nipples, causing her to rub against his erection, nearly ready to come with just that sensation.

"Wait, wait, wait," he'd said against her mouth, as if he knew how close she was.

"Don't want to wait." She'd circled her hips, pressing her clitoris against the seam of her jeans and the iron hardness of his shaft.

His hands had tightened on her breasts. "God, Stevie." His thumbs had scraped over her nipples.

She'd been about to explode.

His hand had slid down the back of her pants again, maybe to halt her enflamed movements. "*Mon ange*," he'd said, his mouth trailing down her neck. "*Mon ange*."

His wet mouth, his naughty fingers, that sweet, seductive French had sent her over the edge. She'd ground against him, coming, coming, and he'd groaned, his hips lifting to meet her halfway.

Their breaths sounded loudly in the confines of the Caddie when it was over. "Hell," Jack said. "The last time I came like that . . . I can't remember the last time I came like that."

"Mmm." She buried her face in the curve where his neck met his shoulder and inhaled the scent that was unique to him. Her bad mood, she realized, was all due to having been cut off from this: the way he smelled, the way he felt against her, the way he could make her lust . . . and laugh.

"I'm going to have to sneak back inside all sticky," he

complained, but his hand gently stroked the back of her head. "You did it again, Stephania. I feel so cheap."

She didn't answer, because all she could think about was how much it was going to cost her when he left for good.

~

The old adage was true, Jack thought, as he unlocked the front door of the "castle" at what he called My Aching Back vineyard. Everybody had an opinion. He'd already heard his mother's view on his decision to purchase the two acres—*I hope this means you're staying long enough in one place to unpack your suitcase*—and now Liam was talking like a real estate agent with a surplus of condos to sell.

"You know," his friend said, "instead of doing the wine-making in this building, you could put up a few walls, put in some different plumbing, and live in the place."

He opened his mouth to explain he wasn't putting down roots. "Look—"

A dark-haired tornado blasting through the door interrupted him. Both he and Liam glanced at each other as the tornado advanced. From a foot away, Giuliana Baci placed her palms on Liam's chest as if to shove him back. But at the contact, they both froze. His friend's jaw tightened.

"Jules . . ." He looked down at the place where she'd made contact. "You haven't touched me in ten years."

The young woman took a breath, then snatched her hands back and tucked them in the crooks of her elbows. "Never mind that," she said, her face reddening. "What's going on between you and Kohl?"

"That's my question," Liam said.

"It's none of your business!"

Liam lifted a brow. "That's my answer, too."

"How could you make Kohl quit Tanti Baci?"

"I didn't make him quit, did I?" Liam said, his voice tight. "I lost the damn bet."

Giuliana vibrated with anger. "How could you wager that in the first place? The winery needs him. *I* need him."

Liam's expression turned stonier. "You have him still, don't you?"

"Yes, but only because of"—she whirled to confront Jack—"*you*."

Jack decided that was his cue to leave. He hadn't won a round with a Baci woman yet and he didn't suppose today was the day that would change. Offering her a charming smile, he backed toward the exit. "I have some, uh, work outside."

Giuliana narrowed her eyes. "I'm worried about how buying the vineyard from Kohl fits in with the game you're playing with my sister."

Instead of answering, he kept on smiling and increased the speed of his footsteps. Still, he only made it as far as the door before he ran into an obstacle. Standing on the front porch was his own beautiful, frustrating nemesis. His smile died as he took in the sight of her. With her painted-on jeans and her blow-job mouth, she was enough to make a man forget his name. But it was her tough talk combined with her romantic heart that really got to him.

The last time he'd seen her, she'd been driving off in the limo, leaving him to make his way into the Bennett house feeling a half-ashamed fifteen. Damn woman.

"What is it you want?" he asked, pretending there wasn't an itch of embarrassment at the back of his neck. And that magnet-pull of attraction. Shit, he should be used to that feeling by now.

"You bought this place," she said, tilting her head as she studied his face. "I don't think—"

"I've already heard plenty of thoughts on the subject." He clapped his hand over the itch and brushed past her. Thank God he'd had the foresight to wear work clothes and bring along some tools to remove the stump of an old, gnarled vine that had been left at the end of one row.

Screaming muscles and a lather of sweat would drown out the opinions he hadn't asked for nor was interested in.

But, of course, it couldn't be that easy. His nemesis dogged his footsteps as he grabbed the digging bar and pick and headed for the southeast corner of the vineyard.

"There are other ways to remove—"

"This is the way I want to do it." The old man who'd conceived of the place had wanted to work the land with his own hands and that appealed to something in Jack, too. Sometimes the only thing that made sense was dirt and hurt.

Upon reaching the offending stump, he started slamming the bar into the ground at its base, prying at the tenacious roots to release their hold. That's what he needed, he thought, a way to release the hold this place and this woman was having on him. He'd escaped to Reno for two lousy days and then he'd been drawn back, powerless against the compulsion to return to Edenville. To Stephania.

He impaled the dirt with the bar, thrusting with a force that radiated up his arms. God damned powerless.

"I feel as if—"

"Look, Stevie," he said, his voice harsh as he glanced at her over his shoulder. "I don't care what you feel."

She jerked back.

And he *felt* like a jerk. Damn it again!

Straightening, he turned to face her as the sweat rolled down his face. It stung his eyes. "That didn't come out right."

One of her brows rose. Yeah, she had his number. He'd spoken the truth, though there was a nuance to it. He didn't *want* to care what she felt. And yet . . .

A car pulling to a stop in front of the vineyard caught his attention. He recognized the man in the driver's seat. Hell. Could this day go any further south?

He headed toward his father as the man stepped from the car. Stevie caught his arm. "I don't know why you're angry with me."

He glanced down at her hand. Even now, in this minute, when he didn't want it to—powerless again—there was something about her touch that arrested him. But that wasn't her fault.

"Of course you don't," he said softly. Jack's father caught his eye and he acknowledged his presence with the lift of his chin. "Excuse me for a few minutes."

Her hand slipped from him. He didn't look back as he walked away, though he knew his voice carried over his shoulder. "And for the record . . . you didn't want Kohl to leave Tanti Baci. So I bought the place from him after he won it from Liam. I did it for you."

Wondering why he'd been compelled to make the confession, he approached his father. "Dad." His other sons and Roxy called him Papa. But Jack had never swayed from the American version and he wondered if that's what made his father see him as so different. So untrustworthy.

"I won't shake your hand, sir," he said, looking down at himself. "I'm filthy again."

His father gave a little shrug. "It looks natural on you, son."

Jack laughed.

The king of Ardenia frowned. "I meant that as a . . . as a compliment, damn it."

"All right."

The frown went fiercer. "Jack, why do you always see me in the worst possible light?"

"Like father like son?"

The other man swore in German, the language he favored when angry. "Can't we have a conversation free of subtle insults?"

Suddenly Jack was weary. Tired of the tension between him and his father and irritated with how this place, this beautiful place, had resurrected so many of his ghosts—his interest in winemaking, the friendships that he'd let lapse, the resentment toward his family that he harbored and couldn't seem to shake.

He didn't want to care about any of it, but now the pervading isolation and loneliness he'd endured during the last decade was exhausting him.

"Then let's cut the bullshit, Dad," he said. "Ten years ago, you believed I had arranged my own kidnapping. Mine and Roxanne's."

"That's not true. I knew for a fact and from the first that Roxanne's involvement was impromptu. She was supposed to be with me and your mother that day and begged off at the last minute."

Jack shrugged. "So instead I took her on that date I had made with Maxine, to that lake in the mountains. Rox became collateral damage."

His father ran his hand over his eyes. "We've all been so damaged by this over the years."

"I know." Weariness dragged at him again. "I'm sorry."

"I didn't ask for an apology," the other man bit out. "Let's be clear about that. I've never asked for an apology from you!"

Jack stared. His father had never raised his voice, not once, in his entire memory.

"It's I who should apologize," the king said, his voice quieter, rougher. He ran his hand over his eyes again.

Jack noted the new lines on the king's face and the folds of skin at his throat as he swallowed. The father had aged in the last decade and there was pain for the son in that, too.

"I somehow gave you the idea that I didn't trust you. That I blamed you, and—" His father broke off. "I can see now that my words aren't working."

They stood together in silence.

His father gazed around the vineyard. "This is a good place, Jack. Edenville, these two acres."

"You think so?" His father's opinion didn't matter to him.

"And don't just credit that old man Ray Crawford for

your interest in it. Plenty of Parinis knew how to grow things, too."

The king of Ardenia looked about him again, then his eyes came to rest on Stevie, standing in the distance. "Your fiancée, I think she's good for you, too, Jack."

"Really?" He said it just to sound interested. Now wasn't the time to be truthful about Stevie.

"Really." His father reached into his jacket pocket and pulled out a set of car keys. *"Bonne chance, mon fils."*

Good luck, my son. Jack shrugged off the well-wishing and instead let his gaze roam the vineyard, where life was waiting to begin again. It *was* a good place, he thought, despite himself. He realized he felt a kind of camaraderie with the dormant vines. For ten years he'd been like them.

His mind wandered and he let his imagination have free rein for a moment. What would it be like to be here beyond Roxy's wedding? Would he be different when the sun warmed the dirt and green growth sprouted from the now-quiet vines? He could almost hear the drone of insects and the rustle of leaves as he walked down the ordered rows. *Would* he change? Could he live with the man he might become here?

His gaze landed on Stevie, who'd taken up the digging bar and was working at the stubborn stump in his stead.

I think she's good for you, too, his father had said.

The king approved of his fake fiancée, and for the first time in a long, long while, Jack let himself care what his father thought.

But could he be anything beyond bad for Stevie?

18

Roxanne glanced over at Emerson as they arrived at her brother's vineyard. "You didn't need to come with me," she said.

"The wedding is scheduled three days from now," he reminded her, taking her hand in his as they threaded the rows of vines in the direction of the small winery building at the rear of the acreage. "You said you needed to talk with Jack before you could make a final decision. I think it's fair that I'm part of that."

Fair? Yes. But the final decision about the marriage ceremony might be something Emerson wanted to weigh in on himself after he learned her last secret—and realized how flawed his fiancée really was and how her bad judgment had ultimately damaged Jack, too.

As if sensing her disquiet, Emerson squeezed her fingers. "I love you," he said.

She could almost smile, understanding him so much better now. When lightning had struck them that first night, she'd embraced the sense of fate—completely dazzled by the flash and heat. Naive of her, she realized today. Emerson, by nature and by experience, had been compelled to take a second look at what they were doing. Though at the moment he claimed to love her and was convinced of their happy-ever-after, she wasn't holding him to "forever" until she finished saying her piece to Jack.

"There he is." Emerson pointed ahead, where she could see Jack sitting on the front steps to the little castle's entrance, a pad of paper on his knee, a pencil in his hand. Disheveled, with a day's growth of beard on his face and dirt on the knees of his jeans, Roxy's brother didn't look anything close to a royal prince.

He looked like Jack Parini, grandson of a salt-of-the-earth Georgia farmer. He looked intent, but content, too, and she had to harden her heart because she suspected she was about to shatter that mood. Maybe it was selfish of her, she thought, pausing a moment. Maybe she should let him be. But this confrontation felt like her last chance to get things right—maybe for both of them. She slid a look at Emerson. All of them.

"Hey, big brother," she called softly.

"Rox." His head came up as he closed the pad of paper. He spared a look for Emerson that wasn't all too friendly. "I didn't hear you two drive up."

"You looked absorbed." She let go of her fiancé's hand to sit next to her brother on the step. "What are you doing?"

"Nothing." Jack put aside the pad and pencil and gave her a small smile. "Do you need me? Is Mom insisting on dressing you up like Marie Antoinette? Is Dad intimidating the staff at the resort?"

"Those things I can handle," she said. "There's just the small matter of you."

His smile died. "I'm sorry the press and everybody keeps chewing on that old story, Rox. Would it help if I left—"

"*No.*" She put her hand on his arm. "No. You can't go

anywhere until you and I talk about that old story, Jack. Until we get some things straight between the two of us."

He rose to his feet. "There's no need."

"Yes, there is." She tugged on the denim of his jeans, forcing him to sit again, then slid her hand in the pocket of her jacket to pull out an object. "Because of this."

Without looking at Emerson's reaction, she showed her brother what she held. Jack stared at the small bride and groom cake topper sitting on the flat of her palm. "Oh, God. I suspected you were tempted again . . ." He passed a hand over his mouth. "I'm sorry, Rox."

"Would you stop saying that?"

He blew out a breath. "So you didn't st—take it, then?"

"Of course I stole it." For the second time, she avoided Emerson's gaze. Would he be disappointed that she still succumbed? "From Stevie's office just yesterday. But you're not the one who should be sorry about that."

Jack was on his feet again. "Damn it, of course I'm sorry."

"This is my problem," she said. "Not yours."

"But it's my fault you have the problem."

There was that burden of guilt she had to lighten. "We need to talk about what happened."

"No." He tried pacing away, but she clutched at his denim pants leg again. "We've both been through it a million times."

"But not with each other, Jack," she said quietly. "We've never been honest with each other about what happened when we were kidnapped."

He dropped back to the step. His gaze shifted to Emerson, standing close, then back to her. "I should have seen Maxine for what she was."

"Beautiful but cold?" Roxanne prompted. "Manipulated by her brother who was evil to the core?"

His hand slashed out. "All that."

"But she covered so well, didn't she? No one suspected that Maxine or Emil were anything but the flashy and somewhat-spoiled progeny of rich parents. Our own brother Henri introduced you to her, right? He didn't exile himself from Ardenia and the family after discovering his peripheral connection to the kidnapping."

"That's ridiculous," Jack scoffed. "Henri didn't lock you in that room. He didn't terrorize you for five days and nights."

"And neither did you, Jack."

"I don't want to talk about this anymore." He scooped up the pad and pencil. "I've got things to do."

She yanked the items out of his hand. "Not until I'm finished. My counselor has helped me confront a few things I've avoided for the last ten years."

He stilled. "You're seeing the doctor in San Francisco again? Good."

"It is good. Necessary." She glanced toward her fiancé but couldn't interpret the expression on his face. "I told Emerson about my problem, you know. It sent him away from me, to Stevie—"

Emerson made a noise, but Jack cut him off with another slashing hand gesture. "I know about that."

She grimaced. "He's lucky you didn't deck him, then. Not that he's a threat in that regard. Stevie's in love with you."

Jack looked off into the vineyard. "Rox . . ."

"Shh. It's still my turn to talk. Ten years ago, remember how—"

"I remember everything."

"Still my turn to talk." She put her hand on his knee. "I told the therapist about the experience yesterday. After years of trying to erase it from my mind, instead I replayed it moment by moment in my head."

"I think the erasing is a better plan."

"But it doesn't work, does it?" At the reluctant shake of his head, she continued. "Ten years ago, we drove up to that house by the lake and went to the door, expecting to see both Maxine and Emil. But she wasn't there. Emil was alone—and surprised to find I'd come along with you." He'd smiled, and to the fourteen-year-old she'd been, it hadn't seemed evil, but exciting.

Jack grimaced. "He was so damn happy to see us."

"Because he thought with the capture of the two youngest in the royal family, he could double the ransom."

"Which he did." Jack's muscles went tense under her hand. "Why the rehash, Rox?"

"Because of the things I've been taking," she said, holding up the wedding cake topper again for him to see. "And what I haven't been taking."

"I don't understand."

"I know." Her fingers curled around the motionless little figures, standing arm in arm, just as she and Jack were linked and frozen by their shared experience. She chanced a glance at Emerson, but his face remained unreadable. "I also know that if it wasn't for me being there that day, you would have gotten away."

"No. I—"

"Yes. I can replay it in my head so clearly now. How you so politely let your little sister precede you through the doorway. Then you walked in, shut the door, and Emil went from smiling host to sinister kidnapper."

"With a great big gun."

"Trained on me." Emerson moved now, his hand landing on Roxanne's shoulder. She had to ignore it. She had to go on. "But I know you, Jack, and I remember Emil. He was small, and nervous. You outweighed him, and you could have overpowered him, too, except he had that leverage."

"Which was you." Jack sighed. "Anyway, what-ifs are useless."

She couldn't let him dismiss her points that easily. "I know Papa had all you boys trained for your own protection. I was so jealous that you got to spend time at the firing range and had been taught down-and-dirty self-defense.

You knew the moves. You would have attempted them if I hadn't been in the way."

"Again, it doesn't matter."

"It matters a lot, if you ask me. It had to be harder for you to be powerless when you knew that if you'd been alone—"

"But I wasn't alone!" Jack half rose from the step, then dropped back down, his voice lowering, too. "Damn it, Rox, this is all so ridiculous. I'm sorry, so sorry about what happened to you. But talking about it doesn't change a thing. I *wasn't* alone that day."

"And *I'm* sorry about that." They'd finally reached the purpose of her visit. It was time to make the confession that she hoped would cleanse the last festering infection from the wound inside her. How Emerson would react—how it might change that date they had at the altar—she didn't know. But she steeled herself to continue. "I coaxed you into letting me go up to the lake with you. I knew you were supposed to be meeting Maxine and Emil there and I wanted in on the fun."

"It was hard for you, being the youngest of all the kids in the family."

"And you were the best big brother in the world for being so patient with me." She smiled a little. "I really missed you when you were away at college in California."

He smiled back. "You're just saying that because Edmond, Henri, and Derick never let you win at Monopoly or Mille Bornes like I did."

"I beat you fair and square every time . . . didn't I?"

Smiling some more, he shook his head. "We had some good times, even in Ardenia, didn't we, Rox?"

"We're going to have some more good times," she said, hoping she was telling the truth. "The best times. But to get to them, I have to put the kidnapping in context for us both. If I hadn't been there, I think Emil wouldn't have managed to overpower you."

"It doesn't—"

"And one of the reasons, I think, I've been taking things is to avoid taking responsibility for that. And for the fact that I was desperate to go along with you that day."

"You were desperate to avoid some ribbon-cutting thing that Dad and Mom wanted you to attend."

She shook her head, then sucked in a breath. It was time, now. Her fingers brushed Emerson's, still on her shoulder, and then fell to her lap, where they rested on that happy bride and groom. "I wanted to see Emil, Jack. I thought I was in love with him. He said he was in love with me."

Her brother's jaw dropped. *"What?"*

Emerson's hand tightened on her. She couldn't look at him. "He'd come over to the house with Maxine that summer. We'd talk, fool around in the pool, you know. Then we kissed a few times, and—"

"He was seven years older than you!" There was outrage in Jack's voice.

Roxanne felt only relief that the truth was finally out—and maybe even a little sympathy for that lovesick girl she'd been. But she kept her gaze lowered to avoid Emerson's reaction. "I couldn't tell the family after the kidnapping. I didn't want to let them down."

"You wouldn't—"

"I was their perfect little princess, Jack, and I couldn't take that away from them. But the truth is, I would have stowed away in the trunk of your car if you hadn't agreed to take me."

He groaned and dropped his head into his hands. "Rox. I don't know what to say."

"I do, Jack." She took up the pad and pencil and flipped it open. It looked like he was redrawing the interior of the winery. Instead of lingering on his pencil lines, she turned to a clean page. Her hand moved swiftly.

"Here," she said, handing it to him.

He glanced at the four words. "Thanks for that, but—"

"Say it out loud," she insisted, giving the pad a little shake.

His gaze moved back to the page. "I forgive you, Jack," he repeated, obviously puzzled.

"Again."

He looked up, a decent man who had blamed himself for too long. "I forgive you, Jack."

Roxanne took a breath. "Now actually do that, best of big brothers. Do what it says. Forgive yourself."

Jack continued staring at her. "Roxanne, I'm lost here."

"No. You've found everything. You found your place." She gestured to the vineyard. "You found what you want to do with your life. You found a woman to love."

She took the wedding cake topper she still held and pressed it into his unresisting hand. "Congratulations, Jack. You found normal."

What she might have given up now, she didn't know.

~

His mind reeling, Emerson silently drove Roxanne back to the resort and just as silently followed her to her rooms and through the door to her suite. He was still himself, the kind of man who needed time to think things through and process them, even though he'd operated on pure instinct and impulse when he'd gone after Roxanne. It was so out of character, he'd gotten that stupid case of cold feet that went even icier when he discovered she wasn't the perfect princess he'd once thought.

Thank God for Stevie, who had pointed out it was his rashness when dealing with Roxanne that proved how strong his feelings were. He'd gone back to his fiancée, convinced of his love, convinced they were meant to be together. When she didn't want to totally commit to the marriage, what could he say? After the way he'd backpedaled, he'd had to respect her wishes.

Yet he hadn't given her too much space, thank God. He wouldn't have wanted to miss her showdown with Jack. When he saw her in action, facing up to her family, owning up to her flaws, he'd been speechless. This amazing woman who had such a clear insight into herself just floored him and he could only be more glad he'd operated on impulse and instinct those months before. Who knew his gut could be so wise? And she'd shown him something . . .

She hadn't wanted to disappoint her family by upsetting their image of her as the perfect princess. His family had an image of him as well, and he was keeping his own silence because of it. Thank God for Roxanne. Without her he might have seen too late that the path he'd been feeling was so wrong wasn't the one he wanted to travel with her, but—

"If you don't want to get married anymore, that's all right. I understand."

He just stared at her. "What?"

"Because now you know all my secrets." She sat down on the couch in the sitting area and folded her hands in her lap, her expression composed, her posture finishing-school perfect. "I completely understand—"

"I can't let you go, Roxanne." He strode over to take a place on the cushions beside her. "You need to understand that. I won't let you go."

"But—"

"I can be as ruthless as any royal princess," he warned.

Her fingers, in their good-little-girl position, turned white-knuckled. "Emerson, I don't know."

"I know. And I know that I need you—"

"What?" She moved suddenly, one hand clutching his forearm. "Say that again."

"I need you?"

"Again," she whispered.

He smiled, knowing that he'd finally found the right words, the right sentiment that would sway this sweet creature. "I need you in my life. I need you in my life so that I remember to appreciate that snap decisions can lead to spectacular things. To understand that my heart knows as much as my head. I need your example—as a person who is owning up to her mistakes and claiming what she wants for her own life."

"Emerson." There were tears in her eyes, but he didn't mind them. "I didn't want our marriage to be a one-way street. I couldn't let you think you were the big strong guy that needed to stand between me and my weaknesses."

Leaning over, he hauled her into his lap so he could hold her closer to his heart, which was beating sure and strong. "Hell, Rox, I've been standing here admiring your strength. I'm going to be thinking of you every time I tell the world who I am and what I want. To do that, I need you, sweetheart. I need you to be my wife."

Her weight was light and warm in his lap and her cheeks damp as he met her mouth with his. The kiss was tender, then not so tender, and next thing he knew his palm was caressing her breast and she was unbuttoning his shirt. Lifting his head, he groaned. "Roxanne . . ."

"Make love to me, Emerson."

"We're waiting until—" But he couldn't think when her small thumb slid across the point of his nipple. Good God, his pants were tight. He took two deep breaths, trying to find that center line again, swerving back from the sweet, dark side of the road. His hand captured hers to flatten it against his thudding heart. "We're waiting until we're married."

"Then let's get married right now." Roxanne had that light in her eyes he was starting to recognize. Militant princess, on the path for a cup of coffee and a man. Him.

Funny how that gleam made him feel a hundred feet tall and strong enough to confront giants—and maybe even a political committee or two. Grinning, he brushed his knuckles down the side of her face. "You want to take a quick trip to Nevada? Is that what you're saying?"

She was already shaking her head and popped off his lap to grab a notebook from the desk. "Let's say our vows to each other, right now. And then we'll make love, Emerson, because in our hearts, we'll be married."

"I haven't written any vows yet." He remembered that day when the idea of doing so had made a cold chill run down his spine. Now he just knew he needed time to find the exact right thing to promise her.

"You said the perfect words to me just the other day."

And she didn't have to remind him more, because he knew the words she meant. He agreed, they were the perfect ones to say. But somehow, they didn't get to their exchange immediately. He stood up to take her in his arms again, and from there it was just a few kisses before half their clothes were gone.

It was a dozen steps to the bedroom and the soft mattress and the cool sheets. She was sleek and so beautiful naked. He left his pants on, knowing it would help him hold back so he could touch every millimeter of her exposed skin.

And he did touch her everywhere, running the edge of his jaw over her pink nipples. Tasting the tender skin between her breasts with his lips. Palming the inner surface of her thighs to open them for his gaze.

"Emerson." Her face was bright with a mix of desire and embarrassment. She tried to close her legs, but he cupped her sex to establish his place there. She was hot and soft against his hand.

God. "No man has ever touched you like this," he murmured.

Her flush deepened and her hips lifted, just the slightest, toward his possession, as if she couldn't help herself. "You know I never dated."

"Until me." Going slow, he caressed with his fingers, opening her folds and finding that she was warmer, wetter, than he thought a virgin could be so quickly. He sought the moisture with his long middle finger, going deep.

Her hips lifted again, her gaze riveted to his face. "Good?" he asked, using his thumb to find the throbbing button at the top of her sex.

She swallowed a little noise.

He smiled. "Good."

Her hand reached up to clutch his shoulder as he continued a gentle glide and press. Then he leaned down to take a tender nipple in his mouth. He sucked on it, his eyes closing at the rightness: it hardening against his tongue, her nails digging into his skin, the flow of heated wetness around his finger.

Her thighs were relaxed now, and he luxuriated in the textures of her body. He bounced kisses off the drum of her belly and ran his teeth over the sharp thrust of her hip bones. His tongue tickled the tiny whorl of her navel. He pillowed his cheek on her thigh and watched his hand dabble in the playground he'd been dreaming of, smiling at how she was moving in counterpoint against his touch.

"Emerson." Roxanne sounded breathless. "Please."

"Baby." He slid up her body so he could sample her mouth again, but she wasn't willing to be so patient now. She plucked at the waistband of his pants, making him suck in air as her fingers brushed against his erection.

"Take these off," the princess commanded.

"Okay, okay." He was feeling a little breathless himself. And it only got worse when his bare legs tangled with hers and his shaft met the silky skin of her thigh.

He groaned, leaning his forehead against her delicate shoulder. "Roxanne . . ."

"Now, Emerson."

Now, Emerson, his libido echoed.

Oh, God, oh, God. His nerves started chattering at him again—she's a *virgin!*—but his body knew what it wanted. He rolled between her thighs and used his hands to draw up her knees against his flanks. The head of his shaft kissed the sweet wet heat at the center of her body.

Her hips tilted. He lowered, beginning to enter the tight clasp of her. Framing her face with his hands, he smiled down at her. "I love you."

"I love you." Her mouth was red and swollen from his kisses. "I want you."

Emerson pushed inside her. She twitched at the intrusion. "Hurt?"

"Not really. It's just . . . new." Her knees tightened on his hips. "I didn't know it would feel like this."

He slid deeper. "We fit together." That was so clear to him now—and something to celebrate.

"You're inside me."

His heart was slamming against his chest. "All the way, baby."

Her voice went husky. "You walked into my life as if I'd wished you there. You made me feel safe and at risk—both at once. I want to take chances with you. I want to stay safe with you by the fireside. I want to keep you close as my own and also share our love with the whole world."

He smiled. "You do?"

A tear slid from the edge of her lashes to her temple, but Roxanne was smiling, too. "I do."

And that was his cue, he knew. He slid out to the tip, then slid back in, connecting them once again. He was besotted, and it was the best damn feeling he'd ever had in his entire life.

"My favorite color?" he said. "You. My favorite flavor? You. My favorite woman?"

He watched another happy tear join the first. "Always you, Roxanne. Always and forever you."

Later, while she slept in his arms, Emerson remembered his father talking during the wine walk. It seemed to fit Roxanne, himself, their relationship, and the bumps and obstacles it had survived these last weeks. *The struggle to grow makes the vine work harder, extending its roots and absorbing elements that make it produce a more interesting fruit.*

Yeah. That.

~

Jack pounded on the back door of the Baci farmhouse. Frustrated when he perceived no response from the other side, he pounded again. Finally, footsteps could be heard crossing the old linoleum. Stevie swung open the door.

He was breathing too fast. It didn't help that she wore a rib-hugging T-shirt and another pair of those thin, low-riding jeans. His fingers were longer than their zipper, which meant he could slide under the waistband and be only a hand span from heaven.

Except she was eyeing him with alarm instead of lust. "What are you doing here?"

His mouth opened even as his fingers closed over the bride and groom in his jacket pocket. *You've found everything*, Roxanne had told him yesterday, and he'd spent hours trying to get the words out of his head. Still, he'd caught himself turning his scratch pad, adding lines, erasing lines, modifying spaces within the castle winery at My Aching Back.

Drawing walls designed to keep him in Edenville.

"I've not been sleeping," he said, his voice guttural. There was that, too. Not that he'd had a decent eight hours in a decade, but he'd kept coming awake the night before, remembering that moment when Roxy walked into that lake house in Ardenia. In his dreams, it would morph into the moment that he'd walked toward Stevie standing by her limousine on New Year's Eve.

In both cases, his mind would be screaming, *Go back! Go back!* In both cases his nightmare self continued onward, unaware of the consequences ahead. Those damn consequences, the worst of which was a profound sense of powerlessness.

When you cared about someone else, you surrendered control. He couldn't let that happen again.

Stevie was still staring at him. "Did you want to come in?"

No. Yes. No.

"Yes." Still, he hesitated as he crossed the threshold. "Were you searching the attic again tonight?"

She yanked on his arm to draw him into the kitchen. "It's cold out there," she said, shutting the door behind him. "And, yes, I was looking again, but I admit defeat.

I don't see any sign of the treasure or anything that looks like it could be opened with the key. I'm about to give up altogether."

He shrugged. "Stevie—"

"I think I've been wasting time in the house. Anne and Alonzo never lived here. But the cottage was thoroughly gutted for the rehab, so it can't be there, either." She sighed, then slid him an assessing look. "How interested are you in wandering the vineyard with a metal detector and a shovel?"

"Tonight?" He stepped toward her and was unsurprised when she stepped back. Her instincts were good and he was feeling particularly on edge. "Not interested at all."

"Okay. So what did you want?" She took another step back.

He reached out to halt her movement, realizing too late he'd reached with the hand still grasping the wedding cake topper. They both stared at it.

"I came to return this," he said quickly.

"Ah." She took it from him, set it aside. "I noticed it was missing from the office."

"Yes. Well." He forked a hand through his hair, agitated. His intention had been to leave it somewhere when she wasn't looking. And then get away . . . from here, from *her*.

"Roxy took it, didn't she?"

Shit. "I—uh . . ."

"I know she has a problem, Jack. Emerson made a comment and then I put two-and-two together."

His empty hand curled into a fist. Ten years had passed and it still cut deep that he hadn't protected his sister in every way. It's why relationships weren't his thing. It's why he couldn't start caring for Stevie. "Don't say anything to anyone. She's getting help."

Stevie half turned from him. "You still think I'd sabotage her, Jack? Great."

"I don't . . . I didn't mean to insult you, but—" Damn.

His mood erupted. He grabbed her by the upper arms and hauled her around to face him. "You've got to stop doing this."

Color flagged her cheekbones. "Doing what?"

"Digging under my skin. Always buzzing around in my head."

She was breathing through her nose like her temper was suddenly running as hot as his. "You asked for it, Jack. 'Fly in your champagne,' you said. 'Thorn on your rose.'"

"All right, then. All right." Muttering, he hauled her closer. "Maybe your way is right. Something's got to get you out of my system."

He slammed his mouth against hers. She bit his bottom lip. His hands raced to the curves of her ass to push her closer, though her mons was already pressed against his rigid cock. They both groaned as her hands dove beneath his shirt and her nails scored the skin at his shoulders.

The sting only further enflamed him. "You make me burn," he said against her mouth. He ran his lips along her jaw so he could nip her earlobe. She shuddered in his arms and molded herself against his chest.

"Sex like a man, but a bed this time," he said, and they careened like two drunks through the kitchen, off the walls, and into the guest bedroom, where he'd slept that other time. The bedside light glowed. Their frenzied dance took them to the edge of the bed, and without a qualm, he pushed her, tumbling her onto the mattress. At the last second, she grabbed the waistband of his jeans and he fell on top of her, his head between her breasts.

She moaned as he took advantage of the position, his mouth latching on to one of her nipples over her clothes. His tongue wet the thin fabric so he could feel the berried crest against his tongue and then take it between his teeth. He bit her there, too, with less care than he might have some other time, but it didn't matter, because she shuddered in his hold and fought him to throw off her T-shirt. He yanked at her bra, its bindings beyond him when he felt this greedy, and finally there was a ripping sound and the sleek bounty of her breasts spilled into his hands.

He held them against his stubbled cheeks, kissing that soft valley until he had to suck again. He ringed her areolas with stinging kisses, then scraped his teeth over her erect nipples.

Stevie had his pants unfastened. She shoved at them, while he kicked off his shoes. Then she rolled on top, and his shirt was gone, he was naked, and she was using that hot mouth of hers to set fires at his throat, along his collarbone, down the center of his torso. She found his cock—oh, God, she took him deep in her mouth in one long slide of molten heat. His heart jolted, his hips rose, even as his hand cupped the back of her head in desperation.

That's what he was—desperate. He had to get her out of his system, pull her loose from him in a quick tear of sinew and bone, whatever it took to be free. Except, of course, this act was just the opposite of that. Instead of out it was in, instead of freedom it was constraints. He had her naked, too, now, and she was so damn tight inside as he slid a finger, two, inside her.

She was on her knees, her magnificent ass in the air as she continued to take him into her mouth, but he tortured her with that same rhythm as he worked his digits inside her clasping, confining, sweet little tunnel.

The orgasm was building in his balls. They were pulling tight, as if seeking to meet that quadruple-score-for-appearance blow-job mouth. He squeezed yet another finger into her slippery warmth and she hummed against his cock.

Gasping, Jack jerked away from her, wanting more before it was over. He shoved her onto her back, and slid down her body, spreading her legs with implacable hands.

She was wide open to him, splayed for his feast, and he slid his tongue hungrily over all the wet and pink flesh, tasting, taking, hoping to drive her into that same crazed state that had his head buzzing and his blood pumping.

His fingers slid inside her again, and he groaned at how the wet walls squeezed him. He lashed at her with his tongue and slid his hand up her belly to palm a breast. Then he found her nipple and pinched it, just as his teeth scraped over the hard jut of her clitoris.

Stevie's body froze. He heard her suck in a gasping breath, but he didn't give her mercy—she'd never shown a crumb of it for him. He pinched tighter, delved deeper, scraped again.

Her body quaked. She cried out. He rode the waves with her, not letting up until the quivers turned to trembles, turned to a tiny whimper. "Jack," she said, her voice sounding drugged. "Oh, God, I need you."

No. No, she didn't need him, any more than he did her. That's what he was here to prove, right? But his body needed release and so he crawled up her damp and heated skin. He'd left condoms in the bedside table before and they were still there. His hands shaking, he rolled one on, then rolled into the cradle of her body.

Lust shot up his spine like a flame up a fuse as she lifted her knees. He took them in the palms of his hands and pushed them toward her chest, keeping her open to him while he thrust against her soft, wet tissue.

His heart slammed in his chest as he pistoned into her body, driving again and again and again, as if each move was a mile taking him farther from her and this indecent desperation.

Her gaze was on him, the light gleaming in her half-closed eyes. There was a flush of color on her cheeks; her mouth and her nipples were strawberry pink. He couldn't look away from them. "Touch them," he heard himself order, his voice guttural. "Touch yourself for me."

And, God, she did, her thumb strumming over one hard nipple. Then her other hand took a meandering path like the snake in the Garden of Eden until it found the glistening flesh of her pussy. As he continued to plunder, she played.

The pleasure was going to kill him. It gathered like a fireball, pressure and heat that built and built . . . and then exploded at the base of his spine. It felt like embers shot from his fingertips, his toes, the ends of his hair. Stevie convulsed around him, finding her own release, and he collapsed onto the pillow beside hers.

Minutes later he made it to the bathroom and got rid of the condom. "I'll leave in just a minute," he murmured to her, but fell onto the mattress and didn't remember anything for hours.

When he awoke, dawn was turning the fog outside the window the pearlized pinks and grays of an abalone shell. Turning his head, he realized he had his wish from the time before—Stevie was still asleep beside him. He watched her breathe, her hair a tangle of waves on the pillow, her lips still swollen from his kisses.

Heat streaked down his spine when he remembered her mouth O'd around his shaft, taking him in, taking everything he'd offered . . . and not asking for any more than that.

Something unfurled inside him at the thought. With a gentle hand, he brushed a lock of hair off her cheek. She didn't move. One shoulder showed, creamy and curved, above the covers, and he traced that, too, reveling in her silky strength.

"Beautiful," he whispered to himself. It didn't seem so dangerous a thought at dawn. She was lovely and luscious, and if he was going to get her out of his system, then maybe he'd have to have her this way, too. Not in urgent demand, but also in soft surrender.

He scooted closer to her, drawing down the blanket and sheet. Her breasts reacted to the little chill, and he took the hardening crests into his mouth, sucking with delicate pressure. She began to stir, and he lightened the suction. She drew up her closest knee, the cap of it brushing his thigh, and he went from half hard to full erection at just that subtle touch.

His breath hitching in his chest, he let his fingertips take a slow path along that sleek thigh toward the center of her body. She was damp there, and as he slowly and tenderly explored the petaled flesh, the moisture increased.

Pressure built in his chest and arrowed to his groin. But he ignored the commands clamoring inside him and continued caressing Stevie's warm skin, for the first time not allowing his lust or hers to order the action.

Now he indulged in that slow lovemaking he'd been after since the first time she'd ground her mouth against his. He drew his lips from her nipple to her neck, pressing soft, open-mouth kisses along her creamy golden skin. *"Mon ange,"* he whispered. She was what he thought there might be in heaven, one of the ranks of seraphim that possessed enough strength to yield swords, enough fire to face down Satan, enough sweetness to comfort small children.

He couldn't even laugh at his own romantic notions. Stevie believed in ghosts and treasure. For this moment, he believed in something he saw in her. Her arm moved, and her hand curled around his head to slide through his hair. He looked up, meeting her sleepy gaze. She smiled at him.

What a way to say good-bye, he thought. Better than last night with its flames and smoke. So he continued making love to her as she stretched and warmed under his touch. He ran his tongue along the curve of each eyebrow, slid his whiskered cheek against the arch of her bicep, sucked her pinkie finger into the heat of his mouth.

She was pliant through all of it, allowing him to turn her this way and angle her that so he might say both good morning and farewell to the nape of her neck and the patch of skin between the dimples on her bottom. He hauled her to her knees so that her cheek was pressed to the pillow and her ass was lifted so he could palm the tight flesh. She was panting now, though, and when she whispered to him, whimpering his name, he reached for another condom.

He curved around her back, fitting his cock to her wet

slit, sliding in even as she moved into his groin. *I could love her*, he thought.

It stilled his rhythm. *I can't love her. I'm leaving her.*

"What, Jack?" She sounded drugged again. "What are you doing?"

"Saying good-bye," he said, his voice thick. "You know that's what this is, right? You know we have to end this."

"I know," she whispered, though her body clenched sweetly on him as she moved her hips backward again, taking him deeper. "I know."

His climax was building again, so he focused on that, directing all his energy to the gathering pleasure. Sliding one hand around her hip, he found her clitoris and rubbed there in light strokes. Tension was gathering in her, too, and he smiled against her shoulder as he felt her tension break.

He followed after.

They stayed like that for long moments, joined. He was relieved she couldn't see his face, though he had no idea what expression it might show. Tenderness? Regret?

"Jack . . . why?" she finally whispered, as they turned to their sides and he spooned against her, his body still intimately joined with hers.

He knew what she was asking. Why was he determined to walk away from her?

"The dark . . . it was the screen that ran my mother's anguish, my father's despair, my brothers' grief. The film of all that played endlessly and there was no light to relieve me of it. I had no control over my surroundings and the blackness was suffocating."

She made a noise and he soothed her with a kiss to her nape. "Parts of me died during those five days—important pieces of my heart. Once we were rescued, too much time had passed to revive them. They were completely cut away when the rumors hit the press—and then I cut myself off from Ardenia, from—"

"Everything. Everyone."

"Yes." He pressed his mouth to her nape again. "I don't see a way—I don't want to try even—to resuscitate it or to forge something new—"

"Or to feel again."

"Not like that." Because he did feel something—relief—that she finally understood.

He waited for her response, but a clattering from the kitchen made them both twitch. "What?" Stevie said. Voices, male and female, could be heard. She jolted now, and it threw him off her. "Oh, God," she groaned. "Allie and Penn."

She was in a robe so fast he didn't get a chance to appreciate her nakedness. He headed for the bathroom as she slipped out of the room, closing the door behind her.

So much for good-bye, he thought. But maybe it was easier not to speak the word again. They'd just go their separate ways. He caught sight of his face in the mirror as he went to dispose of the condom.

That's how he saw his expression shift to shock. *Fait chier.*

The rubber had broken.

Her hair still damp from her shower, Stevie poured coffee for her sisters in the Baci farmhouse kitchen. Amidst the hubbub of her younger sister shuffling around on crutches and her husband bringing in suitcases from their car, Jack had slipped away.

Stevie had left to wash and dress and, when she'd wandered out of the guest bedroom again, found that Penn had gone over to the Bennett house to visit his half brothers and that Giuliana had arrived and was seated at the kitchen table listening to Allie grouse about being laid up with her injured foot. "I'm bored with daytime TV," she said. "And don't laugh, but I hobbled into this shop in Malibu and now I've taken up knitting."

Cups of coffee silenced them for the few minutes it took to doctor their mugs. Then Allie sipped her beverage and smiled at Stevie. "What's been going on with you? How's that fake engagement working out?"

"Fine," she answered. Memories staggered through her head like she and Jack had staggered about this very room the night before. Fiery kisses, rough hands. Tender caresses, whispered words. *Mon ange.*

Her nose tingled, like a sneeze was in the offing. She pressed her knuckles there, hard, to hold it back. Her gaze snagged on Allie's, who was staring. "What?" she said.

"Are you sure you're okay?"

"I'm fine." Her nose tingled again, and she closed her eyes. *Something's got to get you out of my system*, he'd said. But this morning? It had been good-bye and it had been more. It had been unforgettable, though he'd outlined the end of them even as he covered her body with his. *Parts of me died . . . important pieces of my heart.*

She shoved back her chair to reach the box of tissues on the counter. The sneeze was threatening once more. Both her sisters were staring at her now, and Stevie's stomach jolted. They all needed a distraction, she decided, and rushed to the utility closet where she'd stashed the carton she'd lugged down from the attic on that first foray she'd made there with Jack.

Jack . . .

"Don't think about him," she muttered to herself, grabbing the cardboard container and returning to the table. She dumped the container onto the center, scattering the salt and pepper shakers.

"Geez, Steve," Jules protested.

Stephania, do you have to be so rough?

There's no need to yell.

Good girls keep their voices down and their feelings to themselves.

Allie stood on her good leg. "What's this?"

Stevie shrugged. "Things I found in the attic from when we were kids. I thought you might like to look at them."

Her younger sister was already peeling open the flaps. "Oh! My tutu." It was a pink ball of Lycra that had to be turned inside out so that the tulle layers sprang free. "I was a peony in the dance recital."

"I had the only boy part . . . remember? A scarecrow."

Stevie found the battered straw hat she'd worn and stuck it on her head.

"The studio closed the next year," Jules said, rummaging through the box herself.

"Thank God," Stevie replied, tossing the hat to the table. "Then Mom let me join the Bobby Sox softball league instead of insisting I learn to tap dance."

Allie pouted. "I loved being a ballerina."

"Watch out, Jules," Stevie said, throwing a look at her older sister. "The family crier is about to do her thing."

Instead of joining in to tease Allie, notorious for her easy tears, Jules hesitated. Then she took a breath. "Stevie . . ."

Something about her name, in that tone of voice, had her grabbing for the carton. "And look at this. Your baby books." She handed one in pale pink to Allie, another, a ducky yellow, to Jules.

Alessandra raised her eyebrows. "Where's yours?"

Stevie shrugged. "Don't you know? It's the curse of the middle child. Parents never got around to mine."

"Oh." That waterworks-on-the-way look overtook her younger sister's face again.

It made Stevie's nose itch, and she grabbed up another tissue. "Damn dust," she murmured into it.

"But here's something with your name on it," Jules said. She pulled out a thick manila envelope with "Stephania" written on the outside in their mother's handwriting. Turning it upside down, she dumped the contents onto the tabletop.

Allie squealed, as if she were six again. "Look, here are your baby pictures, Stevie."

"Really?" She went for nonchalance as she stirred them with a fingertip. "I didn't know there were any."

Her sister was examining the photos, one after the other. "Looks like they just didn't make it into an album. You could do that yourself, you know. I might have taken up scrapbooking while I was recuperating if I hadn't found the Malibu & Ewe yarn shop."

Stevie made a noise as more handwriting caught her attention. One of the photos had landed facedown and she realized her mother had written notes on the back of each. "Month 2." "First spoon of cereal." "Halloween, age 1."

Her fingers found yet another picture. Their father must have taken it because it showed Stevie sitting on her mother's lap. Child Stevie was somewhere between four and five and it was likely a holiday, because she was wearing a dress and tights. Still, she had a miniature football in her hand. Despite that, the woman was gazing on the child with an affectionate smile on her face.

Stevie turned the photo over, and froze. Her mother had written: "Our stubborn tomboy. I think she's the daughter most like me."

It fluttered from Stevie's hand to the table. With her nose burning, she spun away to grab more tissues. She pressed them against her face.

"Did you know she was a champion pitcher for her high school softball team?"

Stevie turned to look at her sister. "What?" It came out muffled by the tissues.

"Yep," Jules said. "But I don't think girls were encouraged to be jocks in her era. Or at least her parents didn't encourage it. She once said she caught a lot of flack from them about it."

Our stubborn tomboy. I think she's the daughter most like me.

Stevie slid into her seat at the table, nose stinging again. Then, to her deep mortification, she burst into tears. Allie was all over her in an instant. "Steve, what's the matter?" she said, her arms sliding around her middle sister. "What's going on?"

The tears only flowed faster. How had she become so sappy? So soft? "I miss her," she choked out, unable to help herself. "And I could really use a mother right now." Folding her arms on the table, she dropped her head onto them and wished herself, her miserable confession, and the stupid tears a million miles away.

Minutes passed. Her crying subsided to hiccups, but her wish wasn't granted. She remained in the Baci kitchen under the concerned gazes of her sisters. When it appeared they wouldn't suddenly be transported to Timbuktu, either, Stevie lifted her head and scrubbed at her face with the tissue.

"Not like that," Allie admonished, grabbing some from the box. "No scouring. Pat gently."

Stevie allowed herself to be fussed over by her little sister. "You're the expert."

"You can't keep it all bottled inside," Allie said, with the authority of a TV talk-show expert. "You miss Mom. You can say that."

Oh, God. Tears stung her eyes again. She prided herself on keeping it all bottled inside! Keeping it all bottled up inside kept her from being hurt! "I'm fine," she said. "I don't . . ." Again her cheeks went wet.

Giuliana drew her chair closer. As Allie went back to face-patting, Jules slid her arm around Stevie's shoulders. "Allie's right," she said, her voice soft. "Talk to us."

Stevie shook her head. "I can't."

"You can. Try this. What would you say to Mom if she was here right now?"

Was I really the daughter you thought most like you?
Is there more to you than I remember?

Stevie opened her mouth and shocked herself with what came out instead. "I've made the biggest mistake of my life. I think I've fallen in love with Jack."

Allie repeated that six-year-old squeal again. "Love!"

No, no, no. There was no way she was in love with Jack, damn it. That was ridiculous. He was supposed to be her dent-puller, her ego-booster, the guy who restored her dignity. Love didn't lead to dignity.

Desperate again, Stevie sought her older sister's gaze. "Forget I said anything. *Please.*"

Jules's smile was sad. "It's out now."

"Then just promise to stab Allie if she makes that obnoxious noise again."

Allie dropped into her chair. "Loving Jack is a bad thing?"

Jules looked over Stevie's head at their younger sister. "We're talking about Steve."

"We're talking about a *prince*," Stevie found herself adding.

"Oh." Allie slumped against her seat back. "You'd worry about that."

"Yeah. Duh."

"You can't imagine fitting into his world." Allie's eyebrows scrunched together. "Can I tell you how much that makes me dislike Emerson? Oh, let's just save time and extend the sentiment to the entire snobby Platt family."

Stevie propped her elbow on the table and dropped her forehead onto the heel of her hand.

"It's all his fault," Allie said. "Remind me never to vote for his mother again."

"Forget Emerson," Jules said. "Concentrate on Stevie."

"And Jack. Rich, royal Jack." Allie sighed. "Stevie feels like a country bumpkin in comparison."

"And he's known as a player," Jules added. "She doesn't think he'll take any woman, let alone her, seriously."

Allie's fingers drummed the tabletop. "And what if she manages to get up the nerve to share her feelings with him and he laughs it off? That's what she's worrying about."

"But if she doesn't say a word and he walks away, has she lost her chance at happiness? Should she risk being honest?"

There was a moment of silence, then Jules peered at Stevie. "Does that about cover it?"

It would have been good if she'd been able to laugh. Instead, her voice was dry even as more wetness invaded her eyes. "I feel so much better now that I've gotten all that off my chest."

"You forgot the part about how she knows we'll be here for her no matter what," Allie pointed out. "The Three Mouseketeers."

The mention only made Stevie more miserable. She'd distanced herself from their sisterhood when she'd distanced herself from Tanti Baci, hoping to spare herself more pain. That bid for protection had backfired, leaving her feeling so damn alone.

"You can't run from your emotions and you can't run from us, either," Jules said.

"So remember that whatever you do," Allie said, "whatever you decide, sisters come first."

Stevie slid the younger woman a look. "As if you'd ever put Penn in second place."

"I'd heave him over like that," she snapped her fingers, "if it would make you happy."

Stevie burst into tears again. Not because she believed Allie for a moment—or doubted her, either, when it came down to it—but because she wondered whether she'd ever be completely happy again. Jack was walking away and there was nothing she could say or any emotion she could share that would change that.

~

As darkness fell outside the cottage at Tanti Baci, Jack lingered in the well-lit interior. Roxy and Emerson's wedding rehearsal had gone off without a hitch and the rest of the bridal party was already heading toward the wine caves in anticipation of the celebration dinner. He didn't feel the need to rush toward those confining spaces.

Instead, he wandered about the rooms, unsure whether he was hoping Stevie would find him or whether he was here hiding out from her. He'd made love to her as his good-bye, but now they needed to talk about the broken condom.

He hadn't found the right moment yet, because he hadn't found her. Since yesterday morning at the farmhouse, their paths hadn't crossed. His footsteps clapped against the hardwood floor as he made his way into the bride's boudoir. The room held a faint floral fragrance—the memory of wedding bouquets, he supposed. The restful scent lured him farther into the room and he sat on the cushions of the ivory-colored divan. Raking his hands through his hair, he wondered what the hell he was going to do once the wedding was over.

He'd purchased the vineyard but hadn't seriously expected to stay. Yet now he might have made Stevie pregnant.

A child maybe. Fatherhood. Family. Those words hadn't been part of his personal lexicon in a decade of dark, lonely years.

They pierced him now, three painful arrows that had him shoving to his feet again, and the precipitous action knocked askew one of the seat cushions. Something glittered in the crevice between it and the sofa back. Jack plucked the item free and examined it, frowning. Someone had lost a jeweled cuff bracelet of what looked to be diamonds, rubies, and sapphires.

His fingers closed over it. A sign, he supposed, that he should get on to the rehearsal dinner. He'd pass the bracelet to someone from the winery, paste on a party attitude, and contemplate the ramifications of the broken rubber later. Slipping it into his jacket pocket, he moved from the boudoir to the hallway.

The sound of the outer door opening froze him. Stevie? But it was two sets of footsteps clattering on the wooden floor, and he ducked into the groom's waiting room to avoid the new visitors. He needed a few more moments alone.

This room was smaller than the bridal suite. The lamps placed here and there weren't on, but the hall light illuminated the space well enough. One entire wall was the backside of the massive stone fireplace and there was a small wet bar in the far corner. A couple of leather chairs and a matching love seat were arranged in the middle of the room. Another door led to a narrow bathroom.

The footsteps he'd heard before paused. Jack recognized Liam's voice. "Where's Stevie?"

That had been Jack's question.

"She'll be fine." It was her sister, Giuliana, who answered.

She *will* be fine? Jack frowned. Meaning she wasn't right now?

"I thought she was in charge of this wedding," Liam said, "but I saw Allie bustling around on her crutches. Penn thinks it's too much for her."

"Penn would have her travel around on a cloud if he could."

Liam's voice lowered. "Is that what Kohl wants for you?"

Giuliana's reply whipped back. "I don't want to talk about Kohl."

Good, Jack thought. Talk about Stevie instead. Wasn't she feeling well? His chest tightened. Surely symptoms of pregnancy wouldn't show up so fast.

Jesus! Pregnant. A baby. A child.

He braced himself, waiting for the expected dread to hit, now that he was allowing himself another moment to truly consider it.

Pregnant!

But it wasn't horror that filled him. Weird, but he didn't feel alarmed by the thought at all. It just seemed . . . unsettling, as if a seemingly solid wall suddenly fell to present him with a new, unexpected vista. For so, so long he'd been avoiding a multitude of things, including future, including family, and due to one faulty condom, both had caught up with him.

A baby.

But before that was Stevie, her slender body swelling with the child they'd made at dawn in the fallow season of winter. That time of rest before the earth warmed and life broke free again. Maybe it was the Georgia farmer in him, but he realized he was smiling at the thought.

Uncomfortable with that odd sense of satisfaction, he tuned back in to Liam and Giuliana's conversation. Stevie's sister's voice was pensive. "Are we going to save Tanti Baci?" she asked.

"I'll do what I can, Jules," Liam replied. "You know I will, don't you?"

"Yes." Though she didn't sound as certain as the word. "Yes, I suppose I do."

Liam released a short laugh. "What? No barbed remark? No effort to tear the skin from my bones?"

"Maybe this place mellows me."

Liam cleared his throat. "Maybe it's the memories."

There was a charged pause in the conversation. Even from a room away, Jack could feel the sexual tension. He remembered Stevie telling him the cottage had been a popular trysting spot for lovers. Clearly Giuliana and Liam had spent some time here.

Then the other couple was banished from his thoughts as Stevie took front and center again. He remembered her talking to him about another Baci legend. *If you bring your true love to the cottage, the ghosts of Anne and Alonzo will appear.*

Is that what she wished for her future? Did she expect she would bring some other man to the cottage one day and know they were meant for a lifetime? The idea had his hand curling into a fist as if to punch that nameless, faceless lover.

Would any other man see her as he did?

Would anyone else look past her tough, tomboy exterior to discover her soft, romantic center?

Yet, hell, what did he have to offer her beyond that ability to appreciate her inner vulnerability? Nothing but a playboy reputation, an ugly past, and two acres of dormant vines—as well as a heart he'd always assumed was just as dead.

For the last ten years, he'd liked it that way.

His gut was tight and his breath was coming fast as he heard Liam and Giuliana's voices trailing away. Good. He'd take a few more minutes to get ahold of himself and then head for the dinner. When he got Stevie alone, they'd discuss the possibility of pregnancy, but he wouldn't offer her anything beyond his support in however she wanted to handle the situation.

The outer door creaked open.

Then slammed shut—and the lights clicked off.

Just like that, his phobia leapt on him like a wild beast. Jack's heart crashed into his ribs, then fell like a stunned thing to his belly. Cold swept over his skin as the suffocating blackness closed around him.

Breathe. Breathe.

The darkness wrapped him in a tight cocoon. Air couldn't reach his lungs; his muscles wouldn't work to get him out of the cottage.

Lamps. On.

His thoughts moved through his head in panicky gasps.

Lamps on.

Turn lamps on.

As if through sludge, he managed to shift his body. The switch to a source of light was just a few feet away. He must get to it. He had to get to it.

Yet another item on his short list of attributes, he thought, as he ordered his muscles to cooperate. His terror of the dark.

Move.

But rigor mortis had settled in his muscles. He closed his eyes, almost ready to surrender to it . . . and then he remembered his last panic attack. He remembered Stevie in his arms, her warmth, her weight against his aching chest, the sweet comfort she'd offered him that night. The lights she'd left burning through the dark hours.

The pain in his chest eased. He opened his eyes and found the gloom wasn't quite so overwhelming. His feet were in motion and then his hand reached out to locate the base of the lamp. His fingertips slid up cool metal to locate the small knob on its side.

Light bloomed in the room. His heart lifted from its early grave and started beating again.

The panic, already waning, evaporated.

But he still wanted out, and he hurried to the hall and then into the central room, turning lights on as he went. With the exit in sight, he rushed toward the door, and his foot caught on one of the stones of the rock fireplace. As he pitched forward, he caught himself on another of the rocks. It shifted, and he dug his fingertips into the mortar surrounding it.

Which shifted, too. His hand slid, catching on another stable stone.

Now rebalanced, he examined the damage. One of the rocks at shoulder height had twisted in its mooring. It wasn't damage, he decided, but a manmade hiding space. In the gap created by the rotated stone, he glimpsed something metallic. Peering more closely, he saw what looked to be a strongbox. With a keyhole that just might fit a key the size of the one that Stevie carried.

Shaking his head, Jack readjusted the rock, making note of its location so he could find it again. Then he stood, arrested by a sudden thought. "My God," he said aloud. "I'm right. I've found Stevie's treasure."

He didn't know why he was so certain of it—but it had to be true. Nothing short of a miracle, he supposed, but he'd found the lock that fit her key.

Another possibility. Another new vista, perhaps. Jack realized he was smiling again, his chest warming, his anticipation growing like it felt his heart was at the notion that the next time he saw Stevie he'd get to tell her—

—that he loved her. It was yet another sudden, certain thought.

Of course. Of course he loved her.

It didn't even surprise him. It just seemed right.

No wonder the idea of her pregnant was so appealing.

No wonder he'd found the thought of good-bye so painful.

No wonder that he'd begun to see for himself a future beyond running—again—from his own reflection.

He was in love with Stephania Baci.

He'd found what she'd been seeking, and in exchange, he'd found the thing—the person—who had enabled him to strip off the shroud he'd lain beneath the last ten years. Because of her, he'd finally found a way to rejuvenate what once had died inside him.

Stevie. Loving her made him want to no longer be the careless, selfish man of the past ten years. Now he saw a future for himself, lying just ahead. He wanted to spend the rest of his life kissing her awake. Slaying her dragons.

If only she'd let him, he'd be her prince.

It humbled him, how much he wanted that.

20

Stevie had forgotten about the press conference scheduled by Senator Platt between the wedding rehearsal and the rehearsal dinner. Though the politician had yet to emerge from wherever she was waiting, a gaggle of press was already standing in the winery parking area, illuminated by the white fairy lights strung through the trees and along the arbor that connected the administrative offices to the caves.

She skirted the group, avoiding eye contact with anyone. Her intent was to check in with Allie and—hopefully—discover she wasn't needed during the dinner. After Stevie's crying jag, her little sister had volunteered to handle the rest of the Parini-Platt wedding details. With swollen eyes and a red nose, she'd taken her up on the offer. But thanks to a passing time and ice packs, her meltdown no longer showed on her face. Her conscience insisted she at least make sure there wasn't something she could do for her sister on crutches.

A hand caught her elbow. A man swung her into a hug.

"My favorite Baci," he said into her ear as he lifted her onto her toes.

"You big liar." She kissed her brother-in-law, Penn Bennett, on the cheek. Despite the ache in her chest, she found a smile for him. He was a dark blond like his half brothers, Liam and Seth. Rangy and with the same good looks. But what made him most attractive to Stevie was how much he loved her little sister, formerly known as the Nun of Napa. "And you fib with such conviction. That's Hollywood for you."

Everyone knew the crux of the popularity of Penn's TV show was his own good nature and easy charm. Subtract the sunny disposition and he reminded her of another too-handsome man. She looked away, her nose tingling again.

"Steve," Penn said softly. He drew her close once more. "Come with us when we go back to Malibu. We'll wrap you in blankets and prop you up on the deck with a pitcher of margaritas and a stack of romance novels. You'll recover your fighting spirit in no time."

She leaned her forehead against his shoulder. It would be so easy to run away with them. But hadn't she tried that with her whole "sex like a man" charade? She'd been running from tenderness and intimacy with Jack and both had caught up with her anyway.

Drawing free from Penn, she shook her head. "I appreciate the offer, but I've got all those weddings to coordinate—brides to soothe, grooms to buck up—you know the drill."

He spun the gold band on his left ring finger and smiled. "It was the happiest day of my life."

Her nose stung again and she pressed the back of her hand to it. "Penn, don't do that." *Don't make me long for what you have with Allie.*

Reaching out, he chucked her under the chin. "Sorry, sweetheart. But about those weddings . . . Are you sure about that commitment you made to Tanti Baci? I know you did it for us—so Alessandra and I can spend more time together when I have to be in Southern California."

"I didn't do it for you and Allie—or just for you and Allie, anyway." She was wearing an amethyst-colored knee-length wool coat over black trousers and a black sweater, and she shoved her hands in its side pockets. Thanks to her sister's new passion, she was also wearing a lavender hand-knit cloche hat that included a crocheted flower on the short brim. She still felt chilled.

"Tanti Baci is part of me, too." She'd been wrong to try to escape from its hold on her. The winery was not only her legacy, but also the foundation she would need to keep herself steady after Jack left her life. "I need to give it what I can."

Penn swept her into another hug. "It makes your little sister happy to have you part of the team—and Alessandra happy makes me *very* happy."

She clung to him, blessing him for the changes he'd brought into Allie's life. Love didn't have to be totally screwed up, the newlyweds proved, if you found the right fit. She and Jack just didn't mesh in that same way.

"Well, well, *mon ange*," a sardonic voice said. "And here I thought we'd agreed to be exclusive."

Stevie tightened her grip on Penn. "Don't leave me," she whispered to him.

Steeling her spine, she turned to confront the person who had pushed against her barriers and rattled every locked gate. He stood, looking relaxed and elegant in dark slacks, collared knit shirt, and sport coat.

"Exclusively what, Jack?" It took everything she had not to close her eyes and pretend he wasn't there, because if she could have constructed the complete wrong man for herself, it would be him: a gorgeous prince with a wealthy family and a dark past.

He was staring at her. She couldn't read his expression, but she could sense the odd tension in his tall frame.

Her fingers curled into fists that she shoved back into her coat pockets. "What's going on, Jack?"

"I . . . uh . . ." He forked his hand through his hair, a sign of uncharacteristic hesitation.

"Yes?"

"I have so much to tell you . . . I don't know quite where to start." He broke off, speared his fingers through his hair again. His gaze had never left her face. "You're just so damn beautiful."

From behind her, Penn leaned down to whisper in her ear, "Oh, yeah, he's an ogre."

She ignored him. "All right, Jack, I get it. You want something. What is it this time? Because the only thing I'm willing to give you tonight is directions out of Edenville."

"I think we should set a date," he said quickly. "You know, the wedding date."

She rolled her eyes. "Jack, this is my brother-in-law, Penn Bennett. You don't have to pretend around him. He knows the engagement's fake."

He barely spared a glance for the other man. "I don't want it to be fake, Stevie. I want you."

"Ha ha." How sappy was she that even the false words made her mouth go dry? "What is wrong with you?"

"Approximately ten years of debauched and wasteful living—though I swear the worst of it was over within the first two. But even afterward, I confess I never worried what people were saying about me. Now, Stevie, you can't know how much I wish I had better press clippings."

"I hear you, buddy," Penn said, sounding much too supportive. "The gossip industry can be a bitch."

Stevie glanced over her shoulder. "Does he look like someone who needs sympathy?"

Jack acted as if he hadn't heard either one of them. His gaze remained glued to Stevie. "I know I don't deserve you. That's the worst part—I can't think of one good reason why, on the face of it, you'd go into this with me. But

I . . ." His hand scraped over his chin. "I'm in love with you. I'll do everything I can to make you happy."

"What?" The actual sound of her reaction was muffled, however, by that of the reporters as two couples—Emerson and Roxanne, Senator Platt and her husband—stepped out of the entrance to the wine caves. The press surged forward, though Stevie noted that Jack's parents were not on scene. Apparently Emerson's mother was canny enough to know that their glamorous personages would eclipse even senatorial splendor.

"Stevie . . ." Jack started.

She shook her head and pretended to give her attention to the conference a few feet away as the senator began her opening remarks. Stevie didn't really catch what was said, she didn't try actually, because she was using the time to think her way through the muddle in her head. What the hell was Jack doing? Why was he saying these things? Her nose was tingling again but she refused to cry in front of the damn man.

But Jack wasn't accustomed to being ignored. He grabbed her wrist and towed her farther from the activity by the caves' entrance. "Did you hear me?" he said. "Stevie, I love you."

She shook her head, then looked around, desperate to find out who had set her up to be punked.

"I want to get married." His hands came to her shoulders and he gave her a little shake. "I want to marry *you*."

"So not a good idea." Surely, *surely* this was a practical joke. She curved her lips to make clear she understood this was nothing more than a colossal gag. "I'm not cut out for royal life."

"Of course you are." A small smile turned up the corners of his lips. "Think. What's the name of your business? Napa Princess Limousine."

"That's a joke." She turned away from him so he wouldn't see the tears spark in her eyes. "This whole thing is a joke."

He spun her to face him again. "No, no, it's not."

"Jack, you can't be serious." But he looked serious so she found herself answering in that same vein, God help her. "The world of your parents and family . . . how you grew up . . . I don't fit in. I'd always be saying the wrong thing."

"Stevie. You've met my mother. Surely you realize saying the wrong thing isn't such an impediment."

Desperation had her looking around again, still seeking the punch line, the ah-ha.

Jack caught her face in his hand and his eyes bore into hers. "You really don't believe me? You don't believe I can love someone?"

"I didn't say that." Her nose was stinging again. "What's wrong with you? I know you're capable of loving."

A moment passed, then knowledge dawned over his face. His fingers gentled on her. "You don't believe I could love *you*," he said.

She averted her gaze.

"Stevie . . ."

She whispered the truth. "Of course I don't believe that."

"Merde." He was silent another long minute and then his hand dropped. "I thought my biggest obstacle would be convincing you I'm deserving of you."

"You can have anyone you want," she said, stating the obvious. "Anyone would want you."

His laugh was short. "Except you."

"I explained that." Bucking the social order never worked, the debacle between her and Emerson had proved that. "We don't suit—how could we? The chauffeur and the prince."

He was silent a moment, then his eyes narrowed. "Bullshit," he said. "You don't buy that, not really, and neither do I. You're Stephania Baci, the toughest girl in Edenville. Some medieval notion of class isn't going to keep you down. It's just a convenient excuse."

Her throat was closing. "I . . . I . . ."

"So let's get to the real truth, why don't we? If you let yourself believe in my love, if you were willing to have a relationship with me, then you'd have to let me in."

"Jack—"

"Strong Stevie Baci would have to drop her armor and let a big, bad man close." He crossed his arms over his chest. There was a ruthless gleam in his eyes. "She'd have to reveal her innermost secret—that inside she has a vulnerable, breakable heart, just like the rest of us."

She stiffened. "No one can break me."

"Then take me on," he said instantly.

Take *him* on? Prince Jack Parini? He was too rich, too smooth, too elegant, too . . . He wanted too much. "You don't understand," she heard herself say. "It's not that simple."

His expression hardened. "I understand you're a coward, Stevie."

"I don't want to have this discussion with you." If her heart was so well protected, how come it hurt so much?

"Too bad," he said, hundreds of years of royal authority in his voice. "We're going to have to talk anyway."

"I just said I don't—"

"The kicker is, sweet thing"—his expression remained stony—"you can't get rid of me so easily."

"Jack—"

"The condom broke."

She gaped at him. *"What?"*

Strangely now, he looked almost . . . smug. His hands slid into his pockets and he rocked back on his heels. "We might have made a baby."

~

Just then, the crowd by the caves turned noisy enough to yank Jack's attention away from the woman who was twisting his insides into knots. Stevie's brother-in-law caught his eye and filled in the blanks as to what he'd missed. "Emerson Platt just shocked the hell out of people—most particularly his mother from the looks of things—by stating he's not running for any political office. Ever."

Surprised himself, Jack peered over the knot of people toward Emerson. Roxy stood beside him, looking relieved and as ecstatic as a bride-to-be should. The king and queen of Ardenia emerged from the caves' entrance to snare some of the press attention.

But others followed an obviously agitated Senator Platt as she pushed through the small crowd. Passing Jack, she brushed his shoulder, and her high heels wobbled on the pea gravel. His hands shot out of his pockets to steady her and she glanced at him, then froze as something that had caught on his sleeve dropped to the ground at her feet.

She gasped and her voice rose over the hubbub. "My missing bracelet! It's you! It's you who took it."

Qu'ils aillent tous se faire foutre. He might have guessed the piece belonged to her. Rubies, diamonds, and sapphires. Red, white, and blue. And clearly real. Shit!

"You stole my bracelet." Her tone was accusatory as she bent to snatch it up. "It's worth thousands of dollars."

Yeah. Real.

A sick feeling roiled in his belly and time slowed to molasses drips. He thought about finding the bracelet in the bridal boudoir and he thought about Roxy's impulse control disorder. Before, she'd only stolen things of little value, but her stress level these last few weeks had been through the roof.

He didn't dare glance toward his sister to gauge her reaction. She was marrying into the Platt family tomorrow. The senator would be her mother-in-law in less than twenty-four hours and he'd take a bullet before doing anything that might redirect the blame to Roxy.

He couldn't look at Stevie, either. But he could see her in his head, standing in the wedding cottage on New Year's Day. *We're strangers*, she'd said. *For all I know you're a thief.*

And with the old stories and the ugly rumors swirling

around again, everyone from Edenville to Ardenia would believe that.

Another day with Stevie flashed into his mind. Her voice again. *What would you hate to lose, Jack? Is there something you care so much about you'd do just about anything to keep it?*

He turned his head and there she was, her expression stricken, her soft lower lip caught between her teeth. *Is there something you care so much about you'd do just about anything to keep it?*

Good God, no, he'd said then, but now the answer burned in his chest. That something was Stevie. What he'd hate to lose was her.

He was so in love with her, but because of this, she'd be out of his reach in the space of half a dozen more heartbeats. He was about to lose that future that had so recently opened up before him.

Oh, *mon chat*. So this is the real good-bye.

Then his father was at his elbow, his mother glued to her husband's side. "*Mein Gott*," the king said, his clipped German matching his austere expression, "is that bauble yours, madam?"

Senator Platt shifted her gaze to the king. "Uh . . . yes."

"Earlier, I found it myself, over . . . over . . ." his accent had thickened and he made a vague gesture as if he couldn't come up with the proper English word for wherever he'd supposedly discovered the thing. "And then—"

"The king turned it over to me," Stevie put in, stepping closer. "And once I realized it was the one you'd been looking for, Lois, I handed it off to Jack so he could give it to you when he got to the rehearsal dinner." She smiled, brighter than sunshine.

Jack's mother's matched it as she moved closer to admire the gaudy piece of jewelry. "Hot damn, I wouldn't have wanted to lose that fistful of sparkly rocks, either," she said, and her accent was pure magnolia. "We girls gotta stockpile goodies like that in case some dumbass husband decides to trade us in for a younger model."

Lois Platt blinked. "I . . . uh . . ."

The queen linked arms with the senator. "C'mon, now, say thank you to everyone and we can get inside and get ourselves a drink!"

As directed, the other woman stuttered out some grateful words and then was dragged away by Jack's mother. He looked after them instead of looking at the two people who'd come to his rescue. The moment stretched awkwardly. Finally he cleared his throat, his gaze sliding first to his father. "Thank you, sir," he said.

His father clapped his hand on his shoulder, squeezed. "What happened ten years ago . . . we were out of our minds with worry and fear. When it was over, I didn't say the right things, Jack, and I'm sorry."

Now Jack knew something about not getting the words right, too—even when they mattered so very much. Reaching up, he covered his father's fingers. "Thank you for that, too."

He paused now, staring at his feet instead of looking at his second rescuer. So much to say. He'd wanted to promise to slay her dragons, but like always, she'd turned his intentions on their head by stepping up and slaying his. God, he loved her. "Stevie . . ." he began, turning to confront her.

She was gone.

~

The next day, Stevie knew she should have avoided the wedding cottage once evening fell, when the ceremony was slated to begin. She'd advised herself to stay away, and she'd listened at first, ensuring she'd obey by staying in jeans, sweater, her ratty sneakers. As guests climbed the shallow front steps, she'd detoured toward the tent that had been set up for the reception.

Inside, ringing a dance floor, round tables had been covered with embroidered cloths of navy blue on blue satin. The tableware was blue and white china. Blue votives circled the lush arrangements of pink, purple, and burgundy flowers, with fiddlehead ferns curling outward to snag attention.

There were patio heaters and romantic lighting and delicious smells. The bar was being stocked and she knew that plenty of the Tanti Baci *blanc de blancs* was chilling for the toast. Musicians had already set up their equipment and the cake was also assembled, four layers with icing that looked like lace. White roses were scattered around it on the table.

What color roses are your favorite? Jack had asked. She wondered if he'd follow through with his promise to send her a dozen every day.

Of course he would, she thought. She'd never doubted his honor. She would never doubt his word. She remembered that mask his face had donned when Lois Platt had accused him of theft, and a caustic pain filled her chest. He hadn't deserved that.

Rubbing at the spreading ache at her breastbone, she admitted that he deserved more from her, too. He deserved the truth that she'd avoided sharing with him for the last twenty-four hours.

She waited until Roxanne and Emerson's wedding ceremony was over. When the guests began trickling into the tent, she made her way to the cottage. The bride and groom had bucked tradition, she knew, and taken photographs with each other and family before the ceremony so that the celebration could get started right away. Still, they were among the last to leave Anne and Alonzo's former home, and from the shadows, she watched the couple walk arm in arm toward the reception, followed by their parents.

Smiles all around. Good.

Jack wasn't with them. Good, too.

Her feet made no sound as she crossed the porch. The double doors were flung open and it was warm inside, thanks to the previously full house and the fire crackling on the hearth. He stood in front of it, staring into the flames.

The center aisle would take her to him and she stepped forward, even though she felt self-conscious using that route. The ends of the benches were still dressed with satin ribbon and hanging vases filled with flowers that matched those at the reception. Soft music filtered from the stereo speakers. *Here comes the bride*, she thought. *Not.*

Halfway to him, he turned. She jumped, and her feet stopped moving. Maybe he was a vampire after all, because at the thought that this might be the very last time she saw him, her body went limp, as if all the blood had been drained from her veins.

But she couldn't die just yet.

"I have just one thing to say to you." She forced herself to keep walking, because she was, after all, still the brash Baci.

He lifted a brow, and it was elegant, casual Jack who was gazing on her, at home in his tuxedo with a boutonniere tucked in his lapel. A white rose.

Her feet stuttered to a halt again, and she cursed herself for being such a stupid, silly *girl*. Flowers, cake, fancy dresses, the whole wedding business was making her soft. And irritated, she suddenly decided.

She scowled at him. "Do you realize I had to learn what a tussy mussy is? I'm a woman comfortable with carburetors and oil filters, Jack, but now I have to know about tussy mussies. Don't get me started on headpieces."

"I wouldn't dream of it," Jack murmured, sliding his hands into his pockets. "Is that the one thing you wanted to say?"

"What? No." She stomped toward him, feeling much better with a little ire running through her bloodstream. If he'd emptied her of the regular stuff, then indignation would have to do.

Annoyance still edging her mood, she poked him with her fingertip, right between the studs on his tuxedo shirt.

"And what do you mean, even wondering for a second if I thought you capable of loving someone?"

"I—"

"Don't you realize I saw how kind you are to your sister? How far you were willing to go to protect her?"

"I—"

"What about your relationship with your mother? Obviously you care about her deeply. As for your father, well, I think you should wake up and smell the espresso, Jack. I don't have parents anymore so I'm entitled to say you're seriously wasting time by not realizing that man loves you just as much as you love him."

"I'm working on it," Jack said quietly, then paused. "So is *that* the one thing you came to say?"

"No." She stared at his handsome face, his aristocratic beauty almost too much to bear. It leeched away her indignation and she didn't know what was going to keep her standing up now. Her nose started stinging again and she pressed it with the back of her hand. "The one thing I have to say is . . ."

Here it was. The end, the real good-bye, the smashing of the chance that she could have held on to him for a tiny while longer. If she stayed quiet, she could let this play out a few more days, maybe even a couple of weeks. But playing with Jack had only led to disaster.

She took a breath and the air smelled like wood smoke, candle wax, roses. Those damn white roses.

"There's no way I'm pregnant." She forced herself to stay focused on his face, watching for the expected relief. "I'm on birth control."

He flinched, and then he spun away from her, his hand lifting to his face. Taken aback at his abrupt movement, she stared at his broad shoulders.

They . . . trembled?

"Jack . . ." Was he laughing? No. Was he . . .

"Jack?"

He didn't answer. There was something new in the room

with them, charging the atmosphere. A feeling. Sadness? Disappointment? Regret? She shook her head. It couldn't be. "Jack?"

"It was foolish of me, I know," he finally said, his voice thick, his back still turned. His laugh was rough. "In so long I hadn't considered my future, I hadn't thought of having my own family . . . I've been so cut off from everyone. Then to imagine . . ."

Stevie froze, trying to absorb what Jack was talking about, what Jack's reaction really meant. And then, when it sank in at last . . .

Oh, hell. Just like that, it happened. What she'd been running from since New Year's Eve had finally caught up with her. She pressed one palm to her chest and tears sprang to her eyes. "Damn you," she whispered.

Her voice gained strength. "God damn you, Jack Parini." She thwacked him with the flat of her free hand, right between his shoulder blades.

He didn't turn. "What now?"

She thwacked him again. "You just broke my heart."

He froze.

"And you're going to pay for that."

He slowly turned. "How?"

Oh, God. His eyelashes were wet. And there was pain everywhere now, probably all the hurt she'd held on to leaking from her ruined heart. She'd guessed right. Jack had . . . she could hardly wrap her mind around it. Jack had really wanted them to have made a baby.

Which meant his offer of marriage and pretense of love hadn't been a noble act because he'd thought she was pregnant. Of course that answer had crossed her mind the minute he'd said the condom broke. But now she realized he must really want her, or else he'd already be breezing out of the cottage, whistling like a boy let out early for recess.

Which meant . . . Now her eyes were stinging and she reached up to rub her aching chest. She was loved by Jack Parini.

Her shattered heart stayed in pieces, so perhaps it was just the armor she'd built around it that had broken, she thought, as she felt it beating beneath her hand. At fourteen, when she'd lost her mother, she'd started her construction project, desperate never to hurt so much again. But the walls had come tumbling down at the knowledge of his feelings for her.

She was loved by Jack Parini.

She heard her mother's voice again, though not a memory this time. *You're beautiful just as you are.*

Even strong girls can use a hand to hold.

Don't be afraid to love.

Jack thumbed away the tears she realized were streaking her cheeks. "How're you going to make me pay, *mon ange*?" His voice was soft.

"The French," she murmured, trying to work up some righteous anger at him again. "Always with the French."

He smiled a little. "How?" he insisted.

"I only know for how long," she said. Now unprotected and defenseless, the small organ in her chest was starting to thrum with a rhythm she'd never known before.

Jack's shoulders relaxed. There was another little smile. "God, I hope that means for the rest of our lives."

She hesitated. Not so brave, now, was she? Jack had been right about that. But after a deep breath, the words came as naturally as easing her foot into a seamless glass slipper—or winding up for the perfect pitch. "It means I'm in love with you, Jack."

He was silent a moment. His "You don't know how happy I am to hear that," came out cool and calm. Then her sentimental, emotional prince—oh, she had his number now—yanked her into his embrace. She thought she felt dampness as he pressed his face against her hair.

Her poor little heart hiccupped, but then kept right on beating. Maybe it knew what it was doing.

He pushed her away to look into her face. "You believe I love you?"

And she had to smile. "Believe?" She drew his mouth to hers for a long kiss, then held him away again. "You realize you're asking that of the woman who's clung all her life to her faith in family legends, loving ghosts, and lost treasure, don't you?"

He claimed the next soul-deep kiss, then lifted his head again. "I want it all," he said, his voice fierce. "We'll make wine at our two-acre vineyard, we'll make babies that will carry on the tradition, we'll make a lifetime of happiness together."

"You royal types, always expecting to command things," she teased.

"*Bien sûr*," he said, all aristocratic Ardenian prince.

So she jumped him like the tomboy she was, wrapping her arms around his neck and her legs around his waist. He laughed and spun in a circle, hitching her closer against him. "I have such a surprise for you."

She cocked her head. "What surprise?"

He grinned. "I found your treasure."

"There's your arrogance again," she said, shaking her head even as she rolled her hips suggestively. "My 'treasure'?"

"No." He laughed again. "Really."

She speared her fingers in his hair and brought his lips close again. "Tell me later. Right now I've got better ideas for what to do with your mouth."

~

"Come on," Jack said softly. His wife was beautiful to-night, as beautiful as when he'd married her a month before. Their wedding had taken place at seven P.M. in the Tanti Baci cottage filled with family and friends. The room had been nearly pitch-dark, lit only by a smoldering fire as he waited for his bride to join him. Then he'd seen a candle's flame . . .

Her bouquet was a single white taper surrounded by ivory roses. It had illuminated her slender figure in a long, white velvet gown that left her neck and shoulders bare.

His heart had expanded, taking his breath, and tears had stung his eyes as she'd moved closer—so fittingly bringing to him a light to alleviate the darkness.

Her love had banished all his personal shadows. Stevie lit up his soul.

They'd honeymooned in Tahiti, sleeping—or not—in a private cabana built over the water. Now he'd made them a bed on the floor in the wedding cottage's bridal boudoir, but she was hesitating to join him on the pad of quilts and blankets. Candlelight flickered against the walls. "Come on," he coaxed again. "You know you want to."

"No," Stevie protested, even as she sank down beside him and took the glass of sparkling wine he handed her. "It's only a fantasy."

"That doesn't mean we shouldn't give it a try." He kissed the side of her neck, then moved the vase of white roses he'd brought with him farther from the pillows. He'd bought her a dozen every day since she'd agreed to marry him. Practical Stevie kept complaining of the expense, but he knew her secret longing . . . and now she knew his.

Maybe it was the emotional Ardenian in him . . . or perhaps the simple Georgia farmer. Either way, he was eager to plant his seed in this lovely woman and make new life. When he'd mentioned it on their wedding day—which he'd managed to make happen a short six days after Roxy's nuptials, while his parents were still in the States—his bride had melted.

Oh, she was so, so soft on the inside. When they'd unlocked the strongbox he'd found in the fireplace, she'd watched with shining eyes, although the "treasure" had turned out to be nothing more than an old diary. Anne's diary.

"Maybe there's a clue inside," Giuliana had said, her voice wistful.

And his tough girl had handed the leather-bound book to her older sister. "You find out for us," she'd said. Then she'd whispered to Jack, "Maybe she'll find a clue about what to do with Liam and Kohl."

He'd laughed then, swamped by love for her. He was still happily drowning in it.

"Please, Stevie," he said now, kissing her again. "Let me make love to you."

She shivered. "Well . . ."

He tipped up her face to gaze into her eyes, no longer afraid for her to see the emotion in his. "I promise it will be fun."

"Always the fun with you," she scolded, then sighed. "But you can't tell anyone, Jack. Not ever."

"It will be our secret, *mon ange*," he said, smiling. "Our sweet little secret that we conceived our child under Anne and Alonzo's approving gazes."

She glanced around. "That's what makes it feel weird, Jack. I mean, what if the ghosts are really here?"

"They'll close their eyes during the good parts," he whispered. "Come on, Stephania, let's make a baby."

Her hesitation lasted only another second. Then she pushed him down to the blankets and came over him. "Say it in French, Jack," she demanded. "You know I can't resist that."

"Let me show you in French," he murmured against her mouth. *You know I can't resist you.*

AUTHOR'S NOTE

Thank you to my (blushing) reader in France, Emmanuelle, who contributed Jack's French phrases, including the cuss words (hence the blushing). Any mistakes are my own!

As mentioned in the first book in the Three Kisses trilogy, *Crush on You*, there are restrictions to the kinds of events that may be hosted at wineries in the Napa Valley due to its designation as an agricultural preserve. Over the years, the rules have been challenged and then revised. For my fictional purposes the romantic "I-dos" go forward at beautiful Tanti Baci.

Keep reading for a preview of the next book
in the Three Kisses trilogy from Christie Ridgway

Drunk on Love

Coming July 2011 from Berkley Sensation!

1

Giuliana Baci shivered in the June night air even though flames were crackling and roaring just fifty feet away. She clutched the old leather-bound diary to her chest and stared at the spectacle across the street, trying to take it in. A muscle car passed, possibly attracted by the strobing emergency lights, because it slowed to a lookie-loo pace. It veered toward the opposite curb, and she could see the driver's neck crane, his eyes obviously not on the parked obstacle just ahead. "Watch out," she warned, stepping forward.

But it was too late. Two and a half tons of heavy metal had already taken out a headlight and crumpled the hood of a small, innocent sedan. Giuliana's sedan.

Somehow she wasn't surprised to see the overcylindered other vehicle lurch into reverse, then race away from her latest personal disaster.

The screech of tires against pavement was swallowed by the sound of the fire burning up the rest of her belongings in the now-engulfed four-unit apartment building where she'd been living.

"To hell with threes," she said, her voice as defeated as her mood. Her legs folded and she sank to the curb, the cement cold through her thin robe. One set of bare toes crossed over the other. "If you ask me, bad luck comes in batches."

"I'm sorry," the young woman beside her replied. She was perched on the same old-fashioned suitcase she'd lugged into Giuliana's small apartment when she'd offered the woman temporary lodging not long ago. "I'm so very sorry."

"That should be my line," Giuliana answered, though it looked as if Grace had at least saved her possessions. She'd been living out of that very suitcase and sleeping on the—now likely incinerated—living room couch.

"You'll get through this," Grace said, her freckled face earnest beneath her rumpled strawberry blonde hair. "No doubt about it."

Those should have been her lines, too, Giuliana thought. For the last year she'd been repeating them often enough—ever since her father's death and the Baci sisters' takeover of the family's failing one-hundred-year-old winery.

Only a month to go, she consoled herself now. *And then*—

Another car sped onto the scene. Giuliana's nerves went on instant alert, standing on end as she jumped to her feet, still clutching the old diary. Liam Bennett exited the Mercedes even as it rocked to a halt.

Despite her quaking belly, her jellied knees went rock solid. *The girl still has some fight in her*, she thought, relieved. *Now don't let him guess there are any chinks in your foundation.*

Then he was in front of her, the flickering fire and the flashing emergency lights casting reds and yellows over his lean face. Her stomach cramped again, and it was as if the heat of the flames set a torch to her skin. *What is wrong with me?* she wondered for the millionth time. On a daily basis, people encountered their childhood sweethearts and didn't suffer such an intense physical reaction.

But although she'd hidden herself away for a decade, she'd returned only to discover she was still not immune to him.

"What are you doing here?" she croaked out. It sounded more froggy than unfriendly.

Damn it.

He cocked an eyebrow. "This is Edenville."

Yeah, yeah, yeah. Small town of six thousand nosy souls in the northern end of the Napa Valley. Word of what happened had likely run faster through the gossip grapevine than the fire through the clothes in her closet. The mental image made her shiver.

Liam saw it, and he reached for her.

No! every instinct inside her shouted. She swayed back and he froze. Then he stripped off the sports jacket he wore and dropped it over her shoulders, careful that his hands didn't touch her body.

She wanted to grasp the lapels and hug it against her. She didn't. She didn't thank him, either.

The wind shifted, sending smoke across their faces, and she blinked against the sting in her eyes. But it was Liam's scent that was in her nose, spicy, male, and she had to tighten her grip on the diary to remind herself to stay steady. Strong.

When all she wanted was to collapse against him and bury her face at his throat.

"Jules," he said. For a second she thought she heard an ache in his voice that mirrored the one in her chest, but that couldn't be true. Liam's expression appeared as unreadable as it always did.

Only emphasizing the fact that she had to stand on her own two feet. She'd proven she could, all that long time ago, and she wouldn't stumble now. People depended upon *her,* not the other way around, and she was afraid of how she might ultimately be hurt if she forgot that.

Clearing her throat, Giuliana waved away another waft of smoke. "Look, thanks for checking on us. But we'll be fine."

"Us?" he echoed, looking around, and then his gaze found Grace, who offered him a tentative smile.

Giuliana moved closer to her. "You remember Grace Mackey—I mean Grace *Hatch*. I hired her to pour in the Tanti Baci tasting room two weeks ago."

"Hatch . . . ?"

"Yes," Giuliana confirmed. "The dowser." Old Peter Hatch had owned some rocky acreage in the backcountry and eked out a living divining for water and doing handyman chores. Known as a mean drunk and an even meaner dad, those who knew shy and quiet Grace had actually been happy for her when she'd dropped out of high school to marry a boy just home from the Army in the next county. Except he'd been cut from the same cloth as her father, and when Grace had shown up at the winery with final divorce papers and a black eye, what could Giuliana do?

"She's been staying with me for a while," Giuliana explained to Liam.

He glanced over his shoulder at the apartment building that appeared soon to be ashes. "Then you'll both need somewhere to stay. You'll come to my place—"

"No." She shook her head. "Of course not. We're headed for the farmhouse. I've already left a message for Stevie."

He crossed his arms over his chest. He wore a cotton polo shirt tucked into dark jeans. His shoulders had been broad and strong as a teenager, his hips lean, his butt nearly nonexistent. As a man, he'd filled out everywhere in all the best ways. Not that she hadn't tried not to notice.

"That should be fun for you," he said. "Moving in with two sets of honeymooners."

Oh, why bother disguising her grimace? Her youngest sister, Allie, had married Liam's half brother, Penn Bennett, nearly a year before. Though they spent some of their time in Southern California, when they were in Edenville they took over the first floor of the small farmhouse the Baci girls had grown up in. The second story was the domain of her other sister, Stevie, who was camping there with her husband of five months, Jack Parini, while they were remodeling the winery on their two-acre vineyard into a home.

She sighed. "It'll be just like old times."

"Except for the addition of your ardent brothers-in-law. Good luck trying to ignore all the squeals and heavy breathing."

"Surely it won't—"

"They're horndogs, Jules."

Well, duh. It didn't take more than five seconds in a room with her sisters and the men they'd married to realize their relationships were passionate. "I'm sure Allie and Stevie will keep the lid on when guests are around."

"Yeah. You Baci girls are always so good at keeping things on simmer."

The way he said it set her blood on boil. She moved up, toe-to-toe with him. "What's that supposed to mean?"

He looked down his aristocratic nose at her, all golden boy to barefoot peasant girl. The story of their lives. "We could finish this thing, Giuliana. One damn way or another if you'd just give over. Move in, and we could—"

"We couldn't! We won't!" Giving over was exactly what she couldn't do. Rehashing their past had no place in her future.

"Fine. Your choice." His face was composed, his voice steady. "But then it'll bubble and spit and make us both miserable for the *next* ten years."

"No! No it won't." She had a plan, already set in motion, that would bring it, everything for all of them, finally to an end. No more emotional distress, no more poignant pulls from the past.

He quirked that brow again. "How so?"

His calm made her want to murder him. While her heart pounded and her mouth went dry when she shared even the largest space with him, he appeared as unmoved as ice forgotten in a freezer. He might talk about being miserable, but he didn't fathom a damn thing about that emotion or any other.

"Jules?"

His doubting tone had her inches closer and on tiptoe. "Because—" she started. Then she halted, her brain clicking in before her temper got the better of her—hey, she'd matured, too. Telling too soon could ruin everything she'd planned. "Just because," she said, falling back to her heels.

He didn't twitch a muscle, but she could sense his inner mental eye roll.

The temperature of her blood spiked again. "Don't give me that look."

His gaze narrowed. "I'll tell you what I want to give you—" He broke off as a taxi pulled in beside his vehicle. "Oh, hell."

She ignored Liam's disgust as she turned to the figure exiting the cab. At the sight of Kohl Friday's dark hair and rock-solid form, she let her spine sag. The Tanti Baci vineyard manager didn't hesitate to move in and bolster her with an arm around her shoulders. "Okay?"

"Okay." She leaned against him, his presence diminishing a little of the threat she felt in Liam's company. He smelled of cinnamon gum and tequila—which explained why he hadn't driven himself. "Phone lines been working overtime?" she asked.

"I'm here to give you a lift," he said. Then he half turned, his gaze finding the young woman still seated on her suitcase. "Grace."

Her eyes were wide and focused on Kohl's face. Giuliana saw her gulp. "Hi," she said, her voice nearly a whisper.

Kohl turned back quickly, as if aware he was spooking her. "Ready, ladies?"

Giuliana slid a look in Liam's direction. He'd moved away a few paces to lean against the side of his car, arms and ankles crossed. His expression proclaimed he was bored by the proceedings.

"Ready," she replied, tacking on a smile for her second rescuer. Then she walked away from the first one with perfect composure—just as Liam, her very first lover, had walked away from her a decade before.

~

Giuliana peeked through the holes in the afghan she'd thrown over her head last night as she'd tried getting comfortable on the love seat in her office. Sleep had apparently arrived at some point, since early morning sunshine was now in the room, along with something that was rummaging around in the large storage closet located across the tattered Oriental carpet. Drawing the blanket below her chin, she blinked against the light.

"Has the European grapevine moth moved onto paper goods now?" she called out.

A petite brunette peered around the door. "Oh, sorry." Alessandra Baci Bennett, Giuliana's little sister, formerly known as the "Nun of Napa," stepped from the closet, her pretty face contrite. "You're awake?"

Giuliana scooted over to allow the other woman to perch a hip on the sofa cushions and considered the question. "It was all a dream? My apartment didn't really burn last night, my car wasn't bashed in, and I'm not actually relegated to using my office as a bedroom?"

"Not the last, certainly," Allie said, frowning. "You should have bunked down at the farmhouse."

Liam's warnings about squeals and heavy breathing had been hard to forget. "I was perfectly comfortable here," she lied, sitting up. She could smell smoke on her hair and realized she'd have to buy or borrow toiletries along with underwear and clothes and shoes and . . . just about everything. Daunted by the idea, she slid back to prone and closed her eyes. "On second thought, I *am* asleep." If she could manage another hour or two of snooze time, maybe all that lay ahead wouldn't feel so overwhelming.

Pulling the afghan higher on her shoulders, she murmured to her sister, "You don't need me for anything right this minute, do you?"

There was a telltale hesitation. "Of course not."

Even before their mom died when the sisters were sixteen, fourteen, and twelve, Giuliana had been like a second mother to Allie. So there was no way she could ignore the younger woman now. Opening her eyes once again, she rose up on her elbows. "Is there a problem?"

Her sister bounced on the cushions, the dimple at the side of her mouth flickering. "Jules, I've had the most brilliant idea!"

"Does this involve blindsiding Penn with another wedding proposal?"

Allie grinned, unrepentant. "But look how well that turned out." Her arms flew wide. "I'm obnoxiously happy."

It was hard not to smile in the face of all that unrelenting good cheer. And it was hard not to feel that Allie deserved every mote of it after the sad outcome of her first wedding attempt. Love and marriage could work if the couple was the right mix of personality and heart. Allie and Penn, and Stevie and Jack, proved that.

Some pairings, however, clashed, and a woman who worked at a winery understood that, too.

Allie's eyes narrowed. "Uh-oh. What's wrong?"

Giuliana tried shaking off her lowering mood. "Tell me about your brilliant idea."

Her sister seemed to sparkle. "It's about the Vow-Over Weekend."

Of course it was about the Vow-Over Weekend scheduled for the last days in June. "That's what we've all been working toward," Giuliana confirmed. Not only was it the fiftieth anniversary of the sparkling *blanc de blancs* that they bottled exclusively for weddings, but it also signaled the end of the year they'd agreed to give Tanti Baci to get back on its financial feet.

Allie bit her lip. "You know reservations have been a little slow coming in . . ."

Even though they'd been busting their behinds to get the word out that the winery was hosting a series of events to celebrate their wedding wine and the couples who'd toasted each other with it at their nuptials for the past fifty years—up to and including an on-site justice of the peace who would be on hand to help happy couples renew their vows. "You've done the best you can, Allie," she assured her younger sister.

"Yes, yes, but you won't believe what I've found out. What we can really use to create excitement. The legend—"

Giuliana groaned, her hand lifting to cover her eyes. "Not the legend. I'm begging you. Please don't talk about the legend."

"What legend?" It was a new voice. Grace's.

Giuliana dropped her hand to inspect her fellow refugee. The night before, their taxi had dropped the other woman at the small bungalow of Kohl's sister Mari. "You didn't have to come in today."

Grace shrugged, looking fresh and wide awake in a pair of jeans and a simple button-down shirt embroidered with the Tanti Baci logo—a delicate ivy garland with heart-shaped leaves. "Mari lent me some things. So why not work?"

Allie beamed at her. "And as a member of the tasting room staff, you should learn all the Tanti Baci legends."

"If you're going to tell bedtime stories, I'm going back to sleep," Giuliana declared. Suiting action to words, she snuggled back into her blanket and closed her eyes. She could use the twenty, forty, or sixty winks that it would take for her sister to impart the family's tall tales. But she couldn't tune out her sister's voice.

"There are actually three," Allie was saying. "I'm sure you know a little of the winery history. Alonzo Baci—my great-great-grandfather—along with the great-great-grandfather of the Bennett brothers, the original Liam Bennett, were partners in a silver mine north of here. When the ore ran out, they bought this property and decided to grow grapes. They also both courted the same girl—"

"Anne," interjected Grace. "I know that much. And that Alonzo won her. Their original cottage is the one you renovated last year in order to use it as a wedding venue."

"Exactly," Allie said, sounding pleased with her pupil. "That romance caused a big feud between the Bennetts and Bacis that has waxed and waned over the years, because our business dealings are still tangled. To this day, the Bennetts hold some interest in Tanti Baci."

"In the winery," Giuliana felt compelled to point out, though her eyes were still closed. "Not the land."

Allie let the comment pass. "Anyhow, legend number one is that there was some sort of valuable silver or silver-and-gold treasure that's been lost since those early days."

"We found a diary hidden in the rockwork surrounding the fireplace in the cottage," Giuliana said, cutting in again. "If there's a clue about this supposed treasure in the pages, we haven't found it."

Allie sighed. "Perhaps we're looking for the wrong kind of clue."

"So what's the second legend?" Grace asked. The eager note in her voice made Giuliana grimace. She was surrounded by romantic fools.

"Our papa always said that if you take your true love into the wedding cottage," Allie said, "you'll see the ghosts of those great lovers, Anne and Alonzo."

Under the blanket, Giuliana crossed her arms over her chest. "So I'm sure you and Penn have given them a great big howdy, is that right, Allie?"

With her eyes closed, she could still hear her little sister's delicate sniff. "Maybe."

Point scored. Giuliana wiggled deeper into the cushions and let drowsiness envelop her. "Onto load of baloney number three," she murmured.

Her sister sniffed again. "Jules may scoff, Grace, but maybe she shouldn't. You know that we've been retailing our *blanc de blancs* sparkling wine, to be served exclusively at weddings, for fifty years this month."

"On the website it says you keep a record of the name of each and every bridal couple who has toasted with it."

"Exactly," Allie confirmed. "And you know what else the website says . . ."

The women finished the thought together. "Not one of those couples has ever divorced!"

A cute marketing ploy, Giuliana admitted to herself, feeling sleep beginning to overtake her again. She supposed some slick ad man from San Francisco had been paid well for the idea in the days when the winery had money for such things.

"I haven't played that up enough," Allie admitted. "When I've been publicizing the Vow-Over Weekend and drumming up interest from the papers and other local press, I haven't been spotlighting that—and it's a winner angle if you ask me."

Grace's voice sounded as if it came from far away. "I love that story."

Yeah, but it *was* a story, Giuliana thought. And when she woke up next, she'd have to make clear to her little sister that it was a lousy idea to push something so blatantly false. It didn't pack any punch when it could be proved so patently untrue.

"Thank God for the Internet . . . not to mention the meticulous records of some of my predecessors in the winery's PR office."

Giuliana drew her hand under her cheek and hoped she wouldn't drool. She was *so* tired. Surely Allie would abandon this silly idea without her big sister's input.

"I've been checking . . . and my husband Penn has been checking, and Stevie and Jack got in on the hunt, too." Something about the thrill in Allie's voice roused Giuliana just as she slipped into sleep.

Her eyelashes fluttered. "What? What are you talking about?"

"I think it's true. I think no couple that ever toasted each other with Tanti Baci *blanc de blancs* in their glass has ever divorced."

Head muzzy, Giuliana struggled into a sitting position again. She worked her fingers through the tangles in her dark hair and tried straightening the thin cotton lapels of the summer robe she was still wearing over her nightshirt. "That can't be true."

"It *is* true," Allie insisted. "At the twenty-five-year anniversary, a lot of follow-up work was done. It hasn't been that hard to check on those older marriages. Genealogy sites came in handy, too. The more recent ones have been even easier to track down."

"That can't be right," Giuliana declared again. "You can't know all of them are still, um, happy unions."

Allie waved her hand. "I'm not playing marriage counselor here. But I'm telling you, according to the four of us—Stevie and me, Jack and Penn—we've confirmed that the Tanti Baci marriages are still legal and binding."

Voices outside the office door had her little sister on her feet. She cast a look at Giuliana's dumbfounded expression and said, "You need confirmation?"

In seconds, the room was crowded with both her sisters and their spouses. Giuliana's gaze roamed from face to face. "People. No divorces? This can't be . . ."

But they were already nodding.

Giuliana swallowed. "You can't know."

Allie frowned. "We know, okay?" She glanced around to give her husband a little smile. "And all romance-shmomance aside, it is a *great* publicity angle."

Maybe she was still asleep, Giuliana thought. That had to be it. She was dreaming all this. The crowd in the room shifted as another body made his way into her office. Liam. It didn't startle her to see him—he'd been disturbing her sleep for years—nor was she amazed that even while slumbering she'd go dry-mouthed at the sight of him.

"What's a great publicity angle?" her dream man asked her youngest sister.

"You know our books? The ones that list all the Tanti Baci brides and grooms? We've gone through them line by line. None of those marriages ever ended in divorce." Allie sent him a winning smile. "Isn't that fab?"

You'd have to be a keen observer of the man to notice the slight stiffening of his always-cool expression. "You can't know that."

Allie looked disgruntled. "You and Jules. What's going on with you two?"

Giuliana stifled her hysterical urge to laugh. Her gaze met Liam's, and though she thought she should shift it away, it stayed on him as she tried to explain. "We're just, um, uh, surprised, I guess. I mean . . . you've been through *all* those record books?"

"Almost. We're missing one—which is why I was in the closet. But as soon as I find it, I'm going to expose the truth to the world!"

Expose the truth to the world. Giuliana's stomach plunged. She was wide awake now. As a matter of fact, she wondered if she'd ever sleep again.

FROM *USA TODAY* BESTSELLING AUTHOR
CHRISTIE RIDGWAY

Crush on You

First in a contemporary romance trilogy about the bonds of family and friends—and weddings—in the heart of Napa Valley.

The Baci sisters are on a mission to save the winery that's been in their family for generations by transforming it into the perfect wedding destination. If only Alessandra Baci—affectionately known as the "Nun of Napa"—didn't need the help of tempting new neighbor Penn Bennett.

"Christie Ridgway captures the true magic
of falling in love."
—Robyn Carr,
New York Times bestselling author

penguin.com

Dirty Sexy Knitting

From *USA Today* bestselling author
CHRISTIE RIDGWAY

**The conclusion to the trilogy that's
"the perfect combination of humor and heart"
(Susan Wiggs).**

Malibu & Ewe's owner, Cassandra Riley, is about to turn thirty and wants to celebrate with her knitting club and her newfound half sisters, Nikki and Juliet, in a big birthday extravaganza. But with Juliet on her honeymoon and Nikki with her fiancé, it seems everyone's paired up—except for Cassandra. Until a series of near-death accidents causes Cassandra to run straight into the arms of the one man she's avoided most . . .

penguin.com

Who knew knitting could be so sexy?

Don't miss the three books in the
romantic, lighthearted trilogy featuring
the Southern California beachside
knitting store, Malibu & Ewe.

BY *USA TODAY* BESTSELLING AUTHOR

CHRISTIE RIDGWAY

How to Knit a Wild Bikini

Unravel Me

Dirty Sexy Knitting

penguin.com